D0611970

Unforgettable

Unforgettable

Some of life's trickiest steps happen off the dance floor.

TRISH PERRY

Summerside Press™
Minneapolis 55438
www.summersidepress.com
Unforgettable

ISBN 978-1-60936-112-9

Scripture references are from the following source: The Holy Bible, King James Version (KJV).

All characters are fictional. Any resemblances to actual people are purely coincidental.

Cover design by Chris Gilbert | www.studiogearbox.com

Interior design by Müllerhaus Publishing Group | www.mullerhaus.net

Summerside Press™ is an inspirational publisher offering fresh, irresistible books to uplift the heart and engage the mind.

Printed in USA.

DEDICATION

For my dad, Charles Hawley,
former WWII fighter pilot and my hero,
whose unconditional love has always mirrored that
of my blessed heavenly Father.

ACKNOWLEDGMENTS

This is my first novel with Summerside Press, and I certainly hope to repeat the experience over and over. How can you not love a publisher that sends you designer chocolates for agreeing to write a book you wanted to write anyway? Thank you, Carlton and Jason, for tucking me under the Summerside wing. I've enjoyed every step of this process. My thanks to all members of the Summerside family for their collaboration with me on *Unforgettable*.

My special thanks to Susan Downs, my very cool, very kind editor. I've loved getting to know you this year, and I appreciate your classy approach to making my writing better.

And many thanks to editors Ellen Tarver and Nancy Toback for their keen eyes and gracious suggestions to improve this book.

My agent Tamela Hancock Murray has become such a trusted friend, advocate, and counselor. Thank you for always having my back.

Thanks to the USA Dance Central Office in Cape Coral, Florida, (www.UsaDance.org) for help with my ballroom dance questions.

I also want to express my heartfelt thanks to:

My awesome readers, for supporting what I write and encouraging me through your notes, e-mails, and reviews.

American Christian Fiction Writers, Romance Writers of America (FHL), The Girliebeans, and Capital Christian Writers. I'd feel awfully lonely if I didn't know so many equally nutty writers.

Mike Calkin and Vie Herlocker, my tireless critique partners and faithful friends. The scales are way out of balance as to what I owe you in return for your honest efforts on my behalf.

Sandie Bricker, Debby Mayne, and Miralee Ferrell, three of the greatest sources of moral support, reality checks, and laughs I've ever known.

Barb Turnbaugh, Betsy Dill, Wendy Driscoll, and Gwen Hancock. I know you're out there, praying for me. I miss all of you!

The Saturday Night Girls, The Open Book Club, and my Cornerstone Chapel friends, for keeping life fun, challenging, and rich.

Chuck, Lilian, John, Donna, and Chris Hawley, my loving parents and siblings.

Tucker, Stevie, Doug, and Bronx, who make me proud and make me laugh till I cry.

Most importantly, my Lord Jesus, for the constant supply of ideas, blessings, hope, and assurance. You are my Everything.

CHAPTER ONE

June 18, 1951

Rachel Stanhope talked to herself as if such behavior were perfectly normal. Like a lion in a cage, she paced back and forth in front of her Arlington, Virginia, dance studio. When she was stressed, she tended to focus squarely on the cause of her stress. All else—people, traffic, dignity—faded far away. She only *appeared* imbalanced as she muttered. In point of fact, her public monologues kept her sane.

"Should have known better than to count on Betty to get here in time this morning. This is the last time I'll let her lock up the studio at night. The last!"

She checked her watch for the tenth time since she arrived and found herself locked out. The first session of her summer ballroom dance class for junior high school students was due to begin in fifteen minutes. Her budget couldn't handle the loss of these new students, and she had already used up all of her favors with the bank. She stopped pacing, made note of the cars driving past, and huffed out her frustration that Betty's DeSoto wasn't among them.

"Where is she? What an impression this is going to make!" She pulled her long, strawberry-blond hair back from her face and fanned the back of her neck. It was going to be a warm day, even if she managed to cool her temper.

"Is there a problem, Rachel?"

Rachel swung around at the kind voice behind her. She mustered up a self-deprecating smile.

"Good morning, Mr. Chambers. No, I'm just working myself into a lather here. Don't mind me."

Sweet, hunched Mr. Chambers smiled at her, his crooked teeth vying for space behind his wrinkled lips. He and his wife lived in the garden apartments around the corner. She had crossed paths with him so often during his frequent, shuffling strolls over the past three years, he had become a substitute grandfather to her. At times he even acted as her conscience.

"I don't mind you, darling," he said. "But what are you lathered up about?"

She waved off her behavior. Just talking with him about it would help calm her some. It was even better than talking to herself. Because of Mr. Chambers she now associated the scent of mothballs with comfort and assurance. "Betty wanted to stay late last night to work on some choreography. So I left my keys with her so she could lock up. She was supposed to open the studio this morning."

"And she's let you down."

Rachel sighed. "Yes."

He looked away, toward the traffic rushing by. He nodded, and then threw in a few extra nods for good measure. Finally he turned a serious expression on her. "Will you ever be able to forgive her?" He spoke melodramatically.

Which made her laugh out loud. This man could talk a loon off a ledge, of that she was certain. "Yes, I suppose so. Have I told you I love you, Mr. Chambers?"

"Never often enough, dear." He gave her arm a brief pat and started on his way. "You stop on by the apartment if you need to telephone Betty. Nina and I will be home."

No sooner had he taken off than a wood-paneled station wagon pulled up to the curb. The front passenger door opened, and a young boy jumped out, his face fresh and eager. The woman in the driver's seat leaned over to watch him as he ran for the studio door. He shot a polite smile at Rachel and grabbed the door handle right before she called out, "I'm sorry. We're locked out. My assistant is running late."

The boy stopped pulling on the door. "It's locked, Mom."

"Hang on, Jerry." His mother addressed Rachel while checking her rearview mirror for traffic. "I wondered why no one was answering the phone. Are you the owner?"

"Yes. I'm Rachel." She approached the car. "I can assure you this is unusual. And I think we'll still manage to start the class on time. I loaned my keys to my assistant last night—"

"Yes, that's fine. You and I spoke last week. But I'm late for my hairdresser's appointment right now."

"Oh. All right. Do you want to—"

"Can Jerry just wait here with you, you think? Would that be all right?"

Rachel looked at the boy, a well-fed adolescent with a crew cut and obvious confidence. "Is that all right with you, Jerry?"

"Sure." He turned to peer through the studio's glass door. "That would be swell." He gave his mother a quick wave, cupped his hands against the door, and examined the studio as if he were using a periscope.

Rachel shut the car door and Jerry's mother drove off.

At least this student would stick around for the duration. "How old are you, Jerry?" She sat on the bench outside the studio.

"Twelve. I start junior high in September."

"Then you're perfect for the class. Are you excited about learning ballroom dance?"

"Yeah, kind of. I mean, yes. My uncle's a really good dancer. He says the girls love it when boys can do all the fancy dances."

She smiled. Already interested in what the girls liked. "I'm glad you signed up. We never get enough boys, in my opinion."

"Well, here comes another one now." Jerry pointed down the street. "Looks like they're both coming for class too."

Rachel turned to see two kids coming her way. A boy and a girl, most definitely coming for her class. She could tell, because the girl looked thrilled and the boy looked ready to bolt, a far more typical reaction than Jerry's.

Jerry ran up to them. Apparently he never met a stranger. He immediately chatted with the boy and girl as if they were his best friends.

And the man escorting them? Well, he was, in a word, breathtaking. Dressed in a sharp suit and crisp white shirt, dark blond hair cut similar to Cary Grant's, and the kind of keen eyes so blue you could spot their color, even from this far away. Rachel quickly looked away from him, since he was probably their father. She took care with the fathers. Sometimes they had the wrong impression about dancers.

By the time the small group reached her, the three kids had bonded. They ran to the other end of the storefront, where they stood on two benches and stared through the studio windows, chatting like gossips at a beauty parlor.

The attractive man was still attractive, despite the scowl he wore. "Locked out, huh?"

"Yes, I'm afraid so. You see—"

"Exactly what I expected from this type of operation." He nodded at the empty seat beside her. "Do you mind if I sit?"

Rachel struggled to hide her reaction. She swallowed down the gasp brought on by his insult. "Be my guest. Uh, 'this type of operation'?"

He cocked his head toward the building. "The whole artsy thing. Dancing, painting, singing. Usually draws your irresponsible types."

Well he wasn't good-looking at all! As a matter of fact, he needed a shave.

"I can't say I agree with you there," she said. "Do you honestly mean to say you don't enjoy any of the arts? Is that what you're saying, Mr... ?"

"Reegan. Josh Reegan." He put out his hand and gave her a dazzling, genuine smile, and his dark-lashed eyes bordered on pretty.

How could such a stunning man be so stunningly boorish? She shook his hand. "Rachel Stanhope. But—"

"No, I don't mean to degrade all that art stuff. But to devote one's whole life to it? That requires a kind of personality I can't say I appreciate. Kind of frivolous work, don't you think?"

He had absolutely no idea who she was. And no idea what he was talking about.

"Not at all. I happen to believe life would be dull if it weren't for people like—like dancers and other artists, both professional and amateur. Imagine what the world would be like without the beauty and depth of the arts."

He granted her a nod. "I understand what you're saying. I've seen parts of the world devoid of beauty. Berlin and London just a few years ago. Still, there are—"

"You served in the war?"

"Yep. Army Air Corps."

Yes. She could see that. She could imagine him in uniform. The crisp pinks and greens. The broad shoulders. The jaw as strong as his opinions.

"And you're still in the service?"

"No. Newspaper journalist." He patted the pocket of his suit coat, from the top of which a notepad peeked. "But I'm still after the bad guys." He broke into a modest grin.

Rachel sat back on the bench and crossed her arms. "So are you a cynic because of your war experience or because of your newspaper experience?"

His smile dropped. "Cynic? I'm not a cynic. I'm a realist."

"Uh-huh." She raised an eyebrow at him. "That's what the cynics always say."

"I just think—no, I *know*—there are too many dark places and events in the world, too many greedy, heartless people, to warrant some of the more flippant ways people use time they could devote to hunting down evil."

"Wow, I'll bet you get invited to a lot of parties, huh?"

She wasn't sure how to read the look he gave her then. Part amused, part hurt, part annoyed. But she didn't feel right to study his face while she waited for him to respond, so she spoke again.

"I'm glad you're not allowing your disdain for dance to keep you from giving your kids a chance to experience it for themselves. They're just kids, after all. They probably haven't figured out yet how horrible the world really is."

"Those aren't my kids."

"Oh?"

"They're my sister's. I'm not married." He gestured toward the kids with his chin. "They seem to get along well with your boy, anyway."

Rachel frowned and glanced at the trio, who now squatted around a caterpillar as it ambled across the sidewalk.

"He's not my boy. His mother dropped him off."

Josh nodded. "Ah. So why are you here? Not that I haven't enjoyed being insulted by you."

She gave him a prim smile. "Mr. Reegan—"

"Josh."

"Josh. Yes, well, excuse me, but you don't know the first thing about being insulted. Apparently you don't even realize when you're insulting others."

A squeal of panic made them both turn their attention across the street. Rachel's errant employee Betty stood there, waiting for a break in traffic and waving her hands like a jazz performer.

"I'll be right there, Rachel! Sorry! Traffic!" She shrugged with exaggeration, as if she were on stage and needed to communicate befuddlement to the cheap seats. Then she held up a set of keys and shook them. "Don't fire me!"

Rachel squinted at Betty's perfectly upswept Lana Turner hairdo and knew her tardiness probably had less to do with traffic and more to do with a mirror and a well-used curling iron.

No matter. She was here now, and if Rachel lost any of her young students today, it wouldn't be Betty's fault.

Two more parents and their children approached the studio from opposite ends of the sidewalk. Rachel stood from the bench and called to the three kids gathered around the caterpillar.

"Okay, kids, come on in." She smiled at the parents who had just arrived. "We had a bit of a delay getting open. Betty will check your registrations while I get started with the kids."

Finally she glanced back at Josh. He, too, had stood, all six foot something of him. He stared at the ground and rubbed at that stubble on his cheek as if he could wipe it away. When he shot a look up at her, she refused to hold a gaze with those contrite eyes of blue.

True, he was a single man. Possibly he was a war hero. Certainly he was easy on the eyes. But she looked away for all of those reasons. In thirty-two years she had learned to trust her instincts. And instinct told her that Josh Reegan would cause her nothing but trouble.

CHAPTER TWO

Josh crossed the street before the group of people finished filing into the dance studio. The ninety minutes before he had to make a repeat appearance would pass far too quickly for his taste. He wished Mark and Mary could make their own way home so he didn't have to show his face at the studio again. He wasn't fond of making a fool of himself, but sometimes he seemed particularly good at it.

That woman Rachel was quite a spunky little spitfire. He was a sucker for a strawberry blond, but when she finally came clean with him, the warmth in those big brown eyes bordered on scorching. He didn't intimidate her in the slightest—that was clear. Owned her own business. Knew her mind. Stood her ground. And just sat there on that bench and fed him rope while he proceeded, ignorantly, to hang himself.

Well, didn't he mean what he said? Weren't there too many people who had become complacent about corruption around them? Who were eating, drinking, and marrying, as the Good Book says, without paying attention to the slide back toward malevolence and dishonesty in our midst? It hadn't been that long, after all, since the war and all the dark matters it involved.

He rubbed at the back of his neck. Maybe he had been wrong to throw dancing in there with eating, drinking, and marrying, but he didn't really think so.

He walked into the diner across the street from the studio and approached the counter. He caught himself enjoying the mellow voice of Nat King Cole—“Unforgettable,” the song was called—streaming from the radio behind the counter. After his rant at Rachel from his high horse, he felt hypocritical, enjoying one of the “frivolous” arts.

A middle-aged waitress in a pink uniform plunked a couple of plates in front of the only other patrons in the place, who sat at a table rather than the counter.

“There you go, gents. Holler if you need more coffee.”

She gave Josh a quick once-over and smiled with appreciation before he spoke to her.

“Miss, where’s your pay phone, please?”

She fussed with the waves in her dark hair and pointed to the back of the diner. “Right back there, handsome.” She wasted a wink on him before he walked away.

He called his editor and pulled his notebook out of his pocket.

“Sal, it’s Josh.”

He pulled the receiver away from his ear as Sal coughed like the old smoker he was.

“Reegan, where are you? I’ve been looking for you all morning.” His voice sounded like he gargled with sand.

“I called Kitty first thing and said I was going to be late today. She told you, didn’t she?” He knew Kitty would have delivered the message.

“Yeah, she told me. Where are you?”

“I’ll be there in two hours. I have some personal things to tend to this morning.”

“What kind of personal things?”

Josh rubbed his eyes. Sal never missed a chance to interfere in his business, if he could help it. “*Personal* personal things. I was there at my desk till midnight, finishing my piece on Wiley. You saw it, right?”

"That's what I want to talk to you about. Are you sure about these sources?"

"I'm sure."

"Both of them?"

"I'm sure, Sal."

"Because if you're not—"

"I am! Two distinct sources. Neither one even knows the other, and they both swear they've seen the account statements. Both gave me similar reports on them. Trust me."

More unsavory coughing from Sal. "Trust you. We're about to accuse the county treasurer of funneling a sizable portion of the board's campaign funds into his own personal account. You know Wiley has his eye on the chairman's seat. He's not one to go down easily."

"I'm ready for him, Sal. He *will* go down."

From the ensuing silence he knew Sal was weighing the risks of his decision. This piece was important to Josh. He wanted to keep scum like Wiley out of power. But a drawn-out lawsuit could ruin the paper. He wasn't about to oversell the article. He kept his mouth shut and let Sal think.

"All right. It runs in the morning."

"Terrific."

"You better be right, Reegan." He could envision Sal's wagging finger.

Once he hung up he noticed how noisy his stomach had become. He'd overslept this morning and rushed to get Mark and Mary to their class on time. The smell of bacon and other tasty fried foods still lingered from the diner's breakfast rush. Josh walked back into the dining area and took a seat at the counter.

Customers had filled two of the tables while he talked with Sal on the phone, so the waitress approached him from behind, menus in hand. She gave one to him and leaned in enough that he could smell her perfume. Jean Naté. It reminded him of his mother.

"Glad you decided to join us, hon."

He read her nametag once she circled back behind the counter. He flashed the boyish grin he usually used when he needed information from older ladies. Not flirtatious, just aw-shucks cute, as one particularly forthcoming government administrator had once tagged him.

"Can I still get breakfast here, Fran?"

Fran glanced at the clock on the wall behind her, which was odd, considering her answer. "Only twenty-four hours a day, doll."

"Great. I'll take three eggs over light with bacon, hash browns, and toast. Black coffee. Please."

"You got it." Fran jotted on her little green pad of paper and stuck his order on the aluminum ring at the pass-through window to the kitchen. She grabbed the coffeepot and sauntered back over. "I don't believe I've seen you in here, have I?" She turned his cup upright and poured his coffee. "What's your name?"

"Josh. I do live in Arlington, but no, I've never been in here." He cocked his head back to indicate the studio behind him. "I brought my niece and nephew for dance classes across the street."

Fran's entire demeanor softened. "To Rachel's summer classes? Oh, now aren't you the smart one? She's a class act, that Rachel. The kids are going to love her."

"Even the boys?" Josh grinned. "We're talking dance class here."

She snorted a little laugh and swatted at the air. "Honey, especially the boys. Did you happen to look at the girl? The boys will have crushes on her by the end of the first class." She spoke over her shoulder on the way to the coffee station. "I tell you, it's one of the cutest things I've ever seen, the way they look at her, all wide-eyed, when she steps in as their partner." Fran held her arms up as if she were dancing with someone and turned an adoring, cow-eyed face upward.

Josh didn't respond, other than to give her a polite smile. He didn't want to think about how cute and adorable Rachel might be. It just made him all that much more uncomfortable for having insulted her. He felt like a bully. And an oaf.

"Anyway, the classes weren't my idea," he said. "I'm bringing the kids to class to help their mom. My sister Bree. She just started a new job."

Fran used her chin to point at Josh's ring finger. "And you're on the market, are you?"

"Pardon?" He followed her gaze to his hand and then withdrew it and rubbed at it with his other. "Oh. Not really."

"You're married, then?"

Josh laughed. "You're not terribly shy, are you, Fran?"

Fran glanced in the direction of one of the tables. Apparently someone had summoned her. She retrieved the coffeepot again and slipped out from behind the counter. With a quick pat on his back, she spoke. "Shy never got me anywhere, Josh. I'll be back."

Josh opened the copy of the *Washington Tribune* another diner had left behind on the counter. Not that he expected to get much reading done. Fran was one of those hands-on kinds of waitresses, he could see. That was all right, though. It never hurt to develop relationships everywhere in town. In his line of work, you never knew when you'd need to make use of someone else's eyes and ears.

And despite his effort to change the subject, he couldn't deny a scintilla of interest in whatever else Fran might have to say about the "classy" dance teacher across the street.

CHAPTER THREE

Rachel lifted the needle from the record and clapped her hands, both to applaud the children and to get their attention.

"Excellent, all of you! Gracie, your posture is perfect, honey. By the end of the summer, you won't even have to think about it. And, Mark, you see, didn't I tell you the box step would become second nature before the class ended today? I saw you carrying on a conversation there with Cathy, and you didn't miss a step."

The slight, curly-haired Cathy giggled. "He wasn't talking to me. He was counting out loud."

Rachel smiled at Mark after he rolled his eyes. "All of you should be counting out loud at this stage of the game."

Three boys and five girls composed her summer class so far, and she knew at least two more would join them when they returned from their summer vacation. This children's class had been a good idea, after all. If any of their parents decided to sign up for lessons, she might be able to consider hiring another instructor to help Betty and her. Her other two employees, Mel and his wife Connie, worked full-time jobs during the day and taught several evenings a week for Rachel. That kind of growth was exactly what she needed to keep the bank happy.

"All right, your parents will be here any minute. Let's make sure they walk in and see how much you've already learned." She moved one of the boys away from his partner and stationed him in front of another girl. "I want the boys to change partners, and the rest of you girls..." She wiggled her eyebrows at them as she assumed the woman's beginning position along with them. "Imagine Prince Charming is leading you. And what dance begins with this step, the box step?"

"The watts!" Jerry, her gregarious first pupil of the day, called out the answer.

Rachel smiled. "Waltz. The waltz." She gave a nod to Betty, who set the needle back onto the record. Irving Berlin's "Always" filled the room. Betty lifted her arms to an imaginary partner and waited for Rachel's count to begin.

"And, *one* two three, *one* two three."

Once the kids got into a confident rhythm, Rachel broke out of the pattern and moved from dancer to dancer, coaching their posture and steps. From the corner of her eye, she noticed parents trickling back into the studio.

And she wasn't the only one who noticed. Eventually each of the children glanced over at the front door, and in some cases, the distraction of a parent's presence in the studio threw off the footing Rachel taught them. But to the last child, they all refocused on their steps and concentrated with renewed pride at having mastered something their parents might appreciate. Even Mark straightened his posture and supported his partner's arm precisely as taught when his uncle Josh stepped in among the crowd of parents.

At Josh's return Rachel shocked herself with her reaction. She glanced at him, met his eyes for less than a second, and a rush of heat flared over her so quickly, she had to deliberately stop walking amid the children to figure out what was going on inside of her. Embarrassment, yes. But why? Was it because he was so attractive, yet so annoying? Was she fighting his appeal?

No. That wasn't it.

When she realized why she was flushed, she could have stomped out her frustration with herself, she was so incensed.

She cared. She cared what this total stranger thought of her profession. She wasn't just embarrassed. She was nervous. And there didn't seem to be a thing she could do about it. It made her angry as a hornet toward him. She returned to guiding her students, and she danced beside one little couple so they could follow her. But she got so caught up in trying to think of snappy comebacks to any insults Josh might throw her way, she kept dancing well after the music stopped. Betty clapped into the awkward silence and brought Rachel out of her reverie.

Startled, she clapped her hands together, too, so quickly and loudly she looked as if she were trying to kill a bug in flight. "Oh! Yes. All right, good class."

The students headed toward their parents.

She finally got a hold of her wits. "Hang on, students. Another rule in class is to remain on the floor until you're dismissed."

Her students halted where they were.

"You've all done beautifully today. Don't leave without taking the sheet Betty has for you, showing the box step we learned today. I'd like you to practice before our next class so you don't forget what you know. We're going to add turns to the steps next, so stay on top of this. You're going to love it. Oh, and tell your friends to come! The more the merrier."

She looked at the group of parents but avoided direct eye contact with Josh. "Parents, feel free to stay and ask any questions you might have. Remember, we have adult classes too." She smiled at her students. "Class dismissed."

The fact that her students didn't madly dash out of her studio as if it were a torture chamber gave Rachel confidence. A few of the parents lingered to chat and ask questions about their child's capabilities. A few even asked about adult classes. When she finished speaking with them, she realized Josh had stayed behind, as well.

His sheepish grin bolstered Rachel's poise. "Yes, Mr. Reegan?"

"Yeah, listen, I'm sorry." He jerked his thumb over his shoulder, as if gesturing to a past point in time. "That wasn't very nice, what I said before. I wouldn't have said it if I had known this was *your* dance hall."

"We call it a studio."

"Right. Your studio."

"So you're sorry you didn't know to keep your opinion to yourself, is that what you're saying?"

"Well, yes," he said. "I guess that's what I'm saying."

"But your low opinion remains, regardless."

"Oh." He looked around the studio. He appeared to be seeking his response from some corner of the empty room.

"Never mind, Mr. Reegan. Your opinion doesn't matter to me." For the life of her, she couldn't figure out why that wasn't true. And now she had lied, on top of struggling with possibly the most ridiculous pride she had ever experienced.

She walked away from him and chose to ignore how good he smelled. Like fresh soap and expensive aftershave—but she barely noticed, really. She joined Betty at the front desk. She smiled at Mary and Mark and shuffled papers that didn't need shuffling. "You both did so well today. Mary, you have what I'd call natural grace. And Mark, your stance is nice and straight. You look as strong as a soldier out there on the floor."

Mark grinned. "Like a fighter pilot?"

"Yes, okay." She chuckled. "Like a fighter pilot."

"Like Uncle Josh!"

She stopped straightening the pile of papers. She had been horrible and snippy with a former fighter pilot. An American hero, as she had suspected. Couldn't she cut him some slack, as her father would say? Plenty of men had rigid views about artistic endeavors. They just didn't spout off about them right in front of the artists themselves. Wasn't her own father hovering over her shoulder about this enterprise, just waiting for it to fail? True, he didn't *say* that, but she could tell by the worry in his eyes. Yet she still loved him—she did much of what she did for him—for his approval.

Josh approached the kids. Rachel heaved a sigh and made ready to apologize to him for being so rude. "Look, I'm—"

"Okay, kids, let's get out of your teacher's hair." He wasn't even looking at her. Wasn't aware she had even been impolite, from the looks of it, or that she was prepared to smooth things over. He didn't even notice "things" needed smoothing. "There's a really nice lady at the diner across the street. I need to get to the office, but first let's go see what she has for you for lunch, what do you say?"

"Yeah, I'm starving! Woo hoo!" Mark ran for the front door. Mary followed him but turned at the last minute to face Rachel.

"I liked class, Miss Stanhope. A lot."

Rachel returned her smile. "Wonderful, Mary. Practice before our next class. I'll see you then."

She forced herself to look at Josh and was relieved when he gave her a simple nod. "See you at the next class, Miss Stanhope."

"Yes. Good-bye."

He stepped away but pivoted back, a sardonic smile sparking a twinkle in his eyes. "Oh, and thanks for the apology."

Rachel frowned. "I didn't apologize."

"Yeah, I know." He gestured toward her face as if he were drawing a circle around it with his finger. "But I could see you were going to, and it looked downright painful, coming up. Thought I'd spare you the anguish."

She gasped, indignant. She could have stomped her foot, he annoyed her so much.

But she wasn't about to let him see that. The stupid man was surprisingly good at reading faces, apparently, so she turned her back and made herself busy at the filing cabinet. She heard the bell over the door ring, and she braved a glance to watch him walk out the door.

He turned, too, and gave her a wink before he closed the door behind himself.

She huffed out a breath of irritation and darted her eyes away in an effort to pretend she didn't see him. Typical pilot. Too cocky for his own good.

What annoyed her most was her inability to keep a small smile from sprouting, no matter how hard she tried to scowl.

CHAPTER FOUR

Two days later Josh strolled into the office, still expecting to bask in the accolades about his breaking story in yesterday's issue. His exposé on that crook Wiley had caused quite a stir. He already had most of a follow-up story ready for tonight's filing, chronicling the angry reaction of local constituents and Wiley's colleagues. Wiley himself had failed to return Josh's calls, but he'd have to respond sooner or later.

The smoke was thick in the office this morning. The reek of cigarettes was always worse on the news floor, especially as deadlines approached. What was it about reporters and their smokes?

Not Josh. His father had died of emphysema, and the doctors suspected his smoking had something to do with it. Even though his dad didn't quit after his diagnosis, he ranted against cigarettes throughout Josh's youth, even more so when Josh enlisted and left home. And his mom constantly claimed the good Lord expected us to treat our "temples" better than that. So he had remained a non-smoker, but he was one of the few here at the *Tribune*.

As he approached his desk, he could tell by the cautious glances of those he passed that something was afoot. The pounding of typewriters diminished. His assistant, Sheila, handed him a cup of coffee before he even sat down.

"You might as well take this and head right over to Sal's office, Josh. The sooner the better, from what I gather."

"What's the problem?" He took a long, hot drink from the cup and set it on his desk.

Sheila shrugged. "I don't know. But it was mighty loud in there a little while ago, and your name rose to the surface more than once. Kitty just said to get you over there the minute you walked in. So shoo."

Well, that didn't sound good. He grabbed a pad of paper and headed to Sal's office, aware of the stealthy turn of curious heads in his wake.

Although Sal's door was closed, the walls of his office were glass. Josh saw him on the phone, looking far less upbeat than he had yesterday. In fact, he looked especially disheveled and stressed, even more so than usual.

Sal's secretary Kitty stood when Josh caught her eye. "Oh, good. He's been—"

"Reegan, get in here!"

Josh winced. He felt bad for whoever was on the other end of that phone—Sal yelled loudly enough for everyone in the newsroom to hear. But he felt bad for himself as well. Sal certainly wasn't calling him in to pat him on the back.

"What's the matter?" He closed the door behind himself, as if that would do any good. "And I'm right here, Sal. I can hear you just fine."

"Can you? You sure? 'Cuz I don't know if you heard me so good when I told you we had to be 100 percent certain on this Wiley story." Sal erupted in a phlegmy coughing fit that prompted a moment's silence on Josh's part.

Josh crossed his arms. "I heard you loud and clear. What's going on?"

"His attorneys are talking libel, that's what's going on. This paper can't take another—"

"Relax. You know I don't do things halfway. And you can't be surprised that Wiley would take a crack at bluffing about a libel suit. What's he asking for, a retraction?"

Sal hung up the phone—just hung right up on whoever was on the other end of the line. He picked up the stogie in his ashtray but set it back down when he realized it had gone out. "Says if we don't print a front-page retraction in tomorrow's morning edition, they're filing first thing." He paced toward the filmy window and stared blankly outside.

"So let them."

Sal swung around. "You're pretty free and easy with the paper's resources and reputation, there, Reegan."

"I'm just certain of my sources. If I need to produce them, I will."

"You need to produce them." Sal lowered his head and studied him over his reading glasses.

Josh approached Sal's desk and sat on the edge. "I don't want to ask them to come forward unless we absolutely have to."

"You just make sure they know they might have to testify. Or at least make themselves known." Sal pointed a fat finger at him. "Call them. Today. If we can't get guarantees from both of them, we have to print a retraction tomorrow. And I don't know if your career can handle that. Not at this paper, anyway."

Josh swallowed. Sal had threatened him like this before without following through. But it never felt good. He worked to sound nonchalant. "Don't sweat it, Sal. I'll make some calls today."

He walked out of the office, unable to close the door before Sal hollered loudly enough for everyone to hear. "I want answers by three this afternoon."

Of course he didn't even make it back to his desk before a few of his colleagues commented, most of them in a tone of commiseration. Except for his nemesis, Don Stevens, who took his usual adversarial stance with regard to him.

"Looks like you might have been a little overeager on this one, eh, Reegan?"

Josh shrugged off the comment. "You know how it is, Donny. The never-ending battle for truth, justice, and the American way." Then he squinted at Stevens, as if he had just remembered who he was speaking to. "Oh. That's right. You don't know much about that kind of thing, do you?"

Those within hearing chuckled, but the comment struck a nerve in Stevens. "Hey, you're no Superman. And if you're talking about the service, I would have enlisted in a second if it wasn't for my inner ear problem—"

"This again?" Lil Reynolds, the one female reporter on the floor, happened by and interjected reason before things heated up. "Give it a rest, will ya, boys?"

Josh gave her a grin and headed for his desk. He ignored whatever Stevens's next whine-tinged comment was, as did everyone else.

Sheila had already set a fresh cup of coffee on his desk. "Bad?"

"I think it'll be okay." He picked up the phone receiver and flipped his card file to Herman Northrop's card. He pulled it out and handed the card file to Sheila and lowered his voice. "Do me a favor and get Candy Friskin's number out for me, if you don't mind."

Herman answered after two rings, his tone clipped and wary. "What is it now?"

"Herman? It's Josh Reegan from the *Tribune*. You got a second?"

"Josh!" Northrop's attitude changed immediately. "How are you, buddy? I've been meaning to call you about the article. Great job. That'll put the dog in his proper place."

Josh smiled. This was the attitude he hoped for. "That's what I'm calling about, Herman. The dog is biting back. I want to make sure you're still willing to come forward if it comes down to it."

"How do you mean?"

"Wiley's threatening a libel suit against the *Tribune* if we don't retract the story."

"Oh, no, you can't do that. That snake can't get away with this."

Dog. Snake. Certainly there was no love lost between Northrop and his former business partner. In fact, Northrop had been the one to put the bug for the story in Josh's ear with a phone call reporting Wiley's corrupt practices since taking office.

"He won't get away with anything, as long as you're willing to testify if we need you to."

"You can count on it. Wiley knows where you got this info, Josh. I've got nothing to hide. Or fear."

Josh finished the call with a lift in his spirit. This was exactly why he became a reporter. To ferret out the bad guys, one crook at a time.

Now if Candy Friskin would be as cooperative, he'd be sitting pretty. Candy had something a bit different than justice in mind when she agreed to talk about Wiley's second set of books. She had invested the last five years of her life in a personal relationship with Wiley, only to have him dump her for a more socially connected girlfriend when he ran for office. And Candy was no cupcake. The girl knew crooked books when she saw them, and her head for figures—and her desire for vengeance—had proven helpful in Josh's research for his article.

But when Sheila placed the call to Candy for him, he hit his first snag. Her roommate Mitzy answered and asked to speak with him.

"Yeah, Josh, I think I got some bad news for you. Candy took off."

"What do you mean, she took off? For how long?" He broke out in a cold sweat.

"That's just the thing. I don't know. She was pretty tore up, you know, about that dirtbag Teddy."

That was Ted Wiley, the very snake in question.

"Yeah? And?"

"But after she talked with you, he came by. Did some sweet talking with her."

Oh, no. "Where is she, Mitzy?"

"I don't know."

"Mitzy, please."

"I ain't lying, Josh. I don't think he wanted her to tell me."

"He who? Wiley? He sent her away?"

"I think so. She called and told me she was okay, but she wouldn't tell me where she was. I think she was kinda embarrassed, to tell you the truth. You know, that she was caving in like that. He's got some kinda emotional hold on her."

Josh looked up and saw Sheila watching him. He closed his eyes and shook his head, walked around to his chair, and slumped into it. "Listen, Mitzy. This could mean my job, let alone the fact that this creep could get away with stealing from the county coffers."

"I swear, Josh, if I knew, I'd tell you. I think the guy's bad news for her."

He sighed. "Will you see what you can find out, Mitzy? Call me right away if you hear from her? If she calls you, get whatever you can from her. A phone number. An address. Anything."

"I will. I promise. I'm—I'm sorry, Josh."

He nodded. "Yeah. Thanks."

He hung up and met eyes with his secretary. He let out a long, resigned breath. "It's been nice working with you, Sheila."

CHAPTER FIVE

"These Sunday dinners are always a mixed bag for me," Rachel muttered to her sister-in-law Karen while they sauntered up her parents' red-brick front walk. She was blessed that both of her brothers had married women she loved. They were the sisters she had wanted all her young life.

The June evening was still bright and uncharacteristically dry for Northern Virginia. Rachel noticed just enough of a warm breeze to carry the heady scent of her mother's roses from the trellis against the side of the house.

She had arrived moments before both of her brothers and their wives did. By the time she maneuvered her chocolate raspberry cake out from the back of her car, everyone had disembarked, their arms loaded with casserole dishes, Jell-O molds, and breadbaskets.

Her oldest brother Todd, his wife Suzanna, and their twin toddlers were the most manic of the bunch. Todd suddenly grabbed their younger brother Chuck in a one-armed bear hug, and Suzanna chased their toddlers as if one moment out of her sight meant certain catastrophe. To her credit, she prevented little Aaron from trampling over his grandma's tulips near the front porch. The twins were the only grandchildren so far, and Rachel would be glad when they were a little older and less erratic.

"A mixed bag?" Karen dropped her car keys into her purse. "Oh, come on, Rachel, it's only once a month. You can struggle through one day out of thirty, can't you?"

"It's not a struggle, that's not it."

Three-year-old Amanda ran directly in front of them and halted. Rachel and Karen followed suit, creating a three-way standoff. Amanda pushed her adorable little glasses up the bridge of her nose and stared up at Rachel as if she were not quite a normal human being.

Rachel smiled. "Uh, hi, Amanda! How are you?"

Amanda remained quiet long enough that Karen intervened. "Amanda? Honey?" She spoke as if she were trying to snap a catatonic patient from a trance.

The toddler shot her focus to Karen. "Hi, Aunt Karen." She grabbed Karen's leg for a brief hug and ran off, prompting Suzanna to bark out more orders and go back into corralling mode.

"Amanda! Come on. Inside, sweetie."

Rachel's sigh expressed frustration rather than relief. She watched as Amanda ran up the porch steps to Grandma's house. "See, that's one problem with family gatherings. Kids hate me."

"What are you talking about?" Karen pointed at the twins. "*They're* the only ones who hate you."

Rachel gave her a dirty look and Karen laughed.

"They don't hate you, silly. Anyway, I thought you said that dance class for kids you started at the studio was going to be one of your favorites."

"Oh, those kids? They're not really kids. Twelve, thirteen, they're like little grown-ups by that age. But toddlers are weird. They're unpredictable and hard to communicate with. And they're gooey."

Karen bumped her shoulder against Rachel's. "Sounds like it's *you* who doesn't like *them*, not the other way around."

"Yeah, well, they started it." She broke into a smile, despite her cynicism. "You and Chuck don't seem to be in much of a rush in that area."

Karen shrugged. "If God wants it to happen, it's going to happen. But no, we're not in a rush."

The front door burst open. Both of Rachel's parents gushed out.

"I thought you'd never get here," her mother said. In seconds she had a toddler wrapped around each of her legs. Her enthusiasm drew everyone's attention. "And here you all arrive at once. It's like a party!"

Rachel's smile mirrored her mom's. This was one of the items on the positive side of these Sunday dinners. Her mother was the most optimistic woman she had ever known. She energized Rachel whenever they got together. Had it not been for her mother's constant encouragement and hopefulness, Rachel would never have attempted to establish her dance studio. Especially had she listened more closely to her father.

And it was her father who planted a big, whiskery kiss on Rachel's cheek and took hold of her chocolate cake before dashing back inside.

"Hey!" Rachel yelled at his back. "I'll know if you sample any of that frosting, Dad."

He shot a silly, crazed look over his shoulder.

Karen laughed and leaned closer to Rachel. "So where's the mixed bag? I'd kill for parents like yours."

But Rachel didn't get a chance to respond. Her brother Chuck ran up to them, stood between them, and draped his arms across their shoulders. The traces of cigarette smoke in his clothing interfered with the yummy scent of the fried onion and green bean dish Karen carried. After he planted a kiss on his wife's head, he turned his attention to Rachel.

"So who's this newspaper reporter Karen tells me about? Do I need to go bloody his nose for insulting my baby sis?"

Both Rachel and Karen gasped.

"Karen!" Rachel said. "I told you not to say anything."

Karen tried to smack at Chuck, but she held the casserole in one hand and couldn't reach him with the other. "Charles Stanhope! I told *you* not to say anything."

Chuck squeezed them both as they tried to wiggle out of his grip. "Then I'll say no more." He whispered dramatically in Rachel's ear "But Karen thinks you like the guy, so Todd and I are going to have to swing by the studio and check him out."

With that, he released them, took the casserole from Karen, and stood aside for them to enter the house.

"*That's* the kind of thing I dread about these dinners." Rachel scowled, but neither she nor Karen could keep from smiling, really. Still, she gave Karen a little slap on the arm. "And what are you doing, telling him about that guy—"

"Josh. You said his name was Josh."

"Yeah, so? I didn't say I liked him. I said he was arrogant and insulting."

"And a former fighter pilot and attractive."

"I didn't tell you he was attractive."

"But he is, isn't he? I could tell by the way your face looked when you talked about him."

"Karen. We were on the phone. How could you—"

"Like that." Karen pointed at her face. "I'm sure you looked like that. Flushed, bothered, and stirred up."

Rachel sighed and gave Karen a sideways glare. "I don't know the man. And I don't want to talk about him. Especially not here."

Suzanna joined them. She held Aaron in her arms, and he was already gooey. As a matter of fact, he had something on his face suspiciously similar to the frosting on Rachel's chocolate raspberry cake.

"So," Suzanna said, "who's this newspaper reporter Chuck and Todd are talking about?"

Rachel groaned and dashed to intervene before they had a chance to say anything to her parents. She should have known better than to even mention the man.

So why had she?

*****

Dinner involved enough talk about other matters to keep them from coming back to the subject of Josh Reegan. Both Chuck and Todd promised not to say anything about him to their parents, especially after she assured them there was no interest in him on her part.

She managed to relax, until her father turned the conversation around to the studio.

"How's business going, sweetheart? Picking up?"

"Yeah, actually it is. I just started a summer class for kids that's really taken off, and I almost have enough adult clients to hire another daytime teacher."

"Are you managing to save money at all? It's important for you to have something to fall back on if the business fails."

"Walt, leave the girl alone." Her mother's gentle voice was far more effective with her dad than her own exasperated tone could ever be. "She just finished telling you how the business is growing, and you're talking about it failing."

"I know, I know." He looked annoyed with himself. He really didn't seem to be able to help thinking that way when it came to her. He didn't seem to worry like this with his sons. "Don't let me bother you, cookie. I'm just an old worrywart."

Rachel smiled at him. "Don't worry about me, Dad. I'll always land on my feet."

She decided not to mention that the bank had called to caution her about her last mortgage payment being several days late. Nor did she mention the banker's request that she stop by tomorrow morning to meet with him. She honestly *did* think the business was picking up.

"I just don't want you getting hurt again. Over anything." His expression darkened. "Or anyone."

She wasn't sure how everyone else filled the silence that followed that comment, but she most definitely thought about—

"Bill Nawta asked about you the other day."

Yep, that was who had come to mind, and Chuck just put voice to the thought. No doubt everyone but the toddlers had remembered the same person.

"Not interested," Rachel said, a polite smile on her face.

"Yeah." Karen frowned at her husband. "Why would you even bring him up, honey? I'd just as soon you not have anything to do with him anymore."

Rachel stood and gathered empty plates from the table. "No, that's all right. You two were friends long before he and I got involved. Just because he…lost interest in me doesn't mean you have to shun him. That's childish."

"Lost interest in you?" Karen shook her head. "The jerk completely let you down and publicly humiliated you. I know *I* haven't forgiven him."

"I just don't want to hear about him, if you don't mind." Rachel's hands were full, which prompted her mother to stand and collect dishes as well.

"How about coffee?" Her mother had a way of punctuating awkward moments and moving everyone on to more comfortable ones. "And some of Rachel's gorgeous cake. Come on, honey, I'll serve it with you."

Rachel heard Karen quietly chastise Chuck again as she left the room.

"What's the matter with you? Consider your sister's feelings before you speak once in a while, will you?"

While she and her mom got the coffee and cake ready, Rachel could feel her mother's cautious gaze alight on her.

"Don't worry, Mom. I'm all right. It's been a few months, and I've honestly gotten over Billy and that whole horrible night."

Her mother set down the creamer and approached her. She was a nuanced hugger. This situation didn't call for a strong, dramatic, tear-provoking hug. Instead, the embrace she gave her carried her soft Lanvin scent and practically poured strength right into her. "I'm sure that's true, honey. I had to get over a breakup like yours when I was around your age."

Rachel pulled back. "Really? Someone before Dad?"

Laughter. "Of course before him." She placed dessert plates and a silver cake knife on the counter. "I don't think of that fellow often, but the few times I have, I've thanked God for the temporary heartache that prevented a terribly wrong choice of husband."

"Wow. You almost married someone else? You never told me that before."

"There wasn't a good reason to mention it before today. I could have mentioned it right after Bill…um…"

"Dropped the bomb on me? Left me stranded in front of hundreds?"

"All right, yes. But, despite your pain, you weren't ready to hear that he wasn't right for you. Not until now." Her mother tilted her head to look more obviously into her eyes. "At least, you seem ready to hear it now."

Rachel nodded. "Yeah. I've chosen to see this point in my life as the time to concentrate on my business. I'll leave the romance for later." She barely muttered, "If ever."

Mom picked up several coffee cups and headed toward the dining room. “Sometimes that’s exactly when it comes along. When you’re not looking for it.”

Well, then, there was a very good chance it would come along, as far as Rachel was concerned. Romance was the last thing on her mind.

Of course, her next thought was that she might come across a certain brash newspaper reporter tomorrow at the kids’ class. The irony was not lost on her.

CHAPTER SIX

As banker Harper Longworth had requested, Rachel arrived at the Arlington Bank and Trust promptly at eight the next morning. The bank boasted few customers this early. Rachel's clicking heels echoed sharply off the marble floor until she reached the richly carpeted area outside Longworth's office.

Her first Monday ballroom class—the junior high class—didn't begin until ten o'clock, but she still fought against nerves about this appointment. She would have been less nervous had Mr. Longworth been more forthcoming about the nature of the meeting, as well as how long he needed her to be available.

The prim, tight-bunned woman seated at the desk outside his office didn't help matters any. She wasn't unfriendly, but she wasn't the warmest gal she'd ever met either. Her poker face certainly gave nothing away about Rachel's purpose here. Rachel had never been called to the principal's office as a student, but now she knew what it felt like to be summoned by a powerful authority figure. She didn't like it.

Miss Tight-Bun promptly lifted her phone receiver when the intercom beeped. "Yes, Mr. Longworth? Yes. Indeed, sir." She hung up, stood, and walked briskly to Rachel before addressing her. "Mr. Longworth will see you now, Miss Stanhope."

She turned with the precision of a silent drill team member, and Rachel quickly followed.

Mr. Longworth's office smelled of cherry pipe tobacco. He rose from his desk the moment she walked in. His features were easier to read than his secretary's, but she wasn't sure she liked what she read. She saw concern in his eyes. Was he about to yank her mortgage out from under her? She had only been late with her payment that one time, and even then, by mere days. Surely he could give her another chance to prove the financial value of her dance studio, couldn't he?

"Thank you, Mrs. Prinkle. That's all for now."

Once they shook hands and were left alone, he gestured for her to sit. He studied her a moment before he went back behind his desk. The silence while he performed these uneventful tasks was about to drive her insane.

"Miss Stanhope, I wanted to talk to you about the mortgage on your studio. I'm afraid—"

"I'm confident I won't be late with any future payments, Mr. Longworth. That one time was—"

He held up his hand to stop her. "You're not in trouble, dear. Please take a moment to relax."

Relax? Was he kidding?

"Those are comforting words," she said, "but I'm not about to relax while seated across from the man able to destroy my business. Not until I know what you want."

They stared at one another.

What was she thinking? "I—I mean…"

Longworth leaned back in his chair and laughed. "I have to say I wasn't expecting that kind of spunk out of you, young lady."

"Me either!" She laughed, too, but hers was more a shocked reaction than an amused one. "I'm sorry. I didn't mean to be disrespectful."

He shook his head. "You weren't disrespectful. Just frank. And I like that. All right, listen. Here's my idea."

He reached into his back pocket and removed a black eel-skin wallet. He pulled out a dog-eared photograph and placed it on the desk in front of her. She picked it up and eyed the slim, gawky girl who looked back at the camera, her black leotard and pink tutu overwhelming her shapeless figure.

"That's my daughter Mira."

Oh, so that was it. He simply wanted Rachel to teach his daughter some of the finer points of ballroom dance. If Mira had studied ballet, she wouldn't yet have learned the kind of dances Rachel taught.

"You want me to take her on as a student?"

His bushy eyebrows rose and held. "I want you to take her on as a teacher." He raised his pipe to his lips and relit it.

A teacher? Uh-oh. This was bad. Rachel focused on the photograph and wondered exactly how much power Longworth had over her mortgage. Was she going to need a lawyer? This sounded a little like it was headed in the direction of extortion.

"A teacher? But Mr. Longworth, I don't hire kids. I only have adults teaching for me."

He reached over and gently retrieved the photograph from her grip.

"Mira's just turned twenty-three." He held the picture up. "This is a few years old."

"Yes, but that's not the only requirement for my teachers. If she doesn't know ballroom dance—"

"She's been taking lessons the whole time she's been away at college."

"Is—is she any good? I hate to ask so bluntly, but she really has to know her way around a dance floor, and she has to know how to break down the dances and teach them to people who—"

He waved at her comment as if it were smoke. "I don't know if she's any good. That's for you to figure out. I just know she wants to teach, and I thought we might work something out."

Rachel sat back in her chair. She didn't know whether or not he could see she was wringing her hands. "Work something out? Mr. Longworth, this is my business. My livelihood. I've worked hard to get where I am, and I take my work and my studio's reputation very seriously."

He leaned in. "What would you do to enhance your business, if you had the wherewithal?"

"The financial wherewithal, you mean?"

"I do."

She didn't even have to think about this one.

"I'd advertise more than I've been able to do so far. I'd hold some free classes to hook future students. I'd spend more time cultivating teachers who could enter competitions on behalf of the studio. I'd invest in the studio's participation and in providing transportation—like buses—for our supporters to attend those competitions. Win or not, contests can bring name recognition to a studio and always result in a boost in interest and business. I'd also schedule more classes so the calendar would be convenient to more prospective students."

"Sounds to me like you'd need to hire some teachers."

She looked him in the eye and sighed. "I would. But not just any teachers, Mr. Longworth. I don't know whether your daughter would qualify."

"So give her a chance and then you'll know."

Neither spoke for a moment. Finally Rachel said, "What are you proposing?"

He rested his pipe in his hands and studied it before he spoke, as if his proposition were resting there as well. "You give Mira an audition, and I'll cover your next mortgage payment."

She couldn't help herself. She gasped. She tried to cover her reaction by coughing, but she doubted he was fooled.

He wasn't done, either.

"You hire her—I'm not asking you to hire her if she's not qualified—but you hire her, and I'll cover another six months' mortgage payments, to free up some of your business income for some of those investments you just outlined."

"Is that legal?"

He laughed. "I'm talking about my own money, Miss Stanhope, not the bank's. If I want to pay your mortgage, I'm allowed. You just have to say yes."

Rachel had to think. Seven months, mortgage free? She could definitely turn the studio into a going concern with that kind of capital. But did she want Mr. Longworth breathing down her neck for seven months?

He apparently saw her hesitation as something to overcome by sweetening the offer.

"And you say merely competing in those dance contests helps bring in business?"

"Yes. They're like advertisements. People get excited about the idea of dancing as beautifully as the competitors."

"Uh-huh. All right, so if you *do* hire my Mira and you train her well enough that she can compete for you, I'll cover another three months. If she wins? Six more, still."

He toked on his pipe and eyed her through a swirl of smoke.

Rachel had lost track of how many months total he had offered. She tried to review every step he described—

"That's a possible sixteen months, mortgage-free." She saw the twinkle in his eyes. No aspect of this offer had been as off-the-cuff as he made it sound. "Maybe none of these things will pan out, but I'm interested in investing in my daughter."

"But that's quite a lot of money for...well, for not very much return to you, frankly."

"Let me explain something to you, Miss Stanhope. My girl could have relied on my position and financial status when she applied to schools five years ago. Instead she worked hard to gain enough academic scholarships to pay nearly all of her college expenses. *And* she worked for much of the time she was away. I think it's time I gave her a foot up, so to speak."

He put his pipe in his mouth and pulled it back out to gesture at her with it.

"Furthermore, I'm actually comfortable investing in you. I don't expect anything but what I've outlined so far. But maybe you and I will want to do business together in the future. Maybe you'll decide to expand. Open additional studios. Maybe I'll want to get in on that."

The man was quite the motivator.

"And you? The worst you could do is get one month's mortgage paid, just for interviewing my girl, even if you turn her down. So what do you say, Miss Stanhope?"

Rachel's heart raced over the possibilities. She stood and put out her hand. "I say please call me Rachel, Mr. Longworth. You've got a deal."

CHAPTER SEVEN

Monday morning Josh's sister Bree answered the door in her typical rushed manner. She gave her brother a quick peck on the cheek. "Oh, good. You're earlier than last week." And just like that, she dashed upstairs while she fastened an earring.

"Good morning to you too." Josh headed into the kitchen and got more attentive greetings from Mary and Mark. They sat at the kitchen table, finishing cereal and orange juice, as he expected. But he was surprised to see his mother at the sink. She seemed intent on scraping a pan that must have been there since the night before.

"What are you doing here, Mom? Did Bree think I'd forget about the kids' dancing class?"

"Ah, Josh!" She turned her head and stuck out her lips, a kiss waiting for her son's cheek.

He bridged the distance and took the kiss. "Morning." She looked fresh and well rested, ready to take on a day's worth of activities. He gave her shoulders a gentle squeeze. "Did you stay the night or something?"

"No, I—"

"Mom asked Grandma to come by this morning in case you didn't make it." Mark was happy to fill in the blanks.

"She said you just had a lot going on at work, honey." His mom seemed to think he'd take offense at Bree's backup plan. "I have a wash-and-set appointment in town anyway, so I offered to be here just in case."

"Yeah." Josh sighed. "Lots going on." Like getting demoted to the Style and Leisure section of the paper and seeking insipid human interest stories to fill space. Granted, he had kept his job, thanks to Sal. And he knew there were plenty of struggling journalists who would love to write for any section of the *Tribune*. But he had worked hard to attain the position he held before Wiley managed to pull the rug out from under him. Wiley's success in convincing Candy to disappear had been more sly than Josh expected—she seemed so ready to get back at Wiley when she spoke with Josh earlier. What had Wiley promised her to get her to give in like this?

"Can I get you some toast or something, Josh?" His mother had already grabbed a loaf of raisin bread and awaited the word from him.

He raised his hand. "No thanks, Mom. I'm going to grab a bite at the diner across from the dance hall—"

"*Studio*, Uncle Josh!" Mary's voice overflowed with frustrated indignation.

"Studio!" He and his mother exchanged smiles. "I'll get a little writing done and have breakfast across from the studio. It makes more sense than my going into the office and coming back for them." He smiled at the kids. "I'm ready whenever you two are."

They both pushed away from the table. Their grandmother took their dishes from them.

"Thanks, Grandma." The kids spoke simultaneously.

She looked back at him before she brought the bowls to the sink. "You've been a great help to Bree with this, Josh. I know she wouldn't have signed the kids up if she had known Peter had to be out of town these few weeks."

"Yeah, thanks, Uncle Josh." Mary still seemed more appreciative of the chance to dance than Mark did.

Bree dashed into the kitchen. "Kisses, kisses!" She ran from Mary to Mark to her mother. "Hey, kids, go upstairs and brush your teeth before you go, okay?"

She gave her watch a quick glance before flashing a smile at Josh. "Thanks, big brother. You saved my life. Again. Pete gets back from his business trip on Wednesday, so I won't have to lean on you so much next week."

He walked out of the house with her, which prompted her to watch him over her shoulder as she approached the driveway.

"Where are you going? You're going to take the kids to class, right?"

"Yeah. I'm happy to. I, uh, just wanted to let you know I don't mind taking them next week either. It's no trouble. I know it's easier for Pete to be able to go into the store early."

He was certain he heard a snort of laughter from his sister before she got into her Plymouth. The moment she rolled down the window, he frowned. "Something funny?"

Bree lifted her brows and widened her eyes. "Hmm? Funny? No, not at all. That's sweet of you, Josh. I'll mention it to Pete. I'm sure he wouldn't mind driving them, though. Especially after his son has a little chat with him about the teacher."

Josh tilted his head. "The teacher?"

"Yeah." Bree started the car and swiftly turned down the Sinatra blaring from the radio. "My son is twelve, going on twenty-one, apparently. He says Miss Stanhope is a 'real doll.' Mary concurs. Oh, and she thinks Miss Stanhope can't stand you."

"What?" He straightened, arms akimbo, and scowled for an instant before Bree's laughter made him laugh too. "Can't stand me? I don't know what Mary's talking about. I just didn't get off on very sure footing with her at first, but I think we're fine now."

Bree's teasing expression had already softened to something more affectionate. "Good. Really, Josh, we'd all like to see you focus on something besides all that serious, hardboiled political stuff once in a while. Your life is way too serious."

He glanced over his shoulder toward the house and then rested his hands against Bree's car door.

"Then you'll be relieved to hear I've been sacked at the *Tribune*."

Bree gasped. "Josh! What happened? Sacked?"

"Shh. I don't want Mom to hear and get all worried. I haven't actually lost my job. But I messed up with the sources on one of my stories—"

"That crook in the treasury?"

He nodded. "We had to print a retraction. Not good. Rather than firing me, Sal moved me to an opening in Style and Leisure."

"Oh. Well that's not so bad, is it? At least you still have a job, right?"

"Yeah. And now I'll get to write as many fluff pieces as I want. It's only been a couple of days, but I can already feel myself drawn to poodle parlors and pie eating contests everywhere. I can't wait to make my impact on the world." He heard the bitterness creeping into his tone. He straightened and tapped on Bree's car. "Sorry. I'm making you late for work. I'll talk with you later."

Bree nodded, her expression concerned. "Okay. Hey, you never know, Josh. There might be some kind of blessing in this. You don't have to work in a dark environment to make an impact on the world."

She backed out and he gave her a wave good-bye. He shook off the self-pity and marched back into the house, feigning excitement.

"Let's go, ballroom dancers! We're going to be late, and we don't want to make Miss Stanhope mad!"

It wasn't until they had nearly reached the studio that Josh noticed his mood truly had lightened at the thought of stirring up a little trouble—a little fun—with Miss Stanhope. There was no feigning about it.

CHAPTER EIGHT

When Betty walked into the studio an hour later, there was no way Rachel could ignore her disheveled blond hair, pasty complexion, and red-rimmed eyes. Uh-oh. Betty wasn't just an employee. She was a good friend. And even though Betty and Mike had a happy marriage, Rachel knew all couples had their bad days.

Unfortunately, Betty had arrived close to the hour for the kids' dance class. No sooner had she walked in and given Rachel a weak smile then five of their students stormed into the school.

"Welcome, kids," Rachel said. "Go on into the studio and do some of the warm-up calisthenics I showed you last week. I'll be right there."

She put her hand on Betty's arm. "Are you all right?"

Betty nodded and sank onto the stool behind the front desk. "Yeah. I—I need to talk with you after the class, though." She sounded as if she had been crying.

Rachel sent up a silent prayer that nothing serious had happened between Betty and Mike. Betty just adored that man.

"Okay. Why don't you sit out the kids' class until you feel up to joining in? I'll be fine on my own."

"You sure?" Betty clearly welcomed the idea of skipping the class.

Rachel smiled. "See? This is why we need another daytime teacher. We need a little more flexibility in our schedule, don't you think?" Mr. Longworth's offer notwithstanding, she and Betty had talked about the need for another teacher, and Rachel had already placed an ad in the

Tribune. She just hadn't found anyone yet, despite several auditions. Now she wondered if God's hand had been at play in the matter, in light of Mr. Longworth's request.

But for some reason, her comment brought more tears to Betty's eyes. Rachel simply hugged her friend and then headed for the restroom.

Mary and Mark, Josh's niece and nephew, ran in from outside. No uncle with them.

Well, that was fine. She wouldn't have to feel defensive about her "artsy" business today. She couldn't care less if she ever saw him again.

*****

By the time the class neared its end, Rachel was relieved she had taken out that ad for an additional instructor. Regardless of how everything played out with Mira Longworth, she owed it to her students to provide more attention than she could offer all by herself.

Mark's frustration represented the general attitude of today's class.

"I can't get the turn without forgetting my steps. I stink at this."

Commiserating mumbles from the others punctuated his comment.

"Keep confident about this, kids." Rachel saw the possibility of her class making a mass withdrawal from the summer session. "I promise you it's going to click for you, and then you'll be able to do the step without even thinking about it. It's like riding a bike. You're all going to catch your balance in no time."

This situation was partially because the kids hadn't practiced at home as much as they should have. Rachel sighed. She had expected that. It was summer, and she understood the mindset was different when school was out. It didn't help that the weather outside was so inviting. But a large part of the problem was her inability to focus on any one of them long enough before the next student requested help. So the turns and steps weren't settling completely into any of their minds. Despite Betty's obvious distress, Rachel was relieved when she stepped in to help.

"Here, Mark, I'll do the steps with you. It's fun, really. Don't give up." She glanced over at Rachel, sniffed, and attempted another smile.

Rachel could have hugged her. She was the most depressed-looking ballroom dancer ever, but what a trooper.

Rachel walked over to the phonograph and turned it off. "Thanks, Betty. Let's try it again, kids, nice and slowly and without the music. And don't worry if it's not coming to you right away. It's going to happen."

"Miss Stanhope?" Mary spoke softly before Rachel got too far past her. She had been dancing on her own most of the class, since there were so few boys and Rachel had been too busy to switch the partners as often as usual. "I think I get it. The turn, I mean. If you want me to dance with one of the boys, maybe I could help."

"Excellent, Mary! Thanks." She rested her hand on Mary's back and looked around the room. "Let's see, who should I put you with?"

Mary's voice softened until it was barely audible. "Troy looks like he needs help."

Rachel spotted the cute blond boy at the other end of the room. He was trying to walk the steps, even though the class hadn't resumed the lesson yet. Troy and Mary were probably the oldest students in the class, both about thirteen. When Rachel looked back at Mary, her heart melted at the raging blush on the girl's face. Ah, Mary. Rachel had definitely worn those shoes before.

"I think that's a perfect idea." She called across the room. "Troy, come let Mary show you the steps." She clapped her hands and regrouped as many of the couples as she could before they counted through the steps again.

With Betty and Mary both helping, Rachel and the students were far more confident by the time the parents started to arrive.

"You see, it's happening for some of you, isn't it?" She moved to one of the girls who still struggled. "Here Heather, I'm going to dance the boy's part with you. You almost have it."

Minutes later she dismissed the students, who were far more enthusiastic than they had been earlier in class. Crisis averted!

At least *that* crisis was averted. Betty put her hand on Rachel's shoulder just as Josh walked into the studio and made eye contact with her. He looked distracted, but he smiled at her before she turned toward Betty's voice.

"Rachel, I need to talk with you before the next class starts, okay?"

"Sure. Let me just shepherd everyone out and make sure no one has any questions for me. The Latin class doesn't start for forty-five minutes, so we'll have time to talk."

Betty nodded and walked to the back room. This wasn't like Betty at all. She loved people and would normally linger out front to chat with the parents and students. The heavy dread in Rachel's stomach grew and threatened to drag her mood down, as well.

A deep voice behind her soothed her spirits, though, and she turned when Josh spoke.

"I understand Mary picked up the dance steps pretty well today."

Mary stood proudly next to her uncle, clearly awaiting Rachel's praise.

"She did. I was a little shorthanded today, so Mary's offer to help was a real blessing. She managed to teach another student exactly what to do." She smiled at Mary. "Thanks for that." Rachel gave her a wink. There was no way she would tease her about Troy in front of her uncle. She remembered what it felt like to be an adolescent girl. "Keep on practicing, Mary. Maybe help Mark a little."

"Ick. I'm not dancing with my brother." She caught herself. "I mean, I don't think he'd want to dance with me anyway. He's not all that crazy about dance."

Josh chuckled at her. "Well, he *is* a twelve-year-old boy." He abruptly became serious and shot a look back at Rachel. He seemed ready for her to take offense at his comment. The change in his demeanor was so swift, it made her laugh.

"Don't worry. I'm not going to snap at you for that one. I *will* concede lots of boys would rather be shooting BB guns and climbing trees. I just hope Mark isn't going to give up. I think he could get very good. He has a great sense of rhythm and even natural grace."

At that exact moment, she caught sight of Mark. Everyone else had left, so he was alone near the front door. He had started walking through the waltz steps, but now he was embellishing the dance with chicken-like bobs of his head and rushed, goofy footwork. He behaved as if there were no one else around as he performed in his own silly world.

Rachel had to cover her mouth to keep from laughing loudly enough for him to hear. Mary had already wandered in his direction, and she was apparently used to her brother's antics. But Josh turned back to her, and the twinkle in his eyes was certainly the most wonderful thing she had seen all day. He laughed so hard—while trying not to embarrass his nephew—he made himself snort.

"Oh, man." He wiped his eyes. "I love that kid."

Well, that kind of melted her heart, and she wasn't sure what she might have said or done if Betty hadn't caught her attention, desperation in her eyes.

"Ah. Right. I have to talk with Betty before our next class—"

"Sure, sure." Josh stepped away quickly. "Hey, I hope it wasn't rude of me to just drop the kids off at the door this morning. I knew they were running late and—"

"No, that's fine. You don't have to walk them in."

He nodded and turned to leave.

"But feel free to walk them in. Anytime."

He turned and looked at her directly, like he was assessing her. She wasn't sure, but she figured she blushed almost as much as Mary had about Troy.

"Thanks." That was all he said. He rounded up the kids and closed the door behind them.

"Oh, good, finally." Betty sat in one of the chairs up front. Despite those words of relief, her tone hinted at anxiety.

Rachel sat in the chair next to her. "Okay, friend. Something's seriously wrong, I can see that. Everything all right with Mike?"

Betty sighed. *Oh no.*

"Kind of. See, Rachel, it's just… I'm pregnant."

She said it as if she were apologizing, so it took her a while to process what Betty said at first. But then she gasped and jumped up from her chair. "What? You're pregnant?" Both her volume and octave rose with each sentence. "Are you kidding me? This is fantastic news!"

A hesitant smile turned Betty's lips up. Rachel bent down and grabbed hold of her in an awkward hug. "Congratulations! Mike must have flipped, huh?"

Betty's silence prompted Rachel to pull back.

"He's happy, isn't he?"

Betty nodded. "He's happy. But he wants me to quit working."

Ah. Thus the apologetic tone. "That makes sense, Betty." She sat back down and took her hand. "You're going to want to be home with the baby, of course."

"No." Betty shook her head. "He wants me to give my two weeks' notice now."

Rachel frowned. "Already? But you're not even…" She gestured at her friend's stomach and then thought maybe she should shut up. "Oh, you're feeling sick. That's why you've looked so drained all day."

"It's because I'm suddenly feeling sick, but also because Mike's scared the dancing will hurt the baby."

"Oh." Rachel sat back and rested her chin in her hand. "I didn't think of that. I don't really know about the whole pregnancy thing. Maybe he's right."

Betty stood and expelled a heavy sigh. "I'm afraid it doesn't matter if he's right or not. I have to give my notice, Rachel. If I don't and then something happens to the baby, he'd never forgive me. I'd never forgive myself."

"Yeah." Rachel stood and put her arm around her. "I understand."

Betty turned into her half hug, and they gave each other a good squeeze. "I'm sorry, Rachel. I know you really need the help here."

Goodness. Rachel had forgotten about that for a moment. Now she had yet another reason to hope Mira Stanhope was at least trainable. She would need to hire two people in order to replace Betty and add an instructor. What were the chances of her finding two instructors at once?

She steeled herself against panic.

Lord, I think I need to lean on You a little here.

That's what she would do. She had placed the ad in Josh's paper, and she needed to lean on God to send her help. The thought of Josh also brought his cynical view of dancing to mind.

She gave Betty a reassuring smile. She had to believe there was at least one more person out there who had spent the last few years with exactly the opposite view of dance as had Mr. Josh Reegan.

CHAPTER NINE

Rachel shut her mouth as soon as she realized it was hanging open. She sat near the phonograph in her studio Tuesday evening and watched one of her prospective employees—not Mira—audition.

Mira had called to request an audition, apparently at her father's urging. But there had been a few other calls in response to the ad, and it was one of these prospects she now watched.

The woman—with brilliant, bottle-red hair, a blue-satin dress, and voluptuous curves *everywhere*—danced with Mel, Rachel's lone male employee. Mel's wife Connie emitted subtle gasps throughout the routine but looked more amused than shocked.

The woman auditioning apparently had a different kind of experience in dance than this particular job required. Even though she assured Rachel she knew the samba, her version was something for which a fellow might have paid a dime a dance not all that long ago. Mel was a strong leader, so he managed to keep his partner at a respectable distance, but Rachel could never hire her and set her loose on an unsuspecting clientele.

Rachel spoke just loudly enough for Connie to hear over the music but not loudly enough to project across the room to Mel and the applicant.

"Imagine the trouble I'd have with a teacher this, um…"

"Wiggly?" Connie's eyes sparkled with amusement. "Friendly? I think you'd get quite a few men signing up, once word got around."

Rachel widened her eyes at the thought. "That's not the kind of business we need. I'd have a mob of angry wives picketing out front. And I wouldn't blame them." She tilted her head and watched a while longer before leaning back toward Connie. "She *is* awfully sultry, isn't she? And pretty."

Connie nodded. "You'd better end the audition before my poor husband has a heart attack."

Rachel laughed. Mel *did* look stressed, but his stress was clearly caused by the effort it took to avoid impropriety. With a lift of the phonograph needle, Rachel put him out of his misery.

"Thanks very much, Shirley. I appreciate your coming by. I'll be in touch by Friday."

Shirley left the musky scent of her perfume behind.

Mel waited for her to leave before he spoke. "Good night nurse, I smell like an opium den. You're not really considering hiring her, are you?"

Rachel grimaced. "I don't have the heart to turn her down flat. I'll give it some distance and call her Friday."

Mel pulled a handkerchief from his back pocket and wiped it across his forehead. He slipped his reading glasses on and picked up her clipboard. "She's a real handful, that one."

Connie gave him a playful smirk. "And when did you measure that, dear?"

Mel looked at his wife over his glasses. "That's enough out of you, missus. I almost pulled a muscle trying to keep her off me."

"I know exactly how she felt, you gorgeous animal." Connie gurgled a panther-like growl at him and made Rachel laugh. Mel may have been a gorgeous animal at some point in time, but now he carried a paunch in front, very little in back, and he tried to cover his balding head by relocating long strands of hair where they had absolutely no business being.

"Well, we sure better get someone more suitable in here soon," Mel said. "Between the saucy samba dancer and that guy before her—"

"Robot Man?" Connie shook her head. "The man must have been in the military. I've never had anyone dance so rigidly with me in my life. It was like trying to waltz with a member of the Imperial Guard. It almost *hurt* to dance with him." She smoothed her hands down her sides, accentuating her own soft curves. She was nothing like the applicant who had just left, but Connie was still attractive for her age. Mel claimed she put Betty Grable to shame, even at sixty.

"I do have a few more coming in Thursday," Rachel said. "And one more tonight. I can't believe you two don't know people I can hire. Where *are* they all, the dancers from your generation?" Rachel glanced around Mel to see the clipboard before she checked her watch. Mira was due soon.

He handed the clipboard to her. "We're the old folks of the dance world now, Rachel. Most of our cohorts, if they're still dancing, are either in New York or spread across the country, doing what we do. Working part time. More for the fun than the extra income."

Rachel sighed. "You're not *that* old, you two."

"We've worked hard all our lives and have set aside a healthy nest egg, honey," Connie said. "We're just not sprightly enough to dance all day long anymore."

"Yep." Mel pressed his hand against his back, as if in pain. "At our age things start falling apart, Rachel. We're going to get better and better acquainted with our doctors as time goes on." He put a craggy whine in his voice.

They all turned when the front door opened and a young woman with short hair the color of burnt cinnamon peeked inside. Despite the late hour, she glowed like a girl at the start of her day.

"Are you still auditioning for dance instructors?" When she smiled, deep dimples indented both cheeks. "I'm sorry if I'm late. I thought I'd get here more quickly than I did."

This certainly wasn't the stringy girl from Mr. Longworth's photograph, was it?

"You're not Mira, are you?" Rachel asked.

"I am! How nice that you remembered my name."

She certainly didn't act like a spoiled, privileged little rich girl. "Come on in. I'm Rachel, and these are two of my instructors, Mel and Connie."

The girl bobbed her head at each of them. "Mira. I live just down the road." She opened her arms, presenting herself. "And I love to dance!"

Rachel smiled. "All right, Mira. Let's have you dance the foxtrot with Mel here."

She was a beautiful dancer. The heavens could have opened and angels could have broken into song, and Rachel wouldn't have been more certain of God's hand in these circumstances. She said a prayer of thanks before the music even ended. Mira moved into the transitions as if she could read Mel's mind. She kept her shoulders from rising and had lovely expansion in her upper body.

"She positively *melts*," Connie whispered, just as the dance ended.

"That was wonderful, Mira!" Rachel practically hugged the girl. She had to stop from mentioning the girl's father, preferring instead to treat Mira as she would any stellar applicant. "Where did you train?"

The young woman's dimples deepened. "I took ballet for years, but the ballroom was later. I went to college in Los Angeles. I lived right next to an Arthur Murray studio, and I taught for them before moving out here. I heard you were looking for teachers, and I got so excited I called right away. So you still haven't filled the job?"

Not a word about her father's attempt at influence here. Could it be that he hadn't told her? If that were the case, it would mean the girl had no expectation of special treatment. Rachel hoped it would remain that way. But at this rate, she would have offered Mira the job regardless of Mr. Longworth's promises, assuming she was able to teach as well as she danced.

"You know how to teach all the basic dances?"

"Yes. Modern and Latin, both. I'm a little stronger in the Moderns, though."

Rachel took up her clipboard and walked Mira to the door. "If you can come next Monday morning and show me you can work well with my younger students, we'll talk employment."

Mira looked even younger when she jumped up and down with excitement.

"I'll be here! Thank you *so* much!"

Rachel wanted to jump up and down herself after Mira ran out. She grabbed Connie in a hug. She wanted to tell her about how important this development was to the studio, but she felt she couldn't talk specifics. "Connie, I can feel new life being breathed right into the business with this girl."

Mel laughed. "As one of the dusty old dinosaurs in your employ, I take umbrage at that remark, missy."

"Mel, let the girl enjoy herself." Connie pulled back from her. "You still want us for Thursday's auditions? Or are you going to cancel them?"

"I only have a few. Three, in fact. If you two need to get straight home after class Thursday, I can—"

"We'll be here." Mel gave her a quick, decisive nod. "Won't we, sweetheart?"

"We will. We have the early evening class on Thursday, anyway. We'll stick around. Just in case Mira doesn't work out. You never know."

"Right. And I'm thinking I might be able to hire a second person, anyway. So thanks. I'd appreciate your feedback on everyone."

Rachel sighed with relief. If this played out as she hoped, her dad would be so proud of her, expanding the business, bringing in more customers. She stopped at the thought. Here she had silently commended Mira for pursuing her goal free of excessive reliance on her father.

She'd like to think she could say the same about herself.

CHAPTER TEN

Two women came in for auditions on Thursday evening, one of whom had so little experience she ended up enrolling as a student for one of the evening classes.

She laughed as she signed the contract. "I figured I'd give it a shot, the teaching. Kind of a dare between my husband and me. I had no idea it would be that difficult. Ballroom dancers have never impressed me as the great minds of our age, you know?"

Mel, Connie, and Rachel all stared, dumbfounded, at her—possibly adding credence to what she believed—before Rachel shooed her along and raised an eyebrow at her fellow dancers.

"We're going to give *that one* special attention when she begins class."

Connie nodded. "I hope I'm not too stupid to know when she's worn out."

"You two are terrible." Mel laughed. "We've all known teachers who were gifted at dance but barely able to string entire sentences together."

"Mel Friedman!" Connie crossed her arms over her chest. "There are dummies in just about every walk of life. Don't you go giving that woman's ignorant comment your approval." She looked over at the front door, as if the woman were still there. "Great minds. I'll give her a piece of my great mind."

Their next audition wasn't due for a few minutes, so they nibbled on the burgers and fries Fran had brought over before heading home from the diner.

"God bless Franny." Connie dipped a french fry in ketchup and ate it as if it were the answer to her every desire. "Mmm. I thought I'd have to cook when we got home tonight."

"Thanks, guys, for staying late with me," Rachel said.

Mel swallowed and pounded his chest to emit a small burp. "Our pleasure, sweetie. It's not that late. Besides, you and your studio keep us young. That's one of the reasons we like to teach at night."

Connie crossed her still-shapely legs. "Yeah, otherwise we'd be in our pajamas and asleep by eight. I like having the responsibility of getting up and out to teach."

The other applicant who came in was good enough that they might be able to train her to be a teacher, if they didn't get any other prospects. But she brought her two noisy, fighting toddlers with her. Rachel thought the fact that she had the toddlers out in the evening meant she had some freedom to work during the day.

"And your children will stay home with their father if you work here?" Rachel wasn't quite sure how else to ask. "I mean, I'm looking for a daytime teacher."

"Oh." The woman grimaced. "No, he works during the day."

"But we don't have facilities for children here." Rachel scratched her head. Surely the woman wasn't planning to bring the kids to work with her?

The woman waved toward the children, watching as one of them smacked the other over the head just before they both broke into tears. "Oh, they're no trouble. They'll just sit up front and play."

No. They would not.

Rachel didn't want to allow her discomfort with toddlers to color her approach to the audition, but there was simply no way this would work. It appeared she would need to continue searching for another teacher. She sent the woman and her children on their way.

With a glance at her watch she looked toward the front door as it opened. "It's almost seven. This is probably our third audition."

But they expressed surprise over who entered. Here they had just discussed getting older and getting out, and now Mr. and Mrs. Chambers entered timidly. Mr. Chambers spotted her and waved. They walked onto the dance floor.

Slowing his shuffle to let his wife keep up with him, Mr. Chambers smiled. "Fran dropped lunch off for us earlier and mentioned you were auditioning tonight. Are we too late to watch the dancing, Rachel?"

"Not at all! We still have one more person scheduled. Come, sit down. I'm so happy you're both here."

"Oh, you really missed a good one the other night," Connie said. She and Mel opened a couple of folding chairs for their guests. "Like a Vegas showgirl, dancing with Mel here."

"You see, Benjamin?" Mrs. Chambers gave her husband the gentlest shove Rachel had ever witnessed. "I told you to wake me from my nap earlier. It's not right to let sleeping dogs lie so long they miss all the fun."

"The other night, honey." Mr. Chambers spoke loudly enough to make sure his wife heard. "The showgirl was the other night."

Rachel smiled at both of them. "Don't let Connie get you all disappointed. I'm sure there will be other entertaining auditions. This isn't necessarily the last night, anyway. Please, make yourselves comfortable. We have someone due soon."

"Well, we're going to be as small as church mice over here," Mrs. Chambers said. "Just carry on and pretend you don't even see us." The two of them gingerly lowered themselves into their chairs before excited anticipation filled their eyes.

"Isn't it *quiet* as church mice?" Connie spoke under her breath.

"Shh." Rachel gave her head a subtle shake.

As if on cue, a handsome young man, his dark hair combed back in a sleek pompadour, walked in through the front door. Dressed entirely in black, he looked very much the part of an experienced Latin ballroom dancer. The moment he walked in, he spotted Mr. and Mrs. Chambers and approached them, shaking their hands and introducing himself.

Rachel was sure there was no way he thought the older couple was in charge. They simply didn't give that impression. So he was being gracious. Rachel gave him an immediate check on the plus side for that one. "That must be Cruz." She set the clipboard down, next to the phonograph.

Connie rested her chin against her fist and spoke softly. "He's not a very big fella."

"Nope," Mel said. "Definitely the runt of the family litter, I'd bet. But he's young. He still has some growing to do. I'm just wondering if his folks know he's not home playing in his room."

"Hush, you two." Rachel walked toward the front desk. "Give the boy a chance."

He strode toward Rachel with confidence and put out his hand. But when she returned the gesture, she was surprised by his taking her hand and giving it a quick kiss.

"*Senorita. Encantado.*"

"My, my." Mrs. Chambers' soft voice punctuated the silence.

"Oh." Rachel looked behind herself at Mel and Connie and widened her eyes. She turned back around. "No speak…no uh, hablo English?" She had no idea what she was saying, but that had to be close.

"Oh, yeah, I speak English."

The boy had no accent whatsoever. Or rather, he had perhaps a mild New Jersey accent, if anything.

Rachel chuckled. "Then why did you—"

He shrugged and cocked his head. "Goes with the whole look, right? The Latin ballroom look? I mean, my folks are Spanish. From Ecuador. So I can speak it, and I know the stance." He stood at a jaunty, haughty angle that nearly made Rachel laugh. "But I'm as American as Abe Lincoln."

"And you're Cruz, I assume." Rachel looked at Mel and Connie and gave them a slight cock of the head to get them to join her.

"That's me. Cruz Vergara. You still looking for instructors?"

Mel spoke up. "You have experience, do you?"

Cruz nodded. "I grew up dancing, yeah."

"But how about teaching?" Connie asked. "Can you break the dances down and teach them to people who *didn't* grow up dancing?"

"Sure." He didn't hesitate for a second. "I've done it with every one of my girlfriends."

Mel snorted a laugh. "Every one of them, huh? How old are you, son?"

"I'm twenty-one." A hint of defensiveness colored Cruz's response, and Rachel decided to step back in.

"Okay, Cruz. Let's see what you can do. You can dance with me."

He extended his open palm toward her and jumped right back into character. "*Con gusto, guapa.*"

Rachel looked over her shoulder at Connie, raised her brows, and shared a smile. "Music please, Connie?"

Before Connie lowered the needle, Rachel lifted her arms and spoke to both Cruz and Connie at once. "The rumba, please."

Cruz took control the moment the music started. Every movement flowed like water to the next, from the close hold, to a turn, to the close hold again, to the promenades, to the side chasses, to the cucarachas. He led so proficiently Rachel felt she could have relaxed into rag doll status and they would have danced well together. By the time the song finished, with his draping her dramatically over his arm, she was certain she would offer him the job. She was actually a little flustered by the confidence he exhibited during the dance.

Mel and Connie broke into applause at the end of the rumba. So did Mr. and Mrs. Chambers. Mel spoke before Rachel had a chance to. "Son, that was excellent. Your parents taught you well."

Cruz beamed. "Thanks, sir."

"Call me Mel." His voice held newfound respect for Cruz.

Connie put her hand on Mel's shoulder. "He reminds me of you at that age, honey." She smiled at Cruz. "If you can teach as well as you dance…" She shot a look at Rachel. "Well, it's not my decision, of course. I'm sorry, Rachel."

"No, no, that's all right." She smiled at Cruz. "You can see we all liked your audition."

"You too?" Now he looked like a kid again, his eyes full of hope—and possibly a little flirtation—when he met her eyes.

She gave him as motherly a smile as she could muster. "Me too. How about the modern dances—waltz, foxtrot, tango?"

He shrugged. "I'm so-so at those, to be honest. I can do them, but not as well as the Latins. Tango, yes. But to tell you the whole truth, I'm not so good at the quickstep."

Rachel shook her head. "I don't tend to teach the quickstep that often. We do a little swing—"

"I *love* swing!" Eagerness lit up his face.

And that was how Rachel felt, as well. Wow. God had blessed her with two promising teachers, assuming again that they taught as well as they danced. Mira was elegance personified. And this handsome young man was going to draw in the female students like poodle skirts and Frankie Laine. She would just have to make sure she didn't end up with the same problem she'd anticipated with the wiggly bottle-redhead from the other night.

"I'll tell you what. If you can get here Monday for the first class of the morning, at ten o'clock—that's my kids' class—and if you're able to work well with them, you've got yourself a job." She figured she might as well check out both Mira and Cruz together. If everything continued to fall into place, she just might have the two of them dance together in a future competition.

Cruz hollered a whoop, grabbed her in a bear hug, and lifted her off the floor before he seemed to grasp the impropriety of what he was doing. He put her down and stepped away as if he had a disease he didn't want to spread. "I'm sorry. That was bad. I'm really sorry."

Rachel straightened her skirt while Mel and Connie laughed. She smiled at him despite her surprise. He was quite a *physical* young man. She nodded. "Monday, all right? Monday."

With a point in her direction, he backed out of the room, nearly in a run. "You got it. Monday! Ten o'clock! You won't regret this!"

He had barely left the studio before Mr. Chambers' voice rang out. "That was a humdinger!"

Connie's reaction mirrored Rachel's. "A humdinger indeed."

CHAPTER ELEVEN

A few evenings later Josh tossed a package of ground beef into his shopping cart and headed toward the front of the Safeway. A dozen lonely items in his cart. He couldn't think of anything else he needed, but that didn't mean his shopping was complete. There was always something he forgot. One of these days he'd start keeping a list. Ridiculous—a news reporter who didn't jot down everything. If he ran his business life the way he ran his personal life… Well, now that he thought about it, he wasn't running his business life all that well, either.

He got in the shortest line and watched the longer one next to him move along swiftly, while the little old lady in the front of his line methodically counted out every penny of the change the clerk handed her. When he glanced around to decide whether or not to change lines, he spotted none other than Rachel Stanhope, who had nearly finished checking out in the other line beside his.

He grinned at her. "Are you tailing me, teach?"

A moment passed before she recognized someone was talking to her, and then her eyes grew wide as she took him in. Despite a quick attempt at haughtiness, she definitely seemed as if she were pleased to see him, if only a little. "Tailing you? Hardly." She rolled her eyes, but she returned his grin. "I always shop here. But you don't, do you? So I guess *you're* tailing *me*."

"No, I really do shop here. I live about half a mile from here."

"Do you? Hmm. I'm surprised we've never run into each other before." She looked down to count out money from her purse. She would leave soon, and Josh found he didn't want her to. His cashier finally started ringing up his groceries. Josh contemplated leaving half of them behind so he could exit when Rachel did.

He stopped mid-rush. What in the world was he thinking? Was he that desperate? No, he was not. He needed that bar of soap. And that bunch of carrots. He couldn't do without this bottle of aspirin, and he had squeezed every last drop out of his toothpaste tube. Was he going to leave his laundry detergent behind just so he could talk for five minutes to a pretty girl he couldn't quite get out of his mind? A girl who thought he was nothing but a big lug with no appreciation for the finer things of life, like dance and art?

Rachel's voice rang out and interrupted his internal debate. "I guess I'll see you next Monday, then."

He turned and waved. There wasn't going to be a reason for him to show up Monday—not a plausible one, anyway. But he'd worry about that later. "Sure. See you then. G'night."

The moment the glass door shut behind her, he started grabbing items off the belt and setting them on the empty belt in the line next to his. He held up the package of toilet paper.

"You know, I don't really need this. Or this." He set a carton of eggs aside.

The pimply boy behind the register frowned at him. He stopped checking in order to discuss Josh's decision. "You sure?"

"Yep." Josh waved his hand at the remaining items. "Just go ahead with these. Go on."

"But why'd you put them in your cart if—"

"I don't know. I really don't know what got into me. But could we move along now?" He glanced toward the parking lot and could see Rachel loading her few bags into her car.

When he looked back at the cashier, he realized the boy had followed his gaze. He returned to checking out the few items, but he shook his head. "Have a little self-respect, man."

"What? What are you talking about?" Josh felt his face burn. He wanted to knock this kid's block off for calling him out like that.

"Seven dollars and eighty-three cents." The boy lowered his voice and leaned toward him. "She's in here all the time, pops."

Pops? How old did the kid think he was? Didn't matter. He handed him eight dollars and grabbed his bag to go. He was certain he had taken too long.

But there she was, sitting in her car, and she got out as he exited the store. He slowed his step, suddenly filled with confidence. *She* had waited for *him*.

"You still here?" He gave her a lopsided grin.

She didn't smile back. In fact, she looked angry. "It's dead."

"Dead?" He frowned. "What's dead?"

She heaved out a sigh. "My stupid car. I guess it's the battery. It won't kick in. It just clicked the first few times and now nothing. Dead."

Thankyou, Lord.

Now, maybe he shouldn't have thanked God for her misfortune, but at this rate he'd even have time to go back in there and get his toilet paper.

He walked toward her dead Falcon and used his chin to point at it. "Do you have frozen food in there?"

She raised one eyebrow. "You think that's what's causing the problem?"

He narrowed his eyes at her. Surely she was kidding.

Rachel waved off her comment. "Don't mind me. I get mean and sarcastic when I'm under stress. Yes, I have frozen stuff in there."

"We could swing your groceries over to my place down the road, and then I'll give you a jump. I—I mean, we'll use my jumper cables on your car. I wouldn't want your food to melt while we work on this."

She hesitated and looked at her car while she spoke. "Oh. Well, that's really nice of you."

He watched her weigh her choices.

"Okay. I'd really appreciate that."

He nodded and walked over to his Chevy. The mess inside made him think forward. His apartment was a mess too. He wasn't even sure where he had thrown his underwear when he got into the shower this morning. He cleared off the front seat as quickly as he could and tossed loose papers and empty donut bags into the back.

He set his groceries on the floor behind the driver's seat and started back to Rachel's car to help her move her groceries in with his. He happened to glance toward the store and saw the smart-mouthed cashier watching them. The kid held up his hand and made the "okay" sign at him. Josh merely frowned and went on about his business. He hoped the guy was still here when they returned to use the jumper cables. The last thing he wanted to do was hurt Rachel's reputation. As a matter of fact...

"I'll be right back," he said to Rachel. "Go ahead and have a seat in my car. I'll get your other bags and join you in a second."

He walked into the store and tapped the kid on the shoulder. "Listen, do me a favor and keep a watch on that Ford out front. The lady's battery is dead, and we'll be right back to fix it after we get her groceries home, okay?"

He looked pointedly at the kid. This shouldn't matter to Josh, but it did.

"Oh. Sure." The cashier actually appeared embarrassed. That was fine with Josh.

He walked back outside and saw her sitting in his passenger seat, the windows rolled down and a slight breeze lifting wisps of her hair. His car never looked so good. He considered how long it had been since he'd had a woman in his car—a woman other than his sister or a coworker, anyway.

She spoke as soon as he approached his car, the last of her bags in his arms. "You know, I don't live too far from here, either. It might make more sense to bring these bags to my place. We could put your bag in my fridge and then go back for it after fixing my battery. I could maybe even make you dinner when we're done. To pay you back for your trouble, I mean."

He smiled. This was getting better and better. He didn't know when he had decided he wanted things to progress with this woman, but he was feeling as flustered and eager as a teenager. And then it dawned on him. He probably had his jumper cables in the trunk of his car. They could jump her battery, and she could be on her way within minutes. He hated the idea of spoiling what was developing, but he had to be honest with her.

"Uh, Rachel, I'd love to join you for dinner. But I just realized I probably have my cables in my trunk."

He set down her grocery bags, unlocked his trunk, and heaved a sigh of disappointment. The cables lay there, silently taunting him.

He hadn't heard her getting out of his car, but she joined him and glanced down at the cables. "So," she said. "Change of plans."

His brows creased. "I guess so."

"You get my battery working and then follow me home. I'll still owe you dinner, as far as I'm concerned."

She was in total control of the moment, as if she hadn't invested a single sentiment into how this played out either way. Women. He wondered if they all knew how much power they held.

But as for him? He had to restrain himself from breaking into the "Hallelujah Chorus."

CHAPTER TWELVE

Rachel refilled Josh's water glass and rejoined him at her small maple dining table. "Are you sure you don't want something more flavorful? Tea? Lemonade? Soda?"

"No, really." He put up his hand and swallowed his last bite of dinner. "I don't want to spoil the taste of this terrific food."

She laughed. They both knew the chicken she had "sautéed" was horrible. She had been so engrossed in the story he told her about some crook in the county government that she had cooked every drop of moisture out of the chicken before she remembered to check it. She found herself hoping she'd have a chance to cook for him again.

"I promise I'm a good cook, really. It's your fault. I got all caught up in how you exposed that guy." She leaned forward on her elbows. "But now what happens since you lost your witness?"

"Source. Yeah, I lost her. Wiley got to her and convinced her to take off so I couldn't lean on her testimony if they took us to court."

"How do you think he did that? Convinced her to leave, I mean?"

Josh shrugged. "How do men fool women like that? I don't know. This was the second time with the two of them too. He took advantage of her before, and when she acted as my source, she seemed to have him all figured out."

"Are you sure she's all right? I mean, are you sure she left of her own accord?"

"I think her roommate Mitzy would be suspicious if there had been foul play or if Candy had been frightened into leaving. She sounded confident that Candy took off to please Wiley and to avoid me."

She got up to get a tin of cookies from the pantry. "How frustrating. What will you do to prove the story now?" She pried the tin open and set it on the table. Maybe her homemade Toll House cookies would redeem her reputation with him.

"Candy's my only hope at this stage." Josh stood with his dinner plate, but she took it from him and brought it to the sink. He sat back down. "Thanks. Yeah, so since I could only provide one source, the paper had to print a retraction the day after my story ran."

"A retraction? That's serious, isn't it?"

His smile held no humor. "You could say that. It cost me my job."

"Oh, my goodness!" She rejoined him and stopped just short of placing her hand on his arm. "What are you going to—"

"I should be more clear. I didn't get fired from the *Tribune*. I lost my job with the city desk. But everyone knows it's a demotion for me. It wasn't easy working my way up to that position. And now I'll be writing nonsense." He ate a cookie within seconds and didn't even seem to notice it going down. That bothered Rachel a little, but she thought she was being petty.

"What do you mean, nonsense?"

He held up a second cookie. "Okay if I have another?"

"Sure, help yourself."

"These are fantastic, by the way. You make 'em?"

She smiled and nodded casually, as if she just noticed he was eating them.

"My favorite, chocolate chip," he said. "Yeah, but anyway, now I'm with the Style and Leisure pages of the paper."

"Oh, but I love that section!" She didn't say that to make him feel better. She was serious. "I have to admit I prefer reading about—"

Oh. Truth dawned. That was it.

"About what?" He looked up from his cookie.

She fought to keep her lips from pursing. "You think it's nonsense because it's about the arts. That's it, isn't it?"

He seemed to have a hard time swallowing what he'd bitten off. "It's—it's not just the arts."

They stared at each other for a moment. While she was biting her tongue, she thought he was probably doing just the opposite, trying to find something to say. She picked a cookie from the tin, brought it to her mouth, and said, "Go on."

He sighed. "I'm just trying to… You know, it's like a baseball player finally making it to the majors, causing the loss of one game, and suddenly having to play for the minors. It's still playing, so there's a certain amount of appreciation. It's just not as hard a game as he knows he can play."

She chewed on her cookie and on his explanation. She had to admit it. "That makes sense."

His smile was soft but made it all the way to the little creases next to his eyes.

"So what's your latest article about?"

As he described it, she enjoyed the fact that he spoke with animation. He couldn't hate the job too much if his subject made him this upbeat.

"You know how jukeboxes work, right? You put your nickel in, you push the button, and your song comes on."

"Right."

"So I'm writing about wallboxes. Your friend at the diner—"

"Fran?"

"Yeah. Fran gave me the idea. While I waited over there for the kids to finish your class, she was telling me she thinks they're going to be putting these wallbox things in the diner. It's like a remote control, and you can choose songs to play on the jukebox right there at your table."

Rachel grinned. "Yes, I've heard about those. What a fun idea."

"Yeah." Josh nodded. "I figure I can eke out an article about jukeboxes and how they got started and how they're becoming more modern."

"Now, see?" She spoke to him as if she were soothing a boo-boo. "That doesn't hurt so bad, does it?"

He laughed. "Easy for you to joke. You're doing exactly what you want to do, aren't you?"

"I am." She tucked her leg up underneath herself, eagerness making her fidgety. "I know you're not a big fan—"

"No, please don't think—"

"But I love ballroom dancing and I enjoy introducing people to it. It's not as easy as it looks, you know. People feel a real joy when they figure out the steps and put it to music, they really do. And it's so popular I had to put out an ad for more teachers."

As if she needed proof, she stood and grabbed her copy of the *Tribune,* folded open to her ad, from the kitchen counter. She laid it on the table in front of him. "I mean, Betty's leaving so I have to replace her anyway, but I'm probably going to hire two teachers just to keep up. They're coming in to help teach Mark and Mary's class on Monday."

His eyes widened. "Yeah? I'd like to come watch that."

But she was on a roll. Josh's words almost went unheard. "You know, for some people my class is the only movement they make all day, for goodness' sake."

She didn't know when it happened, but when she finally stopped talking she realized she had her hands on her hips, as if she were delivering an angry dressing-down. Maybe she had been.

But there was that twinkle in his eyes again, so she couldn't have been too offensive. Still. Now she deliberately pursed her lips.

"You think I'm *cute,* don't you? That's what that look is. Don't you condescend to me, mister."

But they were both laughing.

He stood and looked around the kitchen. He patted his pockets. "All right, I'd better get out of here before I stick my foot in my mouth again."

She saw his car keys on the kitchen counter and grabbed them up. "Here you go."

His hand met hers more quickly than she judged, so his fingers wrapped around hers for a moment before he pulled back. Something that simple shouldn't have flustered her, but it did.

She grabbed at words. "You're welcome for—I mean, thank you for the car. For fixing my car. My battery."

"Sure. You're welcome. Maybe give yourself some extra time in the morning to make sure it starts all right. But I think you'll be fine."

She nodded. She didn't know if this was going to end in a kiss. Was this a date? Would he be that forward? She had to admit she kind of hoped so.

He glanced around her apartment before he walked to the door. "I like that your apartment isn't too feminine."

She frowned. "Excuse me?" She surveyed what one could see from where they stood, attempting to observe it through a man's eyes.

"It's classy," he said. "I like the modern look of the furniture. Simple lines. Red and gray—bold colors. No frills or doilies." He smiled. "Frills and doilies make me think of my grandmother. Which is *fine,* when I'm having dinner with my grandmother."

She nodded again.

He walked to the door. "This looks like an independent woman's home." He turned and flashed another smile, this one more teasing. "Thanks for dinner, independent woman."

She chuckled. "Thanks for enduring it. I…I'd like to give that another shot sometime. Maybe my car will break down again."

Said the so-called independent woman. Goodness, she hadn't meant to sound so desperate.

"Maybe we won't have to wait that long." His more sober expression made her flush. She needed to change the subject.

"You know, Josh, you might end up getting a lot of new readers, writing for the minor leagues for a while."

A slight frown crossed his expression, but he switched gears with her after a moment.

"Well, I'm hopeful I'll be able to earn my way back to the majors. I don't know if readers of Style and Leisure will be willing to follow me back to the hard news."

She shrugged. "I'd follow you." The moment she said the words she heard how flirtatious they might seem.

He breathed out a soft laugh. "I like the sound of that."

She opened the door and suddenly couldn't look up at him. She felt as if she had thrown herself at him. "Good night. Thanks again."

"You too."

She forced a glance at him and gave him a polite smile right before she closed the door. He was looking at her as the door closed. It was just about the most awkward good-bye she had ever experienced.

She rested her head against the door, annoyed with herself. She was thirty-two years old, not an adolescent like Josh's niece Mary. Why couldn't she be more like Rita Hayworth, all sure of herself and slinky?

She felt, as much as heard, a light tap. She shot upright and looked at the door, a frown on her face. She pulled it open and there he was.

"Oh." That's all she said.

He said nothing. He just leaned forward and brushed her lips with his. Just a soft, lingering brush. He stood back and nodded once. "Better." Then he turned and headed down the walk.

She closed the door and rested against it. She wore a silly smile. Yes. Better.

CHAPTER THIRTEEN

The following Monday morning, Josh shifted in the folding chair and wished his brother-in-law Pete would just watch his kids and mind his own business. They sat together in the corner of Rachel's studio.

Pete had met Rachel, and just as Josh had, he watched her give a few instructions to the class, introduce Mira and Cruz as the studio's new teachers, and begin the first dance exercise. Yet the first thing Pete did when his kids started dancing was chuckle and give Josh a knowing glance.

"So, tell me again why you're here? To watch the new teachers? That cute little teeny ballereeny and the Spanish heartthrob there?"

"Give me a break, will you?" He leaned closer to Pete and spoke as if they were plotting a covert mission. "I didn't set out to meet her, but now that I have, I'd like to get to know her, okay? I don't have the best track record, you know."

"*Don't* I know it." Pete laughed. "It's a good thing your flying record is better than your history with women."

Josh wasn't about to mention the kiss at Rachel's door the other night, even if it was the first thing he thought of when he saw her this morning.

"Yeah, so I'm trying to find chances to just be there, you know? Give her a chance to get to know me. I didn't get off to such a good start. The first thing she heard out of my mouth was that I think ballroom dance is stupid."

Josh realized, by the last word of his comment, that Rachel had stopped the music to give instructions. As far as he could tell, what everyone heard him say, rather loudly, was, "I think ballroom dance is stupid."

One look at Rachel confirmed it. She didn't look angry. She looked downright hurt.

He jumped out of his chair. "That isn't what I meant." He heard a groan of amused disbelief come from Pete and looked down to see him wiping a grin from his face.

By the time Josh looked back up, Rachel had already moved on.

"All right now, class, Mira and Cruz are going to demonstrate the steps we're going to learn. I think that will give you a good idea of what we're aiming for. Ladies, watch Mira's body posture and the fluid way she follows. She'll be guided into natural turns, reverse turns, and forward changes, both to the right and left. I'll point them out so you recognize them. In time you'll recognize them and be able to do them. Gentlemen, watch Cruz's strength and how well he guides his partner. Don't any of you be discouraged by how beautiful they look dancing. They were once beginners too. Be *encouraged* by them. You can learn as they have, if you keep at it. I promise. Ballroom dance is an impressive skill." She shot a quick, icy glance at Josh. "Don't let anyone try to tell you otherwise."

The music started again and Josh had to fight the urge to step onto the dance floor to explain himself to Rachel.

Pete wasn't the most sympathetic companion. "I'm telling you, brother, if you flew like you court, we'd all be speaking German now. It's like you have two left tongues."

The class seemed interminable to Josh, and he did none of what he planned when he came to the class. Here he thought he would charm her socks off by being engaged in how she taught and how she tested her new teachers. With a few words he had fallen back to square one, which, in his case, was a few squares behind your average nudnik. He barely noticed the dancing, except when Rachel was the one doing it. Even then, he focused on her face, her expression, waiting for it to relax. Waiting for her to look at him long enough for him to silently communicate his apology to her.

On the contrary, she didn't glance his way again, even after the class ended and he and Pete approached her.

"You must be Mr. Korinski." She gave Pete a charming, open smile.

"Call me Pete, please." Pete wrapped his arm around Mary and set his hand on Mark's shoulders. "You're doing a great job with the kids." He grinned. "You'd think they were civilized or something."

"Oh, Daddy." Mary nuzzled into his chest.

Mark chuckled, clearly proud that his father still saw him as rough-and-ready enough to be teased as uncivilized, despite the elegant moves he had just attempted.

A nice picture the four of them made. Proud father, loving children, and doting teacher. Josh may as well have been the drunken uncle horning in on a Norman Rockwell painting.

He cleared his throat, and it stood out in the momentary silence like an air raid siren. Everyone looked at him. Everyone except Rachel.

Pete didn't exactly spring to his aid, but he finally transferred his inclusive grip from Mark's to Josh's shoulder.

"Miss Stanhope—"

"Rachel."

Pete nodded. "Rachel, I should explain what happened back there."

"That's okay, Pete," she said. "Ballroom just isn't for everyone. I've known about Josh's disdain since we first met."

Well, at least she called him Josh, rather than relegating him back to "Mr. Reegan" status. As hound dog as he felt, even that was better than nothing. Still, he couldn't ignore what she said. "Rachel, if you wouldn't jump to conclusions—"

Pete squeezed his shoulder.

"What my eloquent brother-in-law means is that what you heard was his telling me what he said to you when he first met you. He was explaining why he probably didn't stand much of a chance with you. On a romantic level."

A stunned silence followed, and Josh was painfully aware of four pairs of eyes turning to him. Pete's eyes held self-pride, as if he had just settled the Cold War. Mary's eyes sparkled, clearly thrilled with the idea of Uncle Josh and Miss Stanhope riding a white charger toward a fairytale castle. Mark's eyes, blank at first, now registered disgust. Or jealousy. Josh couldn't quite tell, and he didn't know enough about Mark's emotional development to figure that out.

Besides, Josh's main concern rested on Rachel's eyes as she responded.

"I see." Although she wouldn't hold her gaze on him for long, the glimpses were soft, even apologetic.

Amen to that! He might have stood still, but inside he didn't even touch ground.

"Miss Stanhope!" Mary spoke with giddy enthusiasm. "You have to come to my birthday dinner tomorrow night! Right, Daddy? Right, Uncle Josh?"

"Oh, I don't know, Mary." Rachel smiled. "It's such short notice. I wouldn't want to interfere with your family plans."

Josh decided it was time to write Mary into his will.

"We're not that kind of family," he said. "We're celebrating at my mother's house. She's a more-the-merrier type of person."

Rachel's two new dancers interrupted. The young Spanish-looking man seemed to speak for both of them.

"Excuse us, Rachel. We wondered if you had reached your decision yet."

The teeny ballereeny added, "We're sorry to barge in." She smiled, and two pixie dimples appeared in her cheeks.

"No, you're not interrupting at all." Rachel stepped back to include them in the group. "Yes, I'd love to talk with both of you. Beautiful job. I think the kids learned a lot with you, didn't you, Mark? Mary?"

Before the kids could do more than nod, Rachel turned back to Pete and Josh. "These are my two new teachers, Mira and Cruz."

Mira's squeak of pleasure accompanied her grasping Cruz's arm, which she just as quickly released. Her cheeks flushed pink, and her dimples kept disappearing and reappearing as she tried to stop smiling.

Rachel gestured toward the front desk. "Why don't you two wait up front? I'll be right with you."

"We'll go." Josh glanced at Pete while the two dancers walked away. "I need to get to the office anyway. But—"

Mary jumped in. "But you'll come to my dinner, right?"

Josh looked at Rachel the way he meant to the entire time he was here today—as a man with hope and interest. "I could come pick you up. At six?"

Pete stepped back, pulling the kids with him. "We'll get out of your way. Hope to see you soon, Rachel."

"Tomorrow night!" Mary called out over her shoulder.

Rachel and Josh turned back to each other and grinned. Rachel crossed her arms over her chest and gave him a teasing glance.

"So."

"So."

"What did you think of my new instructors?"

Startled, he straightened and eyed Mira and Cruz. "Oh. Your instructors?"

Her crooked smile both comforted and challenged him. "Isn't that what you said? That was why you came, even though the kids didn't need the ride?"

"Ah." Josh studied his shoes and waited for inspiration. He shrugged when he met her gaze again. "I think Pete pretty well did away with my charade, didn't he?"

The delight in her laugh gave him courage.

"Come have dinner with us tomorrow night. Will you?"

She nodded. "All right. But I should get back to work. Poor Betty is home throwing up—"

"Betty? The blond teacher? What's wrong?"

"Oh, I guess I didn't mention that. She's in the motherly way. And she's quitting, so I need to get Mira and Cruz helping me out right away. These one-teacher classes are going to be the death of me."

"We can't have that." No sir. He wasn't sure what his future held—he tried to leave that in God's hands. But he hoped the plan involved a deeper relationship with Rachel so he wanted her sticking around as long as she possibly could.

CHAPTER FOURTEEN

Rachel couldn't imagine feeling much better about her life than she did as Josh headed back to work. She tingled all over in anticipation of the evening with him and his family. She needed to get a feel for Josh's stance on a few things—like family and faith—and Mary's party might be the place to do it.

She hadn't been this interested in a man since Billy left her standing alone on that dance floor.

She shook off the memory. No humiliating memories today.

"Well!" She turned to Mira and Cruz, who were engaged in a conversation. Rather, Mira was speaking and Cruz was nodding. Was he even listening to a word Mira said?

How could he ignore the girl? She was delightful. She had shown up this morning in a black ballet leotard and a feminine skirt in pale pink chiffon. She looked like something from a fairy tale, with that gamine haircut and those pixie dimples of hers. And her sweet personality matched her appearance perfectly.

Again, Rachel counted her blessings. Not only would Mira bring talent to the studio, she would bring much-needed cash flow, by way of students *and* her father's generous support. Indirectly, Mira's involvement made Cruz's employment possible.

The boy should pay attention to her.

Rachel looked behind the desk and found the necessary forms. "Let's talk employment. I'm just going to talk openly with both of you, because you're both going to get the same hourly wage, all right?"

They were both so eager, she probably could have offered them less than she did. But she wanted to be competitive enough that they wouldn't be lured away by another studio.

Neither one of them needed to give notice before coming to teach.

"I haven't really been working much since I got back from California." Mira shared an embarrassed smile with her and Cruz. "I'm afraid I've been kind of picky. My parents will be thrilled to know I'm finally going to have a full-time job."

"Especially your father!" Rachel spoke as she glanced over Mira's paperwork, so she didn't give much thought to what she said.

"Why my father?" Mira didn't sound suspicious, but she certainly sounded confused.

Rachel broke out into a sweat. "Oh. What did I say? Your father?"

"You said her father would be especially thrilled she's got a job now," Cruz said, tugging straight the collar of his silky bowling shirt.

Oh, fine. *Now* he listened.

"Right. Well, I know my father is terribly protective of me, even at my age—"

"What *is* your age, if you don't mind my asking?" Cruz interrupted.

And chatty. Suddenly the boy was chatty.

"I'm thirty-two." She watched Cruz's face drop before he could stop himself. She laughed. "Yes, I'm an old lady. But I still have a few good years left in me."

He recovered quickly. "No. You're a mature woman." He stared into her eyes when he pronounced that correction. Was he actually flirting with her? She almost laughed again. Maybe he *was* going to stir up trouble. She would have to keep an eye on him.

"Anyway, Mira. I figure if your father is at all like mine, he'll be relieved to know you're making a decent wage at something you love to do."

Was that a lie? Rachel didn't think so.

"And Cruz, you don't have to give notice anywhere either?"

"Naw. I work for my uncle. Construction. I have a million cousins who can fill in for me. I can start right away."

"Wonderful. Well, if you'll both come in tomorrow around noon, I'll have the schedule done for the rest of the week. My friend Betty is my other daytime teacher, but she's leaving soon. So I'll have plenty of hours for both of you."

Neither seemed in a great hurry to leave, so she pressed on. "I wanted to talk with the two of you about something else too. I'm planning to invest more capital into the business to make the studio more visible to the public. We're going to offer some free classes to get prospective students interested, for instance. And another one of the steps I'm going to take will involve entering us in more local competitions—"

Mira gasped and nearly grabbed Cruz's arm again. This time she caught herself, quickly drawing her hand back.

Rachel smiled at her. "And while we haven't been able to be very active in that regard lately, I think now we might be able to compete on several levels, assuming we manage to win locally. So what I wanted to ask you both is whether you'd be willing to put in the extra work, between teaching classes, to bring yourselves to the point that you could compete."

"Yes!" Mira nearly jumped out of her seat. "Yes, definitely!"

Cruz played it more coolly, but there was no denying the interest in his smile. He nodded. "I would, yeah."

"Have either of you competed before, then?"

They looked at each other before responding, as if the other had the answer.

Rachel chuckled. "It's all right if you haven't. I just want to gauge how much work we have ahead of us."

They simultaneously admitted no experience.

"Okay." Rachel stood and walked onto the dance floor. "Then, before I let you go, why don't you both come on in here and just let me watch you once more together."

They walked in after her, but Cruz asked, "Don't you ever compete?"

"Not anymore, no. I haven't for a while, anyway."

"But why not? You're so—"

"I'm just not in that frame of mind anymore." Not only did she not want to hear whatever complimentary word young Cruz planned for her, she didn't want to explain about Billy and how his behavior had led to her fear of competing publicly. How she'd allowed him to dampen her confidence. Not when she was about to embark on her efforts to raise *their* confidence and get them competition-ready.

"Now, you two looked lovely waltzing together for the kids' class. But you have to become more than lovely. You have to become amazing. Do you both dance the tango?"

They nodded.

She walked to the phonograph and pulled out "El Día Que Me Quieras," one of her favorite tango records. "Let's get a feel for how you look together."

The violins and distinctive accordion notes from the bandoneón cued up, and both Cruz and Mira transformed into romantic characters before her very eyes. Even though they hardly knew each other, they danced as if they had loved and argued and forgiven each other time and again.

Rachel had to rub the goose bumps away. Before the dance was even over, she offered up a silent prayer of thanks. Her direction now was crystal clear.

CHAPTER FIFTEEN

When he returned to the office, Josh quietly reached Candy's roommate on the phone. He hoped for good news about his missing source, but he was supposed to be working on his next story idea for Style and Leisure. His editor was looking over his jukebox story now.

"Have you heard anything, Mitzy? Any calls from Candy? Any requests to forward her stuff?"

"Nothing since that first call after she took off. I have a feeling she's going to lie low until it's too late for you to use her testimony."

Too late? Did Wiley think Josh would just give up on this after a few months went by? Then it dawned on him. His article had alerted Wiley to possible charges before it was retracted by the *Tribune.* All Wiley needed was time to find and destroy any hard evidence that might exist. Once this became nothing but Wiley's word against his old partner's, the case was too weak. If Wiley could keep Candy hidden or at least mollified, he'd never be charged. And the longer Candy's corroborating testimony was kept out of the picture, the weaker her accusations would seem, and the less vivid her memory would be.

Josh sat back in his chair and pressed his palm against his forehead. "How about family members, Mitzy? Are her parents in the area? I can't imagine they're happy about her being shipped away to help a crook."

"She didn't like to talk about them. I don't know where they are."

He sat up. "You think she might have gone to live with them?"

"I don't know. Maybe. I could… Well, I probably shouldn't, but I could root around in some of her stuff and see if I can find anything."

How he wished he could just go over there and root around himself—but that wasn't going to happen. "Anything you can do to help me reach her would be great. I don't want you to do anything illegal, though."

"Like what?"

"I don't know. Don't break into anything that's locked, for instance. But if something happens to be out in the open, yeah, I'd appreciate it if you'd just give it a look. See if it leads to any information. Family addresses. Photos that might show familiar places she would consider comfortable for hiding out. Anything like that."

"To tell you the truth, Josh, I'm pretty curious myself. We might not have been bosom buddies, but I thought we were getting to be pretty good friends. I'd like to know she's all right."

"Hey. What about her share of the rent?" He glanced at his desk. "It's July 2. Didn't she have to mail you her share? Where'd she mail it from?"

"No good. She paid me her share in advance for three months. And I can tell you right now, the girl didn't usually have that kind of cash laying around."

Josh scowled. Probably came out of the county treasury.

He heard his editor's door open, and he lowered his voice. "Okay, gotta go. Let me know if you find anything, okay? Even if it doesn't seem like much. I might be able to figure something out from the littlest thing."

"Gotcha, Josh."

Lou Tutera, Style and Leisure editor, stormed out of his office, no-nonsense purpose in his stride. His rolled-up shirtsleeves hinted that he had been hard at work for hours. He tossed the jukebox article on the desk as Josh hung up the phone. "Got some rewriting to do there, Reegan."

"What's wrong with it?" Josh picked it up and frowned at all of Lou's markings.

"I like the idea," Lou said. "Good topic. Good setting—diners and malt shops. But it's missing something. No one's going to read past the first paragraph—no one who reads Style and Leisure, anyway."

Hmm. This article was chock-full of interesting information. "Why not?"

"Too dry. It has no human element to it."

"It's about a machine. There *is* no human element to it."

Tutera was done. He leaned forward on Josh's desk. "Find one and put it in there, hotshot. I want it back by tonight." He turned his back on him and moved on to his next victim.

Josh ran his hand through his hair. This fluff stuff was harder to write than he expected.

"Human element. Human element." He drew his hand across his jaw, rubbing at his stubble. Jukeboxes. Diners. Malt shops. None of that stuff was human. Here he thought he got off easy, getting his first idea handed to him like a free serving of bacon from Fran during breakfast.

"Fran." He sat upright. *She* was about as human as they came. He stood and grabbed his hat and his article. He didn't know if she worked the dinner shift, but she struck him as a hard-working woman who would be there till the bitter end each day.

*****

"Me? You want to include me in your article?" She leaned against the counter and laughed wryly, but he could see she liked the idea.

He tapped his pen point on the article. "You could be my human element."

She put her hand on her hip. "Well don't *you* know how to turn a girl's head?"

"Come on, Fran. I'm having a tough time going from writing hard news to writing this kind of piece. Apparently I wrote the thing like a research paper for a high school electronics class. Let's just talk about why you think your boss is putting the wallboxes in, how you think they'll affect patrons, that kind of thing. What *you* think about them. And then maybe I could talk with a couple customers. Maybe even your boss. Is he around?"

"Artie? No, he's out of town for the weekend. Our short order cook's in charge. He's Artie's brother."

"I could interview him, then."

Fran chuckled. "Not on your life. Artie would kill me if I let you print anything Eggie has to say. The man can't get through a sentence without cursing like his thumb is in a vise."

"Eggie?"

"Edgar, but believe me, he's more of an Eggie. You know, Josh, if you mention the diner in a positive way, Artie will love this. And then he won't mind that I chatted with you between customers."

Josh stifled a grin. Fran had certainly never worried before about chatting too much.

He spent the next hour or so peppering her with questions. And she was so chummy with the customers, he got plenty of colorful input from them as well. One thing was clear. The wallboxes were going to be a hit. And now he had a more human angle to the story. Somewhere along the way, the customers shared their favorite songs with him, along with a few stories behind their fondness. He thought he might actually manage to spin another article out of the stories they told.

"Warm you up?" Fran stood by with a coffeepot, ready to pour.

"No thanks. I've had plenty. And I think I have enough for my article too. Thanks, Fran. I'd better get back to the office and write this up before my new boss cans me."

He slapped his money on the counter and stood up from the barstool. But he stopped in his tracks when the door opened and Fran greeted the next customer.

"Hi, Rachel, honey. You done for the day?"

Josh turned around and met eyes with her. Still in that pretty little polka-dotted dress from this morning. The fact that they were slated for an official date—at least that was the way he saw tomorrow's dinner—added a more exciting dimension to this casual encounter. Neither one of them spoke for a moment, but they both stared at each other until Fran spoke loudly into their silence.

"Ahem."

They both started and looked at Fran, who wore far too knowing a smile. She had returned the coffeepot to its burner, but now she picked it back up, looked pointedly at him, and said, "You want to reconsider your response about that coffee, hon?"

Before he could answer, Rachel walked up to the counter. She gave him a shy smile. "Hi."

"Hi, Rachel."

Fran returned the coffeepot and grabbed a couple of menus. "Would you two like to share a booth, maybe?"

Josh looked back at her and caught her wink.

"No thanks, Fran," Rachel said. "I actually stopped by to pick up the dinner Mr. and Mrs. Chambers ordered. I told them I'd bring it by for them."

"Oh, now, are they feeling poorly again?" Fran folded her arms across her waist, her head tilted with concern.

"No, they're all right. They just stopped by the studio on their evening walk, and when Mr. Chambers said they were going to call in for dinner, I offered to save them the second trip out."

"Mr. and Mrs. Chambers?" Josh sat back down on the bar stool.

Rachel pointed over her shoulder. "They're this sweet older couple who live in the apartments around the corner. They're kind of my third set of grandparents, I guess you could say."

"Let me see if their order is ready." Fran walked away.

He had hoped Fran would find a reason to leave, but now he wasn't sure what to say. "So how's the car holding up, anyway?" Smooth, Josh. Sweep the girl right off her feet.

A quick, confused frown flashed across her features. "Uh, great. I think you were right. The battery needed water."

He nodded. All right, they had talked that subject out.

"How about your jukebox article? I've been watching for it."

That made him grin. She had honestly listened to him when he talked about his work. After he had been such a lunkhead about her business, here she was, showing interest in his. He held up the red-slashed copy from Lou. "It wasn't exactly award winning."

Her eyebrows lifted. "Sort of like going back to school sometimes, huh?"

"Yeah. I think this editor is going to be even tougher than Sal, my editor on the city desk. And that's saying a lot!"

She laughed. "Just as long as you don't get fired again!" She gasped right after she spoke. "Oh, heavens! I can't believe I just said that!"

He had never seen a woman turn red quite that quickly. She was a lighter shade of the dots on her dress. He laughed out loud. "Don't worry about it. I hope he doesn't fire me too."

Fran walked out with two brown bags that already showed a

few spots of grease from whatever the Chambers ordered for the evening.

"Two fried egg sandwiches to go."

While Rachel, still looking flustered, dug through her purse for money, he reached out and took the bags from Fran.

"How about I walk with you to the Chambers' place? Let me just drop my stuff in my car outside first."

Fran grinned. "That's a great idea. A girl can't be too careful out there."

He waited for Rachel to look up from her purse. When she did, he knew the grateful look in her eyes had more to do with his shrugging off her comment about his getting fired than it did any chivalry on his part.

Even as they walked to the door together, she muttered as much to herself as to him, "Ugh. I'm such a dumbbell. I can't believe I made that 'getting fired' crack."

He placed his hand at the small of her back as he held the door for her. "Rachel. Listen."

She glanced up at him. Man, she was a pretty thing.

"I'm listening."

He looked off into the distance. "Hearken back with me—"

"Hearken?" Now a smile started to return.

"Yes, hearken. And don't interrupt. Hearken back to a day not so long ago when a clumsy but ruggedly handsome newspaper reporter—"

She tsked out a little laugh.

"—sat next to a lovely ballroom dance instructor and called her life's work…"

He couldn't remember what he had called it that first day.

"Irresponsible? Frivolous? Flippant?" Rachel easily filled the silence while he tried to remember.

He frowned. "Yikes. And then there was this morning's charming display."

She laughed. She stopped walking and put her hand out to him. "All right. Even?"

"Even." He shook her hand. Her small, warm, soft hand. "Although, if that's what I really said, I think I might still owe you a little more kindness as payback."

He wasn't so sure about that, really. He just liked to suggest they had a reason to stay involved in each other's lives. So her simple response pleased him.

"Maybe so," she said.

CHAPTER SIXTEEN

The air outside was far more humid than it had been this morning. Looked like the evening would turn rainy soon. Rachel glanced up at the gray sky, not too thrilled about heading home and spending the drizzly evening alone.

Josh said, "So how did you get involved with this old couple, the Chambers? Are they in any of your dance classes?" He carried the Chambers' food, his hand supporting the bottom of the bags as if they contained fragile sculptures rather than fried egg sandwiches.

Rachel chuckled. "Oh, no. Neither one of them is all that able-bodied. But they're big dance fans. They stop by and watch the classes and they come to every event we have, when they're able to."

"Events? What kind of events do you have?"

She shrugged. "You know, performances for family members to come watch." She gave him a sly smile. "Sometimes family members decide they want to sign up for lessons too."

"Smart girl."

"And sometimes there's a dance competition with other studios. I mean, there are more and more studios opening all the time. And now there are local, regional, and even national competitions each year."

"I had no idea there were so many people interested in this stuff. And your students compete?"

"Well, no, we haven't participated a lot yet. I competed a few times with my boyfriend—"

"You have a boyfriend?"

She saw him catch himself after he blurted his question. She tried not to smile.

"Had. We broke up months ago. But we danced in a few competitions when we were together. It's really good for business when a studio competes, even if it doesn't win. Gets the word out. You want to build your reputation any way you can. The two people who teach for me in the evening used to win a lot of competitions in their day. Now they just teach part-time. And they're excellent at it."

"And you hired those two young ones this morning, right?"

They crossed the street and Rachel pointed ahead. "Just up to that next corner. Yes, and not a moment too soon. Betty leaves in a week. Even sooner than that, really. And I was already at a point where I needed another full-time teacher."

"That's good, right? You have lots of customers?"

She liked that he truly seemed to have shrugged off his distaste for "art" as a business. She hoped that was genuine. "Yeah, as long as I have enough teachers to teach them. If I have to turn away any students, that will be business I lose to another studio. There's another one in Falls Church, just one town over. Here we go." She started up the concrete walk to the Chambers' door.

Josh chuckled. "They have a bit of a June bug problem."

It was true. For a few warm months each year, the June bugs could be invasive around the D.C. area. The Chambers' front porch was especially bad.

"That's because of their hummingbird feeder." Rachel swatted one of the shiny green beetles away from the pretty porcelain pot hanging from the porch ceiling. "The bugs like it as much as the birds do." She smiled at Josh before she rang the doorbell. "I tried to convince them to take it down. But they get such joy from the occasional hummingbird, they don't care about the beetles. The neighbors usually sweep the porch for them, but I think they're out of town this week."

"It's a small porch," Josh said. "If they have a broom, I could sweep it in a matter of seconds."

Rachel looked at him again. Well, didn't *he* just get even better looking all the time?

Even though darkness hadn't yet fallen, the porch light went on, and the front door opened. Mr. and Mrs. Chambers were both there at the door. You would think a celebrity had come to visit. Rachel smiled. She just loved these two.

"It's Rachel!" Mr. Chambers spoke to his wife as if she couldn't see with her own eyes. "It's Rachel, dear, come with our dinner like an angel."

Rachel laughed softly. "Hi, Mr. and Mrs. Chambers—"

Mrs. Chambers looked at Josh. "And she has a handsome young man with her!"

Josh smiled and extended his hand to Mr. Chambers and then his wife. "Josh Reegan. Very nice to meet you both."

"Come in, come in," Mr. Chambers said. "Let's back up, Nina, and let them in."

And they did exactly that, shuffling backward for a while before they finally turned and walked into their close, cluttered little home. Because of her visits here, she would always associate the smell of Vick's VapoRub with the Chambers.

"We're not going to stay." Rachel took the bags from Josh. "We just wanted to drop off your dinner. I'll put it out for you. You should eat it now, while it's still hot."

"And if you tell me where you keep your broom, I'll sweep those June bugs off your porch before we go."

Mrs. Chambers smiled at both of them. "Look at you kids, killing two stones at once."

Rachel shot a glance at Josh, who looked puzzled for a second before he smiled and cast his eyes down. Such dark lashes for a fair-haired man.

They all went into the Chambers' kitchen, where Rachel quickly set their small Formica table and put out their food. She pointed at a closet off the kitchen. "Josh, the brooms are in there."

As soon as Josh stepped back outside with the broom, Mrs. Chambers sat at the table and grabbed Rachel's arm, her bony, veined grip far stronger than she would have expected. "He's a wonderful young man, Rachel. Don't you let him get away, now."

Rachel laughed. "We barely know each other, Mrs. Chambers."

"I barely knew Benjamin when we married. Look at us now." She reached down and smacked her husband's hand as he tried to take one of her french fries.

Mr. Chambers planted a kiss on his wife's head before sitting down. "You see? The honeymoon never ends." The couple looked at each other and started laughing so hard Mrs. Chambers fell into a coughing fit. Once she was breathing normally, she took a french fry and fed it to her husband, still chuckling. "How are things at the studio, Rachel?"

"Good! I've hired my new instructors—"

"That wonderful young man? The one we saw dancing with you?" Mrs. Chambers' eyes were as eager as a child's.

"Yes. He's one of them. And a girl I auditioned earlier in the week."

Mrs. Chambers jerked her thumb toward the front of the house. "You sure he won't mind?"

Rachel looked at the front door and back again. "Who? Josh?"

"Mm-hmm." Her tone suggested Rachel was up to something naughty.

"Uh, I can't imagine why he would mind my hiring new teachers."

Mrs. Chambers leaned forward to whisper. "No. I mean you and that dancer. Won't your young man out there worry about the hanky-panky?"

"Oh! You mean with Cruz?" Rachel chuckled. "No, Cruz is an employee. Not a boyfriend. And he's *very* young."

"I'm three years older than Benjamin." She got a saucy twinkle in her eyes.

Josh walked back into the kitchen. "Spick-and-span!" He held the broom beside himself like a trident.

"I thank you, Josh," Mr. Chambers said. He started to push himself up from the table, but Josh stopped him.

"No, don't get up." He returned the broom to the closet. "Have your dinner. I have to get back to the office anyway and finish some work. Were you going to stay a little longer, Rachel, or can I walk you to your car?"

She opened her mouth, but Mrs. Chambers answered for her. "Yes, you most certainly can walk her to her car!"

Rachel smiled at Josh, her eyes wide. "I guess I'm leaving too."

They said their good-byes to the old couple and left.

"I'm parked just down the street." She pointed ahead. "I'm sorry. I didn't realize you had to go back to the office."

"Yep. Got my electronics term paper to rewrite."

Her brow furrowed briefly and then awareness dawned. "Oh. Your article. Well, I appreciate your helping me. Helping the Chambers."

"My pleasure. They're a sweet couple."

She nodded. "They have what everyone wants."

"Bacon and egg sandwiches?"

She smacked his arm. "You're quite a romantic, aren't you?"

He looked straight ahead when he responded. "Maybe a little more so now than I was a few weeks ago."

Goodness. That definitely shut her up. When she finally had the nerve to look at him, he gave her a very attractive, very amused sideways glance.

Goodness again. Did this guy realize how charming he could be? She certainly hoped not.

They reached her car. She wasn't sure what to expect, so she carried on as if she expected nothing, kiss-wise. "All the best with your rewriting tonight."

He opened her door for her, and she got in and started the engine.

"Thanks. And I hope everything works out well with your new teachers."

"I think it will. What? What's that look for?"

He shrugged. "I just wonder how long you'll be able to hang onto the kid."

"Cruz?" What was it with everyone focusing so much on Cruz? "Why wouldn't I be able to hang onto him?" Did Josh think Cruz was going to be a problem? Sometimes guys could see things in other guys that women simply missed.

"I just think he's actually...well, pretty much a *guy*."

"So?"

"So how long do you think it's going to be before he realizes he doesn't want to be doing all that..."

She could see it. He just realized he was saying the wrong thing.

"All that what, Josh? Silly dance stuff? Are you really that unaware of how many men teach ballroom dance?"

He frowned, and then he made a face as if something smelled bad. "Grown men?"

She felt way too much irritation coming on. "Of course grown men. I already told you I have a married couple that teaches for me in the evenings."

He shook his head and rested his hand against the top of her car. "I think you said a couple of *people*."

"Men are people!" She turned off the engine. "What's the problem, Josh? What exactly are you insinuating? That no *real* man would ever do something as frivolous as teach dance?"

He sighed. "I'm sorry. It's just hard for me to fathom."

Hard for him to fathom? What a caveman he was! Rachel swatted at him so he would step back. "Excuse me." She pulled her door closed and started up her car again. She was tempted to roll up her window.

"Oh, come on, now, don't get frosted about it. I didn't mean anything insulting."

Now it was her turn to sigh. "You know, your attitude just shows that you still have no respect for what I do. Of *course* men teach ballroom and they dance it too. I just finished telling you my boyfriend and I used to dance together in competitions. Did you think he was less than a 'real' man?"

Josh shrugged. "How do I know? I know he must have been a stupid man, to—"

"No, don't even try to flatter me right now, all right? Look, you're entitled to your opinion, so please don't pretend to have a different one, just for my sake."

"But you're mad at me for my opinion!" A few drops of rain fell around them.

"I'm sorry about that. Maybe I shouldn't be mad at you, but I am. And I think it's best that... Well, I've got to go. You have work to do, and I have a very busy day ahead of me tomorrow."

"Rachel, come on."

"Thanks for your help with the Chambers."

"What about tomorrow night? You don't want to let Mary down, do you?"

She had forgotten about Mary's birthday dinner. She could have growled. "No, I don't want to let her down." She sighed. "All right. I'll see you tomorrow. But I have to go let off a little steam right now, okay?"

The rain came down more heavily, and she sighed with more force. "Do I need to drive you to your car?"

He just shook his head and pointed ahead. "I'm right up there."

She nodded and rolled up her window. She pulled away from the curb and fought the impulse to look in her rearview mirror as she left. She gave her steering wheel a tight-fisted little punch. It really was best that she not cultivate her attraction to Josh any further. She had enough weighing on her mind what with her dad's fears that she couldn't be as successful as her brothers. And if Cruz got a whiff of the kind of nonsense Josh was spouting, maybe he *would* think it was unmanly to dance. Then what would happen with Mira? And Mr. Longworth's financial backing?

The last thing she needed was to fall for some guy who didn't support what she loved and did for a living. No man was good-looking enough for that.

She'd just have to keep telling herself that until she could embrace it as truth.

CHAPTER SEVENTEEN

Several hours later Josh sat at his desk in the relatively dark, quiet office. The bulk of the support staff had gone home, and most of his fellow Style reporters had turned in their copy hours ago. He worked under the glare of his solitary desk lamp. He finally had what he considered an article with enough of a human element to make even the most people-loving editor smile. He had tucked away all thought about the tussle he had with Rachel before he came back to the office. He couldn't afford that kind of distraction when he was under the gun to produce acceptable copy for tonight's print. There was nothing he could do about it now, anyway. The damage was done.

He gave his article one last scan and got up to put it on Lou's desk. Lou would be back from his brief dinner meeting any minute, and he preferred that Lou think the rewriting effort had been a walk in the park, finished quickly after he began work on it.

He paused at Lou's office door and gave the article another look. Maybe he should call his sister Bree and read it to her. She had a soft, womanly heart. She'd be able to tell if he had fluffed it up enough.

He dropped to the edge of his desk, picked up the receiver, then dialed.

"Josh? What are you doing, calling so late?" She spoke almost as soon as he said hello. "Are you all right?"

"Oh, sorry. Were you asleep?"

"No, I was about to chase the kids to their bedrooms, though, so

Pete and I could have a little time together. I'm just not used to hearing from you at night. What's going on?"

"Nothing serious. I just thought you might be able to give me some advice about this article for the Style pages. My editor wanted me to make it less technical. More people-like. Okay if I read it to you?"

"Sure. Let's hear it."

He nodded and stared at the paper in his hand. "Let me ask you something, Bree. How would you feel if Pete wanted to take up ballroom dancing? What would you think of him?"

"You wrote your article about ballroom dancing?" Bree chuckled. "You're jumping into this Style and Leisure job with both feet, aren't you? I never would have thought you'd be willing to—"

"No, the article is about jukeboxes."

Silence.

"Jukeboxes," she said.

"Yeah."

"So why are you asking me about Pete and ballroom dancing? Do they use jukeboxes at the dance studio? I didn't think—"

"Two different things, Bree. I'm talking about something other than the article right now."

Bree's sigh was a quick blast of noise in his ear. "Okay, big brother. You're going to make me nuts here. This must have something to do with the lovely Miss Stanhope. Right?"

"I just don't think it's all that strange for a grown man—I've seen war, for Pete's sake. Is it so strange that I think ballroom dance is a little silly? I don't mean to be insulting. It just seems…awfully feminine for men."

"Josh, what did you do? Sometimes you're like a big dumb ox, you know that?"

He ran his hand through his hair. "I know. I'm a moron."

She laughed. "Tell me what happened."

She uttered little groans here and there as he described the conflict with Rachel. He explained that they had gotten off to a bad start when they first met, patched things up—as far as he could tell—and then he had fallen back into trouble this evening.

Bree spoke off to the side before commenting, saying something to the kids about getting ready for bed.

"Okay, Josh, listen to me. You need to loosen up, big brother. Yeah, you've been through the war, but so have a lot of other people. Gene Kelly served during the war, you know, and he's slightly fond of dance. Nothing feminine about him. And you're just being stupid about dance, to tell you the truth. Women *love* a man who can lead them across a dance floor. Don't you want women to love you? You bathe daily, don't you?"

He frowned. "Of course I bathe daily."

He heard a snort and looked up to see Lou listening to him. Josh covered the mouthpiece. "Do you mind, Lou?"

"Yeah, I mind. Where's the article?"

"Oh." He looked at the article and figured he'd give this version a shot. He handed it to Lou. "Let me know what you think."

"You know I will." Lou walked into his office and shut the door.

Josh rubbed at his eyes. "So why are you asking me about bathing?"

"You like to smell nice and clean, right?"

"Yeah."

"But if you didn't bathe, you'd smell more like a real man."

"A real smelly man."

She sighed. "My point is that there are certain things you do because you're not an ape, okay? So even if you never dance the cha-cha, you don't *need* to spout off about how silly you think it is. How it's too feminine for a real man to do. Everyone knows you're a big tough guy, Josh. It would actually be a good thing if you took a few lessons yourself. Learn enough to be able to dance at your own wedding. You know, with your bride? Do you want a bride someday?"

"Sheesh. Cut me some slack, Bree. I've barely kissed the girl."

After Bree gasped there was nothing but silence from the other end of the phone.

"Bree?"

Again, he heard her talk off to the side. "Honey, give me a few minutes, okay? I've got Josh on the phone. I'll fill you in later."

"Hey, come on. Pete's already riding me like crazy about Rachel. Don't be telling him this stuff."

"Ha! You should know better than that. You lived with us for a year. You know how I am with him. I tell him *everything,* so you might as well think about that before you call me next time. And *when* did you kiss her? You Casanova, you!"

He smiled. He forgot for a moment that Rachel was angry with him. "*Barely* kissed her. Barely was the key word there. And at this rate I doubt it will happen again. I just helped her when her car battery died a few nights ago, and we got comfortable enough around each other to..." He frowned. "Anyway, that's all different now. I think I've used up all my chances."

"It's all because of Daddy, you know." Bree's voice had softened.

"What's all because of him?"

"Sometimes I notice how much Pete is like Dad, in lots of ways. Especially the good ways, you know? Like he's hardworking and puts family first and he's probably the most honest man I know. Losing Dad when I was an adolescent—well, I think I looked for someone like him from then on. Pete's his own man, but he fills that gap for me."

Josh scratched at a spot of something that had dripped and dried on his desk. He didn't want to insult yet another woman, but he had no idea what she was going on about.

"Uh, okay."

Another exasperated sigh from Bree. "I'm saying that losing Dad affected you too. You were so young. What, sixteen? You lost the most important man at a time in your life when you were just becoming a young man yourself. I think sometimes you try too hard to, I don't know, to be like him. He was awfully manly, I'll admit."

"It's been almost twenty years, Bree. I've been through enough to make my own judgments and decisions."

"I know. You're right. But I don't think you're happy with the judgment you passed a few hours ago, when you were talking with Rachel. Believe me, no one is going to question your masculinity just because you show respect for what Rachel does for a living. Dad wouldn't, even."

His brows knit together. "Man, you make me sound so unsure of myself."

"Yeah." She laughed softly. "Show me someone who's completely sure of himself, big brother, and I'll show you someone who's faking it." She spoke off to the side again before she said anything else. "Okay, listen, you'd better read me that article so I can go. My husband needs some attention, or he's going to feel unsure of himself."

Josh chuckled. "Never mind. Lou took it while we were talking. He hasn't stormed out of his office asking for another rewrite yet, so maybe I got it right this time. Thanks for your help, sis."

"You're coming to Mom's for dinner tomorrow night, right? And Mary's expecting Rachel, so you'd better patch things up quick. Six o'clock."

"Yeah, I'll be there. Love you, sis."

He hung up and looked at the closed door to Lou's office. Was the article all right or not? He wanted to head home.

Images of Rachel filled his mind at the moment, and he pulled his wallet out of his pocket without a great deal of awareness. He flipped it open and looked at the photograph of his father he had carried for nearly twenty years. The picture had been with him through plenty of hard knocks, from the war, to working his way through college, to late night after late night, nosing around in risky quarters to catch the news and claw his way to the city desk at the *Tribune.*

Until Bree mentioned it, he hadn't really thought about how vividly he felt his father's presence, his influence, over every decision he made. She was right about another thing too. He couldn't picture his father dumping his own critical feelings on a sweet, hardworking young woman the way he had with Rachel. Twice. Plus what Rachel had overheard him say to Pete in the studio. Granted, he was simply misunderstood that time, but she had looked so hurt.

He picked up the phone but then considered the hour. Tomorrow. He'd call Rachel in the morning and try to make things right.

His dad couldn't advise him, but Josh wasn't averse to a quick prayer to his heavenly Father.

What do You think, God—You want to give me a little help here? Should I call her in the morning?

Lou stuck his head outside his office. "That's the right idea, Reegan. Let's run with it." He held the article aloft, and Josh wondered if two questions hadn't just been answered at once.

CHAPTER EIGHTEEN

Rachel's comment on the phone the next day made Josh cringe. "I should have told Betty to tell everyone who phoned that I'd call back later. I feel bad you thought you needed to call so many times this morning."

He regretted having called four times. He attempted to brush aside the fleeting image of himself, forever apologizing to Rachel. He was going to start thinking of her name as Sorry Rachel.

Still, now that she finally called him back, those words fell familiarly from his mouth.

"Sorry, Rachel. I didn't mean to come across as pushy." Or desperate. He had no idea Betty had made note of each of his calls to the studio. He *told* Betty he would try back later, that she needn't tell Rachel he had rung. Now he realized his having called four times might have shaken up Rachel. In a bad way. He was good and embarrassed.

He tried to explain. "I kept calling because I hoped to catch you between classes or something."

"Don't worry about it."

She sounded calm and friendly, if a little reserved. That was better than he expected. He let her carry on, knowing he could only mess things up by interrupting her.

"I told Betty not to put any calls through, because I wanted to focus on my new plans for the business. And then I needed to set up a new schedule and look into upcoming competitions, change my payroll records, stuff like that. But there was no way Betty wouldn't have told me you called…"

He sat up, especially when she stopped in midsentence. Hmm. Did that mean his calls in particular merited mention, or all calls Rachel received today?

"I mean, of course she would tell me you were trying to reach me," she said. "Otherwise, what would be the point in her answering the phones for me? Right?"

Ah, well. He was one of many, apparently. "Right. That makes sense." But did Betty *have* to tell Rachel he had tried four times?

"Josh, about tonight—"

This time he couldn't help himself. "Wait, Rachel. Please don't let my ignorant comments last night keep you from being there for Mary's birthday. My sister tells me she's talked of little else since she invited you."

"No, I'm not cancelling. It's just that I'm going to be a little busy up until then. I asked Mira and Cruz, the new teachers you met, to come in and work with Connie and Mel—"

"Connie and Mel?"

"The older couple I mentioned. Last night. They teach for me part-time. And I want them to start working with Mira and Cruz, to help them think about competitive dance."

"Okay. And?"

"And it would actually be easier, if it's all right, if I just drove to Mary's birthday dinner myself. From here."

Josh held back a groan. He had looked forward to that time alone with her on the drive to and from Bree and Pete's house. And then he realized this could be his chance to show more appreciation for ballroom dancing. He wanted to be more supportive of Rachel, even if they never became anything other than friends. She had been supportive about *his* work.

"Rachel, I'd actually prefer to drive you so you don't have to find your way there the first time."

The insinuation hung in the air that she would become involved with him enough to go to his sister's house again in the future. She said nothing, so he jumped back in.

"Hey, maybe I could come by a little early and meet Mel and Connie and watch for a while." That wasn't too hopeless sounding, was it? His plea, coupled with the multiple phone calls?

"Sure, feel free. But don't come by just to try to convince me you enjoy dance."

The bitter edge of her comment was not lost on him.

"Look, Rachel, I'm sorry about that—my being so rude about male dance teachers."

"Thanks. I guess I'm a little oversensitive sometimes."

Well, that was an olive-branch comment if he'd ever heard one. "I don't think so. My sister tells me I'm an ox."

He heard a soft laugh on the other end of the line.

"I think I like your sister, between the fine job she's done with Mark and Mary and her astute ability to judge character."

"She's also a very forgiving woman, which is another fine quality. Wouldn't you agree?"

"I suppose so." He heard the smile in her response.

"Yep. They say forgiveness is divine. So I'm happy to provide you with another chance to behave divinely."

Her silence stretched before she finally answered. "Speaking of divine, what church do you attend?"

Well *that* was like a bird hitting the windshield. "Uh, church?"

"You know, those pretty white buildings with the pointy tops on them?"

He laughed. "I guess I don't have a regular church. I go to my mom's every once in a while. It's a Christian church, but no denomination."

"Perfect! I'll make a deal with you then. Commit to come with me to church this Sunday morning—I go to Arlington Bible—and I'll accept your offer of a ride, and you can come early and watch my dancers."

"But you already told me I could come watch."

Another brief silence.

"You have a problem with my proposition, Josh?"

He smiled. If he had a problem with it, there was no way he would cop to it now. And he really didn't have a problem with it—if she lived in the same general area he did, she probably went to a church fairly close to his house. It would do him good to start going to church again. He had let work take over his Sunday mornings, and his attendance had become spotty even before then. But skipping church really wasn't necessary, especially not until he got back onto the city desk.

"No problem at all," he said. "As a matter of fact—"

"Josh!" Rachel's gasp stopped him midthought.

"What? Are you okay?"

"I just opened today's paper! To page E-1, actually."

He smiled, glad she couldn't see how happy he was that she finally noticed. "Oh." He chuckled.

"Why didn't you tell me your wallbox article was in today's Style and Leisure section? If it'd been me, it would have been the first thing out of my mouth, I'm sure." She gasped again. "Aww, Josh, was that why you kept trying to reach me this morning?"

He laughed outright. "Credit me with a little more modesty than that, young lady."

"All right, I will. Why, then?"

He frowned. "Why then what?"

"Why did you call my studio a hundred times today?"

"Oh," he said. She brought a smile to his face. "I called to tell you that you're a shameless exaggerator."

"No, really. I never gave you a chance to tell me why you called."

He sighed. He thought that had been clear. He hated to say it again. "Just to tell you what a bad-mannered clod I was when we spoke last night."

She chuckled. "That's so cute."

"My humility?"

"No, that you thought I hadn't already figured that out on my own."

He laughed. "Are you drinking vinegar over there, all by yourself?"

"Buckets of it. But I have to go now. I have a very important news article to read. I'll see you here around five, five thirty, then?"

"I'll be there."

His smile lingered long after he hung up the phone. He pictured Rachel sitting in her office, the newspaper splayed out in front of her, with his article her sole focus. Now he was glad Lou had insisted on that so-called human element being added to the piece. It made for a friendlier story. And it gave him a chance to show Rachel a little something about himself in a way she'd be more likely to appreciate than had the story been another hard-news piece about that snake Wiley.

Not that he didn't still prefer the satisfaction of using his writing to expose corruption over writing to expose the latest in gadgets and fads. But if he had to write this stuff, he might as well find some advantages to it. He didn't plan to use his Style writing to woo Rachel—he wasn't even sure if wooing Rachel was something he wanted to do, considering how often he seemed to upset her. But he had a feeling it would be a good thing to imagine he were writing each article specifically for her.

His smile deepened, and he opened his copy of the *Tribune* to attempt reading the article from her viewpoint. "My muse."

He decided she would like it—the mention of Fran and the diner, the quotes from the customers—and he folded the paper away. He needed to get to work on his next article so he'd be able to head to the studio in time.

He and his muse were going to dinner.

CHAPTER NINETEEN

"My wife tells me you've brought new spring to my daughter's step, Miss Stanhope. I trust this month's mortgage payment will go to good use for you and the studio."

Rachel didn't need to see his face to know he was pleased. She could hear it in his voice, even over the phone. She couldn't help but squirm about the secrecy of her arrangement with Mr. Longworth, for a number of reasons. She stepped away from her desk and casually glanced out her office door to make sure no one was within listening distance. All the teachers were looking over records and talking music selection. She gritted her teeth before coming clean with Mr. Longworth.

"I have to be frank with you, sir. Mira is a beautiful dancer and a very promising teacher."

"If you say so, that's all that matters."

She frowned. Why was it all that mattered? Didn't the man have any interest in his daughter? She may as well be a show dog under a trainer's care, for all the involvement he had with her. Why hadn't *he* noticed the spring in his daughter's step?

"You should..." No, that wasn't the way with a man like Longworth. No unsolicited advice. "Feel free to come by the studio anytime. I think you'd be very proud of her. And what I was going to say—to admit, really—is that even if you hadn't made the offer you did, I would have hired Mira. I just can't sleep at night without telling you that, okay?"

He chuckled at the other end of the line. "I like your honesty, young lady. But I'm as good as my word, always. A deal is a deal. And part of our deal was that you didn't have to hire Mira if she wasn't qualified. You're not telling me anything surprising. I knew you wouldn't hire her strictly for the money. So you're covered for this month and the next six, regardless of what else happens."

Rachel released her breath in relief. She hadn't realized she was perspiring, but now she patted at the tiny beads of sweat on her forehead. "I do appreciate that. I have plans for the studio that will very likely involve Mira."

"Yes, well, I look forward to hearing about that at some point, but I have to get to a meeting at the moment. Good-bye, now."

"Oh. All right. Thank you, Mr.—"

But he had already hung up. What an odd man. Despite the fact that he seemed to have confidence in Mira's capabilities, he simply didn't seem interested in knowing anything about the very thing that gave his daughter joy.

Rachel thought of her own father. He didn't have an abundance of confidence in her capabilities, but at least he demonstrated some interest in… Oh. No, actually, her own father didn't seem terribly interested in what went on at her studio, either. What *was* it about men? Maybe her father would find the studio more interesting once it turned the kind of profit she hoped it would, thanks to Mr. Longworth's investment. But that wasn't quite the same thing as interest in what gave his daughter joy, was it?

And it was with these thoughts in mind that she walked out of her office and saw Mel and Cruz working together with Connie and Mira. She broke into a smile. There were a couple of men who appreciated how attractive ballroom dance could be.

Betty stood at the edge of the dance floor and watched. Her purse, flung over her shoulder, showed she meant to leave but got caught up in watching the dancing. She turned and grinned at Rachel as she approached. This was the best Betty had looked in a week. Maybe the morning sickness was starting to abate.

"Rachel, you're going to do just fine without me. I'm even a little jealous to be quitting and missing out on what you're going to accomplish with those two. Mira and Cruz."

Rachel draped her arm around Betty's shoulders. "You're not going into hiding, Betty. Come by anytime. You're part of the family. And you know you're welcome back to teach in the future, assuming I'm still in business."

"Oh, you will be."

The front door opened, and Josh stepped in. Rachel smiled at him and waved him over. "Come on in, Josh. You know Betty, right?"

"Sure I do." He shook her hand.

"You're Mark and Mary's uncle, right?" Betty studied him as if she had never looked at him closely before. "And you're taking our girl here to a birthday dinner, I understand."

Rachel could tell he appreciated that she had talked with Betty about the evening.

"Yes, that's right. Mary's fourteenth." He looked at Rachel as he spoke, and his fondness for her was especially evident. "Mary's really looking forward to Rachel's being there."

There was no disguise in Betty's discerning comment. "I can see *Mary's* very excited about the evening."

Rachel's eyes widened at Betty before she shook her head. "Don't you need to get home to your husband or something, lady?"

Betty laughed. "Yep. I'm going. You two kids have fun tonight."

Rachel motioned toward some chairs on the periphery of the dance floor. "Have a seat, Josh. We're only going to work another thirty minutes or so, and then we can head to Mary's dinner. Is that all right?"

He nodded and looked toward the dancers. "That's what I'm here for."

She left him then and mingled with the others, giving tips, observing, stepping in to demonstrate. She almost forgot about Josh sitting there, she got so involved in the choreography they all discussed. Before she realized it, forty-five minutes had gone by. She glanced at the clock and panicked.

"Oh! Josh, I'm so sorry. Hey, everyone, we have to call it a night, okay? At some point tomorrow everyone's on the schedule at the same time. There's a bit of a gap between the four thirty and six o'clock classes. Everyone willing to work through?"

She got their agreements and hurried them all out. No one appeared to mind the rush except Cruz. And he seemed less perturbed by the rush than he did by the presence of Josh. Maybe he had a problem with being watched while he worked. If that were the case, he'd have to get over that. Rachel made no mention about his frown and let him take it outside with him. She grabbed her purse, keys, and Mary's gift.

"Please forgive me!" She put her hand on Josh's arm, breathless. "I lost track of time."

He smiled and presented his arm. "Nothing to forgive. But I'm glad we have another apology on your side of the scale."

She locked the door before looping her arm through his. "That's awful. If I'm going to make you late, I guess I'm going to have to work on holding my temper. We can't have the scales tipping too far in your favor."

She considered that as they neared his car. Josh might repeatedly step on her toes, but he always made the effort to apologize when he did. She didn't want to compare him with anyone, especially Billy, but she couldn't remember a single time when Billy had apologized to her. Especially not for that last thing.

CHAPTER TWENTY

"Yeah, so this big lug lived with us for, what? Five years was it, Josh?" Pete passed a bowl of mashed potatoes to Rachel while he addressed his brother-in-law.

"Oh, honey, stop. It was one year." Bree shared a laugh with Josh.

Rachel hid a smile. Josh looked ready for the dinner topic to change. But she wanted to hear a bit more about him.

"When was that?"

Josh shrugged. "The year after I got home from the war. I just needed—"

"Josh already had his college degree before the war started," his mother said. "So he just needed a little time to get his feet on the ground with the newspaper. And I had just moved into my smaller place, so Bree and Pete came to the rescue."

Mary piped up. "I loved it when Uncle Josh was here. He used to read bedtime stories to me sometimes. And make me pancakes. Remember, Uncle Josh?"

"And he wrestled harder than Dad did," Mark said. "Dad always let me win."

Pete laughed. "Hey, you weren't supposed to know that. Uncle Josh is just more competitive than I am." He shot a wink at Rachel.

"That's not true." Josh came to his own defense. "I just wanted Mark to know you don't win every contest in life, that's all."

Bree reached over and gave Josh's hand a squeeze. "My serious brother." She smiled at Rachel. "We loved having him here. Gravy down this way, please, Mary?"

Josh nodded. "I had to make sure my little sister was being treated right, chained as she was to this guy." He cocked his head toward Pete.

Josh's mother sat back, her arms folded across her chest, and addressed Josh. "You were always looking out for Bree. Even when you were both little." She sat up and accepted the plate of roast chicken from Rachel. "He was three when she was born, and he called her 'my baby' for the longest time."

Bree laughed. "Until he discovered girls, I think."

Rachel cast a glance at Josh to see if he was comfortable with the conversation. She caught him watching her, but he didn't look away. He slowly closed his eyes and shook his head over Bree's comment before giving Rachel a broad smile.

"Now, now," his mother said. "Let's not be rude. Rachel doesn't want to hear about all of that."

She did, a little, though.

"No one wants to hear all that." Pete grinned at Josh. "Least of all Josh."

Mark sat up abruptly. "He had so many girlfriends! It was like a new person every time."

"That's an exaggeration, Mark." Bree frowned and then slapped on a smile when she turned to Rachel. "He's exaggerating."

Josh cleared his throat and said, "So Mary, how do you like turning fourteen? You look all grown up in that new dress."

"It's a poodle skirt, Uncle Josh." Mary needed no further prompting to carry the conversation away. She interrupted her meal to stand and spin around for everyone. "It's what I wanted for my birthday."

"I love it," Rachel said. "You'll have to wear that to dance swing."

"Will you teach us swing?"

"Come on, honey, sit and eat." Bree waved Mary back to the table.

Rachel looked at Mark to include him in the conversation. "Sure, you'll both learn swing if you keep coming to class."

Mark nodded. "Yeah, yesterday Cruz said he'd teach me swing as soon as you let him. That's pretty cool, I guess."

By the time they finished the meal and made themselves ready for Mary's birthday cake, Rachel nearly felt like one of the family. She didn't know if she'd ever met a woman as open and welcoming as Josh's mother. And she could tell they all loved Josh. Even though there was plenty of teasing going on, they seemed to hold him in special regard.

"Why is that?" she asked Bree. They were putting candles on Mary's cake when she mentioned her observation.

Bree tilted her head in thought for a moment. "I think it's because of his being gone for those years during the war. We really came to appreciate him." She leaned in and whispered, "Mom was so afraid she would lose him too." She eyed her mother, who busied herself putting out coffee cups. "You know, as well as my dad. She never quite recovered from that, and he died almost twenty years ago."

And yet Josh's mother didn't show a hint of resentment toward Rachel for her apparent involvement with her son. She wasn't one of those clingy mothers, apparently, even though she had every reason to be. Billy's mother had been the *worst*.

There she went again, comparing. She needed to stop doing that or she might come across a comparison that cast Josh in a bad light. That wasn't really fair.

The cake lit up the darkened dining room and cast a rosy glow on Mary's face. She playfully refused to tell her father what she had wished, and she nearly cried with excitement when she opened Rachel's gift to her.

"It's called a four-layer chiffon skirt." She knew Mary would love it, and it was the only gift she could get together on such short notice, since she stocked them at the studio. "You can wear that when you practice. And it has an elastic waist, so I think it will fit you for quite a while. You should see how those layers flare when you spin."

Mary ran to Rachel's side of the table and gave her a warm hug. "I love it! Can I go try it on, Mom?"

Bree laughed. "Definitely. Come down and show us once you have it on."

It occurred to Rachel that she might have accidentally misstepped with her gift. She studied Bree's face. "I hope that's all right. I didn't realize you were getting her a poodle skirt. Did I—"

Bree waved the issue away. "Nonsense. I can't believe how considerate you are, to have brought a nice gift like that on such short notice. Anyway, as I keep trying to tell my hubby, a woman can never have too many clothes."

"Josh, that reminds me." His mother had slipped into the kitchen and brought the coffeepot out. She warmed everyone's cups. "Are you still planning to come put that extra shelf in my bedroom closet for me?"

He stretched as he answered, and Rachel realized she hadn't noticed before how strong his arms looked. "Yep, I'll be over on Sunday. Oh, but not too early. I'll come after church."

All movement and conversation stopped. Rachel watched them all turn to stare at him. He laughed.

"What? I'm going to church with Rachel. Arlington, what is it again, Rachel?"

"Arlington Bible."

"Right," Josh said. "It's not that big a deal."

But she could see it was a big deal to the rest of his family, even if Josh hadn't been aware of that before. His mother looked at her as if she had just landed from outer space. Then, as a sly smile spread, she walked right over, took her face in her hands, and kissed her on the forehead. "Rachel. Bless you, my child."

They all started laughing.

"Don't pay any attention to them, Rachel." Josh rolled his eyes. "I just haven't gone for a while, that's all. And Mom's been bugging me lately."

"Only since you came home from the service, that's all." His mother had her hands on her hips. She pointed her finger at Rachel. "You, young lady, get brownie points."

They certainly knew how to make her feel special. If Josh had dated so many women, she wondered why she was the first to take him to church, especially since his family was clearly churchgoing. And the prayer Pete said before their meal definitely honored Jesus as Lord.

Mary ran downstairs to model her skirt, and the subject changed before Rachel could learn anything else about Josh and church. She needn't have worried, though. She only had to wait for the drive home before a few more answers came.

CHAPTER TWENTY-ONE

"So tell me about it." Rachel spoke almost as soon as they left Bree and Pete's house.

There were so many things she might be talking about, after that rather informative dinner. "Uh, tell you about what, exactly?" He opened the passenger door for her, and she got in. She flashed him a cute little smile and he closed her door.

At least she seemed happy. And why wouldn't she be? They loved her. That was obvious. He found that her being happy—especially about his family—made *him* happier than he'd been in a long time.

He matched her grin as he got in the car, but he narrowed his eyes at her. "Tell you about what?"

She turned toward him as he drove away. "What's the big deal about church with you?"

"Oh, that." He shrugged. "It's not a big deal, really. I got out of the habit when work heated up at the paper. I mean, I found myself so busy all the time, and the next thing I realized, I hadn't gone for quite a while."

"But your mother said you hadn't gone since you came home from the war."

"That's a bit of an exaggeration. Like I told you before, I went with her on occasion. Just not regularly."

She nodded. "Well, I hope you enjoy Arlington Bible, but please don't feel I'm pressuring you to go."

He chuckled. "I thought that was *exactly* what you were doing."

"What do you mean?" She frowned, but she couldn't hide her smile.

"I seem to remember this whole evening being held as ransom." He pointed to his steering wheel. "This very *drive* together rested on the requirement that I go with you to church on Sunday." He grinned at her. "Am I remembering right?"

She dusted off her lap and pursed her lips primly. "Oh, well, perhaps."

He laughed out loud and so did she. "Perhaps, she says."

"But after Sunday, it's completely up to you, Josh. Honestly. There's nothing worse than a man going to church under duress. Well, there are plenty of things worse than that, actually. But I'm not going to be responsible for your spiritual life. That's all I'm saying."

"What if I never go to church again after this weekend?"

"Not my business. That's between you and God."

"No, I mean, what will you think of me?"

She sobered and sighed. "I can't say it wouldn't be a problem."

Silence. He cast a sideways glance at her. "And what if I enjoy it?"

"You very well might." She tilted her head and raised her brows. "The teaching is wonderful and the people are friendly—"

"How about the women?"

A small gasp escaped before she was able to stop it. "The women?"

"Yeah. A lot of single women attending, are there?"

"Well. I don't know. I suppose so."

"And what happens if I really like it there and start going regularly, and you and I—"

"You and I what?" He could tell she was leaning forward, studying his face. He tried to keep it straight.

"You know. What if we don't work out? And there I am, going to the same church as you. And all those desperate single women—"

"Ha!" He couldn't tell if she was still joking with him or not. "They'd *have* to be desperate."

He threw back his head and laughed. "You can be downright mean when you want to be."

She sat back. "I have my moments. Anyway, it's a big church. If you and I don't 'work out,' as you say so romantically, I'm sure we can avoid crossing paths. And if we can't, you can just go somewhere else, because I got there first."

"Quite the little evangelical, aren't you?"

She turned toward him again. "And what's up with you and all the girlfriends? You certainly made quite an impression on Mark. Do you have a problem with monogamy?"

"No, I just stink at dating. You may have noticed."

"Nonsense. I have a hard time accepting that. You haven't done so badly with me. And anyone with eyes can see you're..."

How he loved remaining silent at that moment. Whatever she had been about to say was clearly going to be flattering. So flattering that her pride kept her from saying it. He waited just a second more before speaking.

"Anyone can see I'm what? You're not going to be mean again, are you?"

"Of course not. I was—I was just going to say that you're... Well, you're not completely hideous."

"You're right. That wasn't mean at all."

She laughed. "So obviously you have no problem getting women to go out with you. So why so many? You don't really strike me as the playboy type."

He sighed. "Honestly, it's just that for the longest time I would meet someone I found remotely attractive and then ask her out before I knew anything about her. So I went on a lot of first dates."

"You're not one for second chances, then? One date, and if they don't measure up, adios?"

"Not exactly. But if I can tell on a first date that a woman isn't the one—you know, *the* one—it seems like it wastes both our time to date, just to have something to do."

He glanced at her and saw her nod.

"Anyway, I haven't dated like Mark described for quite a while. I've learned not to be so quick. Too frustrating."

"Mm-hmm. I agree with you there."

"And what about you? What happened with the guy you said you broke up with a few months ago?"

She didn't answer right away. He eyed her and she shrugged.

"He was just a guy I met through my brother Chuck."

"What happened?"

"We broke up. That's all."

Hmm. He suddenly wanted to know just how far out of the picture this guy was. "So… I take it you're still hurt."

"Why would you assume that?"

"You don't want to talk about him."

"That might just be because I don't care about him enough to talk about him anymore."

"Is that the case?"

She didn't answer right away and he knew not to fill the silence.

"No. It was pretty bad. My brother introduced us because he, well, he played ball with Billy, and then heard he was pretty good at ballroom dance. So he introduced us, and Billy started taking lessons where I worked. I didn't have my own studio yet, but I was working on it. I was teaching in Annandale."

"How long were you together?"

"A little over three years."

Josh whistled. "That's definitely not someone you didn't care about."

"Yeah, but you know, Josh, I don't really want to talk about him right now. It's been such a fun evening. I'd rather not think about all that stuff. Do you mind?"

"No, that's fine." He wanted to know, though. It didn't sound as if the guy had gone away, at least not based on what little she had told him. The last thing he wanted to do was get involved with a woman who carried a torch for some other guy. He had enough problems right now, business-wise. He didn't need personal concerns too.

By the time he pulled up to her car outside the studio, he had come to a decision. No, he didn't want to date someone who wasn't definitely *the* one, but he didn't know yet about Rachel. She just might be the one. He wasn't ready, not by a long shot, to write her off. But he was going to have to take it very carefully with her. Not get too attached. When she could talk more comfortably about the other guy, and he could be sure this Billy was permanently *out* of the picture, he'd put more of himself *into* it. Not before.

He walked her to her car. He thought she might expect him to give her a good-night kiss. And he wasn't made of stone, so he couldn't just salute her and walk away.

He bent forward and gave her a little peck on the cheek. "Good night, Rachel."

"Oh. Uh, good night."

Yep. She had expected more. Shoot, he had been more romantic with her when he knew her less. He made a point of giving her a broad smile. He didn't want her to think anything was wrong. Ah, and they had church on Sunday. He'd nearly forgotten.

"So, I'll come pick you up for church Sunday, right?"

She recovered and returned his smile. There was a politeness about her that hadn't been there before. That was his fault, he knew it.

"Sure, that would be good. Nine thirty, okay?"

"It's a deal." He had to look away from her to keep from kissing her again. He knew if he kissed her a second time, he wouldn't hold back. It just wouldn't be right to get too passionate if there was a chance they weren't going to work out. He walked back toward his car and talked over his shoulder. "I'm going to wait until you pull away, okay? Just to make sure your battery is all right."

"Thanks. See you Sunday."

He got into his car and watched her start up her Falcon and pull away. He saw her silhouette and her dainty hand come up and wave.

The evening had gone so well up until the awkwardness of these last few moments. As his brother-in-law liked to remind him, he didn't handle women nearly as well as he handled aircraft. Tonight he had definitely gone off course, despite his best intentions. He didn't like to admit it, but he feared there was a possibility he was headed for a crash.

CHAPTER TWENTY-TWO

Before Josh arrived at her home Sunday morning, Rachel had two concerns on her mind.

One, she couldn't help but notice how he changed his tone with her after they had talked about Billy the other night. That was one of the reasons she preferred not discussing him. But Josh would just have to accept that she didn't want to dwell on what happened with Billy. That was her business and no one else's. The fewer people who knew about the details the better, as far as she was concerned.

Secondly, she anticipated she would need to give him plenty of attention at church, since he didn't know anyone there. That might be awkward, if he kept up his reserve toward her.

But when he showed up and they made their way to church, Josh acted as though nothing uncomfortable had happened the other night. And when they got to church, you'd have thought he'd been a member of Arlington Bible for years. He knew at least half of the hymns and sang them in a confident bass. He sat through the service in total comfort and in rapt concentration, and then he worked the crowded, noisy fellowship hall like a celebrity among fans. Not cocky. Just self-assured. She had to admit she hadn't seen that in many men. She also had to admit she found it awfully attractive.

Even though Betty's morning sickness kept her home, her husband Mike was there. He tossed his empty paper coffee cup in the trash and sidled up to her while Josh chatted with some church members she didn't even know.

"He seems like a nice enough fellow, Rachel. Betty's spoken pretty well of him."

Rachel cocked her head and smiled. "Has she? I'm glad. I wasn't aware he had even made an impression on her."

"She said he seemed like a good uncle to his niece and nephew and that he was taken with you."

She felt her cheeks heat up. "Oh, we're just friends."

"Yeah, well, your friend is coming back." Mike pointed toward Josh with his chin.

"Really friendly people here, Rachel." Josh's grin would draw in anyone. Before she had a chance to introduce him to Mike, he spoke directly to him, a twinkle in his eye. "So Mike, how are you feeling about the whole fatherhood job coming up?"

Rachel smiled but gave Josh a frown. "How did you know—"

Mike said, "We chatted over by the coffee machine. But I don't think Josh realizes my wife is Betty."

"Betty." Josh looked as if he were doing quick math in his head before he looked at her. "Your Betty? From the studio?"

She nodded.

Josh laughed and shook Mike's hand. "Well, congratulations again. I didn't realize. I know she hasn't been feeling all that great." He accidentally bumped into a couple behind him and turned to apologize. Within moments he positioned himself to include the couple in his conversation with Mike and her.

"I'm Josh Reegan," he told them. "And maybe you already know my friends, Rachel Stanhope and Mike…"

"Verano." Mike shook hands with the couple.

"No, we haven't met," the husband said. His hair looked prematurely gray compared to all but the sleepy bags under his eyes. "The church is getting too big for its britches, I guess. There are so many unfamiliar faces here now. We're Craig and Margaret Friskin." He pointed at Rachel. "I definitely recognize—"

"Friskin?" Josh widened his eyes, and his jovial smile softened. "Did you say Friskin?"

"Yes." The wife finally spoke. She had that same tired look to her. "Have we met before?"

Rachel could almost hear the increased level of adrenaline in Josh's tone. "Are you, by any chance, Candy Friskin's parents?"

Both of them gasped. "Do you know where she is?" Mrs. Friskin spoke, desperation in her voice.

"Are you a friend of hers?" Mr. Friskin acted just as concerned as his wife.

Rachel's heart ached for them. What must these poor people be going through if they asked a near stranger if he knew where their daughter was?

Josh sighed. "I'm so sorry. I mean, yes, I'm a friend. Or at least we know each other. She helped me with a newspaper story I wrote."

"Candy did?" Mrs. Friskin wrung her hands.

"Yes. But I was hoping *you* knew where she was. I need to speak with her—"

Mr. Friskin was suddenly more wary. "Is it because of your story she took off the way she did?"

Rachel watched a number of emotions quickly play out in Josh's expression.

"I certainly wish she hadn't taken off. Her leaving was the last thing I wanted her to do, believe me. I've been trying to find her. Her roommate—"

"Mitzy," Mr. Friskin said.

"Right. Mitzy says Candy's been in touch—"

Mrs. Friskin said, "Yes, we've heard from Candy. We know she's fine, or so she says. But she won't tell us where she is, and that has us worried."

"It's that boyfriend of hers." Mr. Friskin pursed his lips. "A real—"

"Craig." Mrs. Friskin rested her hand on his arm. She looked at Josh, Mike, and Rachel. "We're just praying about whatever she's gotten herself into. We want her to come home."

"I'd set the police on her trail if she gave me the slightest hint of being in trouble." Mr. Friskin tightened his lips. "But she insists she's all right. I'm concerned a call to the police might lead to trouble for her."

Rachel nodded. "I can't even imagine your worry. I'll pray about it too."

Josh shook Mr. Friskin's hand again. "Craig, I promise you, if I find out anything about where she is, I'll let you know."

Josh and Mr. Friskin exchanged contact information. Once the Friskins moved on, Rachel saw Mike study Josh with increased interest.

"That was one of the more intriguing fellowship hall conversations I've heard in a long time. What kind of story are you working on?"

Josh shrugged. "Actually, I'm currently writing a story about A&W root beer."

Both Rachel and Mike eyed him skeptically.

Mike scratched his head. "I had no idea root beer was such clandestine stuff."

"No." Rachel laughed and wagged her finger at Josh. "You're not looking for Candy for your root beer article. It's for the one that you told me about before. The one you got in trouble for. Because of her, right? Because she's your corroborating witness and she took off."

Mike rubbed his hands together. "Man, this is juicy stuff. You've gotta date this guy, Rachel, so we can live vicariously through him. I'm telling you, life as a car salesman just doesn't have this kind of mystery."

Rachel's eyes bored into Mike's, and she knew Josh would see that. But what in the world was Mike thinking, to pressure her about dating Josh? Right in *front* of him? Didn't she tell him only moments before that they were just friends? Mike didn't know about Josh's change of tone the other night, but did that really matter?

One quick glance at Josh and she knew he had shifted back to his playful self again. His quick eyebrow wiggle about Mike's dating comment actually filled her with relief, and a laugh nearly bubbled up.

"You men are really *something*, you know that?"

"Hey," Josh said, "I'm just an innocent bystander here."

Rachel gave him a sardonic smile, and he spoke again, his palms turned up to the heavens.

"I haven't even asked you out or anything. Not officially."

She couldn't help but laugh. "Well, that makes me feel so much better. And maybe a little insulted, I'm not sure." She turned to Mike, who sputtered in his attempt to smooth over his comments. Rachel pointed at him.

"You need to go home to your wife, Michael. 'Live vicariously,' my eye. Go home and think about what you've done, young man."

Mike laughed. "Whatever I did, don't tell Betty. She'll never let me live it down." He shook Josh's hand. "Good to meet you, man." He cocked his head toward her. "You could do worse, you know?"

Rachel gave him a playful shove. "Go!"

She tried to give Josh a serious look, but his wry smile was too infectious.

He shook his head ruefully. "After this kind of pressure, I suppose I'm obligated to ask you out to lunch."

"Well, don't feel obligated." She put her hand on her hip. "It so happens I'm not free for lunch, because I'm a very important person."

He nodded. "I knew that. The part about your being important, I mean." Now he looked at her more seriously. "Really, though? You can't come to lunch with me?"

"No, but thanks. I'm getting together at the studio with Connie and Mel. And Mira and Cruz. Choreography."

"All right." He smiled. "Sure I can't come watch? Would I be in the way?"

"*Can't* come?" Rachel feigned shock. "Josh Reegan *wants* to come watch people dance? How can this be?"

"Okay, now."

She ignored him. "Has the world stopped spinning on its axis?" She closed her eyes and reached out in front of herself. "Auntie Em! Auntie Em! I'm lost in a strange land far, far away. Auntie Em!"

When she opened her eyes he was no longer in front of her, but a little girl stood there, staring up at Rachel, her equally fascinated mother directly behind her. Rachel gasped and searched the crowd before Josh tapped her on the shoulder. She laughed and smacked his arm.

"You had that one coming," he said. "Come on, I'll drive you home, crazy lady. I should get to work on my A&W article anyway."

On the way to her house, their conversation turned to her concerns about the studio. Rather, her father's concerns.

"He loves me and I've never doubted that. But lately I've noticed he seems to be so sure I'll fail. He worries about me much more than he ever has about Chuck and Todd, my brothers. I guess it's because they both served in the war and got college degrees and dug right into their careers. I barely took any college courses, I never did anything as gutsy as fighting a war—"

"I don't think that's it. I think he worries because you're a woman."

She shifted in her seat. "So?"

He glanced at her and smiled. "Let me put that another way. I think he worries because you're *his* little girl."

"I'm thirty-two."

Josh shook his head. "Doesn't matter. I think sometimes it depends on the parent's gender. *And* the child's. You know what my mother's name is for me? *Baby.* I'm a thirty-five-year-old fighter pilot, a reporter who until recently hung around some pretty dicey environments researching my stories. I've taken perfectly good care of myself, on my own for, what, seventeen years? But to her, I'm still Baby."

"You see, that's what I'm saying. *My* mom… Well, actually, she's kind of like that too. With my brothers, I mean. Maybe you've got a point there. With me, Mom was gung ho on my opening the dance studio. She's always had every confidence in me and spurred me on. Really terrific. But yeah, with Chuck and Todd, she acts like they're kids sometimes. And they're both married and everything. One of them even has kids of his own."

"But she never treats you like you're still a little girl, right?"

"No, not like that. I mean, she's affectionate, but now that I'm an adult, we're almost like—"

"Girlfriends?"

"Yeah. I love that. I wish my dad would treat me like that."

"I think lots of parents work with what they know. A father knows what a son is capable of, because he's been through life as a son. As a guy. My father probably would have treated me more like your dad does your brothers. I still remember when he was alive—"

"Do you mind if I ask how he died?"

"Emphysema. They think it was because of his smoking. I was a teenager. During those last years he acted like I was able to do anything I set my mind to. And he expected me to be responsible for myself. I'm not so sure he was like that with my sister. We men don't understand you women. *Or* what you're capable of."

"Maybe I should try to get my father to stop by the studio once in a while. See that I'm able to run a business just fine."

"Your parents don't visit your studio?"

She shrugged. "They went to competitions I was in, back when I did that kind of thing. But I don't think they—well, Dad—I don't think he... It's hard for my dad to think of dance as a serious business."

Josh frowned. "Not think of dance as a serious business?" He pulled up in front of Rachel's building and sighed. "What is it with some men? I'm telling you."

She laughed. "Maybe that's why your attitude bugged me so much. You're like my father." Josh narrowed his eyes in thought. "What? Why are you looking at me like that?"

"My sister said something similar to me the other day."

"She said you were like my father?" Rachel smiled and got out of the car.

Josh did the same. "She told me that her husband Pete is a lot like *my* dad. She meant it as a compliment. She thinks Pete fills a void in her left when my dad died."

She wasn't about to make a teasing comment about not having such a void in her life. But Josh's thoughts went in the same direction, apparently.

"And I know your dad is still around," he said. "But I'll bet he's a great guy." He held her apartment door open for her. "Just like me. Which is why you like me so much."

She laughed. She found she wasn't eager to send him away, but she had to get to the studio.

Josh didn't walk into her apartment with her. "You can never have too many great guys in your life."

Rachel lifted her eyebrows and waited for him to consider that comment more fully. "Is that what you think? Maybe I should be on the prowl for more great guys, then."

She watched his thoughts fall into place. "Oh. I mean, great guys like fathers. And brothers. But you certainly don't want to clutter your-your personal life with a bunch of—"

"Great guys?"

He opened his mouth and then closed it. He shook his head, as if frustrated with himself. "I give up."

"Oh, don't do that." Rachel spoke before she really thought. But when Josh met eyes with her and they both broke into appreciative grins, she was glad for her impulse. She spoke softly. "You know, I didn't tell you this, but I really loved your article about the jukeboxes."

"Did you?" His voice had softened too.

"The way you wrote about people's memories stirred up by certain songs—if I didn't know better, I'd suspect you of being a romantic."

They still stood at her door. He leaned toward her. "But you think you know better, huh? That I'm far from romantic?"

She tried to act cool, but his closeness blew that. This was so much nicer than how they ended their last drive together. And he smelled *so* good. When she spoke, her voice nearly squeaked. "Maybe."

He slowly leaned forward, but he didn't kiss her as she expected. Instead he whispered to her, his breath warm on her ear, and his lips barely brushing against her skin. "Maybe I'll prove you wrong."

He straightened up and smiled. He tilted his head and studied her, a spark unmistakable in his eyes. Then he took a step back. "I'll see you later, Rachel."

She swallowed and nodded. "Mm-hmm. Okay. Later."

She closed her door, walked into the kitchen, and splashed cool water on her cheeks and behind her neck, dripping water onto the linoleum.

You can't have too many great guys in your life, he said. Too many like him, and she'd absolutely melt. She'd be that little puddle of water on the floor.

CHAPTER TWENTY-THREE

That evening Rachel helped her sister-in-law clean up the kitchen. Suzanna couldn't have picked a better night to invite her to dinner. After working all afternoon with her dancers, Rachel hated the idea of cooking, especially when it was so muggy out. And, despite her aversion to the barrage of questions she often experienced at her mother's larger Sunday dinners, she liked the idea of a family meal tonight, even one with two crazy toddlers in attendance.

"I'm so glad you decided to join us tonight." Suzanna wiped the table down after the insane meal they had just finished. Macaroni and cheese may as well have been shot from a cannon onto the table and floor, and at least two cups of juice had been spilled during the meal. Yet Suzanna cleaned in apparent oblivion to the daunting task at hand.

"I don't know how you do it." Rachel rinsed the suds off dishes and stacked them in the draining rack.

Suzanna looked up from the table, her hair limp around her face. A full-body apron still covered her clothes, and the green substance smeared on her shirt collar had nothing to do with what they had eaten for dinner. "How I do what?"

Rachel laughed. "Maybe God blesses parents with some kind of tunnel vision or blindness, just to get them through the whole toddler experience. Am I *ever* going to want kids of my own?"

"Oh." Suzanna waved her comment away. "That. Yeah, when they're yours, they're always better than when they're someone else's. You'll want them once you fall in love and all that."

She said nothing to that. Her plans had been to spend the evening alone. She did love her own company, but after the exchange with Josh at her door that morning, she felt tempted to call him. But she didn't want to come across as one of those brash, lonely women. Yet another reason Suzanna's call was timely.

Suzanna broke through her silence. "Speaking of which, what's going on with that guy you told everyone about at your folks' place last Sunday?"

"*I* didn't tell everyone about him. Our chatty sister-in-law did."

Again, Suzanna waved her comment away, and this time a few noodles flew from her sponge. "Oh. Lovely." She spoke as she hunted down the errant noodles. "Doesn't really matter who brought it up, does it? You? Karen? All I want to know is, have you spoken to him since dinner at your mom's?"

Todd's voice called down the hall. "Honey? I need a towel for Aaron."

Rachel smiled, touched that her big brother was giving a bath to the twins so Suzanna could chat with her. Granted, Suzanna was cleaning up the dinner mess with her, but typically, she'd do that *and* bathe the kids. Rachel knew her brother.

Suzanna called back. "Under the sink."

"What?" The energetic squeals of the toddlers competed with their parents' conversation.

"Under the sink," Suzanna called.

"What? Pink? Yeah, pink, blue, I don't care. I just need it right away."

"Sink! Agh." Suzanna threw her hands up and grimaced at her. "I'll be right back." She marched toward the hall to solve Todd's crisis. She slipped on a noodle on her way and barely avoided a fall.

Rachel shook her head. Her life was so nice and easy. So ordered, compared to the sloppy chaos Todd and Suzanna tolerated.

She heard Suzanna laugh and couldn't help but saunter down the hall to investigate. She quietly poked her head around the doorway and saw the little family simply enjoying the moment, the scent of baby shampoo in the air.

Both Amanda and Aaron were covered in suds and making a soapy mess—everywhere they went, they made a mess. But they were pretty doggoned cute, and her heart melted at the way Todd and Suzanna looked at the toddlers and then at each other.

Okay. *That* she could do.

Suzanna glanced over her shoulder and saw Rachel. She pushed herself up from her knees. "Okay, gang, you finish up. Come into the living room to give Aunt Rachel and me good night kisses once you're in your jammies. Daddy's doing storybook and prayers tonight." She gave Todd a kiss on the cheek and batted her eyes at him. "And there's more where *that* came from, hotcakes."

Rachel opened her mouth to say something fun and auntie-like to Amanda and Aaron, but she was at a loss. And, despite the suds all over Amanda, she still gave Rachel that blank stare she always reserved for her. Just as dogs could smell fear, Amanda seemed to smell inadequacy on Rachel's part.

"Time for coffee." Suzanna wrapped her damp arm around Rachel's shoulders and led her out of the bathroom. She whispered once they were in the hall. "And Boston cream pie."

Suzanna had already percolated the coffee, so Rachel poured while Suzanna removed the pie from the refrigerator and cut two thigh-widening slices for them. Rachel laughed.

"Ah, so this is how you survive motherhood. Sugar and caffeine."

"You said it, honey."

They curled up on the couch, and she barely got her first bite down before Suzanna returned to their earlier topic. "So. The reporter. Spill the beans, Rachel."

Rachel smiled around a small forkful. "We've crossed paths a few times over the past week or so. At the grocery store, where he fixed my dead battery—"

"I'll bet he did."

Rachel used one raised eyebrow to chastise Suzanna. "And his niece invited me to her fourteenth-birthday dinner. And he swept the June bugs from Mr. and Mrs. Chambers' front porch."

Suzanna stopped chewing. She swallowed so she could speak. "That's one of your less common dating rituals."

"We're really only friends at this point."

"At this point." Suzanna used her fork like a baton for emphasis. "But you're both going in the same direction? And that direction is huggy-kissy?"

A shrug. "I can tell he's attracted to me. And he keeps coming back, even though I've gotten a little snippy with him a few times."

Suzanna nodded. "Snippy is what landed your brother."

"Really?" She glanced down the hall toward the bathroom. "He actually found that attractive?"

"I'm not saying I set out to play hard to get or anything like that. But he kind of stumbled all over the place when we first met. Too blunt. Too cocky."

"That's my brother."

"That's plenty of them, especially ex-servicemen. Consider what they went through just a few years ago. I think a lot of them decided life was too short to namby-pamby around. So they just charge toward whatever they want. Sometimes that's us."

She considered Josh's friendly, assertive behavior in the church fellowship hall earlier that day. "I kind of like that attitude in a man sometimes. That confidence, I mean."

"Mm-hmm. It has its appealing side."

"The only thing that's bothered me has been Josh's opinion about what I do for a living. He doesn't have a lot of respect for it. But I think that's improving."

Suzanna took a long drink of coffee. "Don't let that slide, Rachel. I have *tremendous* respect for what you're doing. So does Todd."

"You do? Todd too?" She couldn't help grinning.

"There aren't many women running their own businesses out there. You've got gumption. And you're a hard worker. And talented. If Josh's attitude doesn't improve so you can be certain of his support, that's a big deal. I don't care how cute he is."

Now she felt a little unfair in how she presented Josh, considering his request about attending today's choreography meeting.

"He wanted—well, he offered—to come watch my choreography session this afternoon. And he came with me to church this morning."

"Well now." Suzanna set down her coffee cup. "Little sister doesn't waste much time, does she?"

Rachel smiled. "Don't be silly. I'm not doing anything to move things along. Most of our interactions have been happenstance, really. I'm not even sure how I feel about Josh or the idea of dating him. We need to get better acquainted before taking that step."

Suzanna sighed. She glanced down the hall, as if she wanted to verify that Todd wouldn't overhear.

"I know Todd's your big ol' stinky brother and all, but I can tell you. Despite his stumbling approach in the beginning? I knew he was the one—well, maybe I didn't *know*, but I was pretty well sold—when he gave me that first kiss." She scrunched up her nose and shrugged.

She looked like a giddy sixteen-year-old. "Silly, huh? But that's how it was."

Rachel scooped another forkful of pie into her mouth to avoid the need to respond. Did that soft, feather-like kiss at her door count? Or the brush of his lips when he whispered in her ear? Was it all right that she didn't feel the certainty Suzanna described when he did those things? She was certain he was the one who gave her goose bumps. The one who brought a flush of warmth all over. The one whose face and voice kept invading her thoughts. But goose bumps, warmth, and obsession did not eternal love make, in her mind. She had felt that for Billy, and look how wrong she had been. She wanted more than those infatuation-type reactions.

So she kept to herself the info about the kiss, the whisper. If she and Josh had a future together, it was obviously going to take a path of its own.

CHAPTER TWENTY-FOUR

"Human element. What's the human element?" Josh muttered to himself as he glanced over his notes for the A&W article. He sat in his Chevy outside one of the drive-ins, tapping his pen against his notebook in time to the song filtering through the windows of the car beside him. "How High the Moon," by Les Paul and his wife, Mary Ford. The tune was so catchy he couldn't concentrate. He figured he might as well go inside and talk with the franchise owner, even though he was five minutes early for their appointment.

"Take your order, sir?" A young carhop with a crew cut approached him before he had a chance to exit his car. The boy wore a crisp white, short-sleeved shirt and bow tie.

"Oh, no thanks, son. I have an appointment with your boss."

"Yes, sir. You just let me know if there's anything I can do for you, sir."

Josh smiled as he walked to the front door. The kid had a great attitude.

Within minutes he stood at the counter inside, nursing an icy root beer float. He figured he might as well enjoy the assignment if he had to write about something as simple as a food chain.

The owner, Frank Bowry, dressed similarly to his employees. If he cared about customers recognizing him as the relative hotshot in the operation, he certainly didn't show it. Frank continued to work on orders as he spoke, answering questions with a cheery brightness. "I couldn't have opened the place without the GI loan. But business has been so good, I'm about to open another one on the far side of town, near the D.C. line."

"That good, huh? Is it the product, you think?"

"Everybody loves root beer, right?" Frank grinned. "The food is tops too. And people love the carhop service. But I think the best thing to happen to the company was last year, when Allen sold the business—"

"That's Roy Allen?" Josh jotted on his notepad.

"Yeah. He was the *A* in A&W. So he sold last year to Gene Hurtz. And let me tell you, that Hurtz is one aggressive businessman. I'm hoping to emulate his success in my own little way. 'Scuse me, just a sec, will ya?"

"Sure."

Frank walked away from him the moment a couple of customers came in to order. Josh watched him work the people, not in a feigned politeness, but in what seemed like genuine pleasure to serve them.

"That's fine, now," Frank told them. "You folks go on out and relax in your car. One of my carhops will bring your order right out to you just as soon as it's ready. Nice and hot. Nice and frosty. And if you like, next time just pull up. We'll come to you, don't even have to leave your car."

Frank gave him a wink when he returned. "People these days are looking for convenience, right? The economy's picking up, everyone's driving everywhere they go, and if you're not going to sit down in a restaurant, why not relax in your car? When folks come inside to order, I try to encourage them to sit still next time and let us serve them." He tapped a finger against his forehead and pointed it at him. "Service. That's the key. That's what brings 'em back over and over." Frank shrugged. "Along with good food, of course."

It *did* smell awfully good in there.

And when he left Frank, a bag heavy with french fries and a Papa Burger in hand, he thought he might have found the human element for this one. Frank had a humble and genuine appreciation for the attitude of service. Not only had it made him a relative success, it seemed to make him personally happy. And his employees showed the same outlook. Maybe he could slant the article to draw readers to that quality—kind of inspirational. Lou would probably like that.

By the time he got back to the office, his mind started to wander back to his ill-fated story about that snake, Ted Wiley. He fished out the phone number Candy's father had given him at Rachel's church and gave him a call.

"Yes, hello, Craig? This is Josh Reegan from Arlington Bible. Or, we met at Arlington Bible—"

"Right, I remember you. The reporter with the *Tribune*."

"Yes. I was—"

"Have you heard anything about Candy's whereabouts?"

Poor guy. He could hear the heartbreak in his voice.

"No, I'm sorry, Craig. I haven't. And frankly, my paper hasn't allowed me time to look into the situation or where she might be. I'm not on the city desk anymore, thanks to...I mean because—"

"Because Candy's gone. I got ya. Josh, just how involved with your story was she?"

Josh sighed. "Look, it's hard for me to talk here. I'm—I'm supposed to be writing Style pieces, and my editor isn't going to be happy if he catches me talking with anyone about the Ted Wiley story. Could I possibly come talk with you?"

Silence.

Craig finally responded. "Maybe I could meet you somewhere."

"Uh, actually, I was hoping to meet you at your house. I might be able to figure something out just visiting Candy's family home. Maybe look over any mementos she might have left behind. *Did* she live there, or have you and"—he glanced at the paper in his hand—"have you and Margaret moved since Candy struck out on her own?"

"No, this is Candy's childhood home. But I'm hesitant to have you come here. I'm concerned about endangering my wife. My home."

"Endanger? Oh. No, listen, I can assure you that Ted Wiley is small potatoes, Craig. He isn't important enough to be dangerous to anyone. Except the taxpayers, that is."

He sat through another moment of silence before Craig answered.

"All right. Let me give you the address."

Josh was up and out of the office before Lou had a chance to catch him. He'd get the root beer article done in time for tomorrow's press. But the idea of getting a good night's sleep, thanks to toppling that crumb Wiley, was too great a draw to put on hold.

Frank Bowry and his love of service was an inspiration indeed, and Josh was sure he was meant to serve the public by getting this Wiley story straight.

CHAPTER TWENTY-FIVE

"That's beautiful, Mira." Rachel lifted the needle from the song she had chosen for Cruz and Mira's cha-cha. "Now, remember to keep the pressure on your toes. We want that nice Latin swing in your hips to happen more naturally, and the proper foot placement is going to help. Otherwise it looks too forced."

"It's my ballet training getting in the way." Mira shrugged. "Sorry about that. Sometimes I'm a little too formal, I guess."

"You look lovely. It's going to fall into place before the competition," Rachel said. "We still have two weeks."

Connie stepped up to Mira and Cruz and nudged them back into position. "I think we need a shoulder-to-shoulder right before that first a la mano. What do you think?"

"Yes." Mel joined Connie and took her in his arms to demonstrate. "And Cruz, you can move a little more into her shoulder. Like this."

Rachel watched from her spot by the record player. "Are you comfortable with those moves? Cruz? Mira?" Cruz was a given, since he had obviously mastered the Latin dances, so Rachel already knew he was comfortable with the choreography. But she didn't want Mira feeling she was the only one being watched, so she kept checking in with both of them. It was best that Mira feel confident. She really was a wonderful dancer.

Both Mira and Cruz nodded. Mira said, "Are my hands better now when we do the New York?"

"Perfect." Rachel smiled. "That little flick of tension was all you needed to add to your fingers. Let's try it again from the top."

After several more run-throughs, she let them take a short break. "Take five, and then we'll work on the waltz. Mel has a few little lifts he wants to incorporate into what we've worked out so far."

Mira ran off to the ladies' room, and Cruz joined Rachel, Connie, and Mel in the front room. He sat next to Rachel and stretched, his back bent and his arms pressed forward.

"Do you really think we're going to be ready in two weeks?"

"Definitely." She patted his shoulder. "You two make such a handsome couple out there. You balance out each other's strengths and weaknesses. She's stronger in the Moderns, and you're stronger in the Latins. And you're both quick learners. I have so much confidence in you both."

Connie winked at Cruz. "And that little spark between the two of you doesn't hurt the dance-floor chemistry."

"Spark?" Cruz frowned. "What do you mean?"

Rachel gave Connie a private grimace. As far as she had seen, the spark only went in one direction, from Mira to Cruz. The boy hadn't yet realized what a charming creature Mira was. But Mira clearly found Cruz's dark, exotic looks and behavior attractive.

Connie laughed as if she had been joking. "Oh, don't mind me. I'm forever poking fun at my students. You just look perfect together out there, that's all. As if you really enjoy dancing with each other."

Cruz nodded. "Yeah. Mira's a good kid."

Rachel exchanged a sardonic smirk with Connie and Mel. As far as she could remember, Mira was older than Cruz. Good *kid*, indeed.

Mel chatted briefly with Cruz about the lifts he had in mind. "Mira's so slight, I think these will require very little effort on your part."

"I'm all for it," Cruz said. "I like the idea of jazzing it up."

"Okay, I'm ready for more!" Mira practically pranced back from the restroom.

Rachel loved her attitude. Mira had taught several classes already today, one of which was a group of retired people who had very little ability or energy. Yet she was as lively and fresh as when she had arrived that morning.

"Terrific," Rachel said. "Let's have Mel work with the two of you for these lifts." She headed back over to man the phonograph. "Connie and I will plant ourselves over here and watch."

Mel's ideas were a terrific improvement. The competitors weren't allowed to stray far from the standard steps in the competition, which made sense, considering how crowded the floor could become at times. But Mel's lifts were subtle and didn't require any more room than had Mira and Cruz stayed floor-bound throughout their performance.

They had already accomplished the lifts and performed them twice. Rachel and Connie both applauded at the end of the second run-through. Rachel approached Mira and Cruz and draped her arms across both of their shoulders.

"Okay, you two have worked hard enough. I want you to take it easy tonight to rest your muscles. All right?"

Mira hesitated. "Do you mind, though, Cruz, if we go through it once more before quitting for the day? I felt just a little wobbly on the landing on that last lift. I'd like to leave feeling more certain about it."

"Sure," Cruz said. "I can go one more time."

"Really?" Rachel studied their faces carefully. "I don't want you overdoing it."

Mira shrugged. "It's just a three-minute dance."

Cruz struck a muscle-man pose. "She's like tissue paper in these arms." And for the first time that night, he shared a laugh strictly with Mira.

Who was Rachel to stand in the way of progress?

"Okay. Once more from the top!" She nodded at Connie, who lowered the needle onto "Tenderly."

Sheer perfection. Until they reached the point Mira had deemed wobbly. Cruz provided plenty of support, but when Mira touched down, her ankle gave way under her. She cried out and fell, much more heavily than tissue paper, to the floor.

Cruz cried out, too, clearly concerned that Mira's fall had been his fault. "I'm so sorry, Mira!"

Mira, in tears, managed to answer between whimpers of pain. "No. It was me. My fault."

She, along with Connie and Mel, ran to the center of the floor and knelt around her.

"You see," Cruz cried, the melodrama thick in his voice. "I knew something would happen today. It's Friday the thirteenth. Didn't I tell you?"

"Oh, Cruz, hush with that nonsense." Rachel frowned as she tried to hold her panic at bay. "Mira, you must have been unsure the last time through because your ankle was getting tired. I shouldn't have let you try it again. Mel, could you run across to the diner and ask Fran for some crushed ice?"

"Right." Mel was up and out.

Connie headed to the front desk. "Should I call an ambulance?"

"No!" Mira certainly wasn't so distracted by the pain that she couldn't pay attention to what was going on. Still, tears continued their stream down her flushed cheeks. "I'll be fine in a minute. I just need to rest it, that's all." She looked up at Cruz. "Oh, don't feel bad, Cruz, really. Your arms held me up just fine. It's these stupid ankles of mine." She looked from him to Rachel. "Could you two help me to a chair?"

Cruz immediately scooped her up. He definitely had been strong enough to support her in their dance.

Mira smiled at him as if he were a prince saving the day. “Let me try standing on it.”

Rachel tried to stop her, even as Cruz lowered her with care. “No, Mira—”

She fell to the floor again. This time Cruz was able to break her fall, but Rachel saw surprise flash in her eyes and her teeth grit with the pain.

“Oh, heavens!” Rachel said. “Okay, that does it, Mira. I think that ambulance is in order.”

“No, please don’t make it such a big deal. If my father finds out…”

Rachel stopped in her tracks. She hadn’t thought of that. Still, they had to do what was best for Mira.

Mel ran back in the front door, a towel full of ice in hand. “Franny said not to put the ice directly against her skin.”

“I can drive her to the hospital.” Cruz strode to the front desk. “Mel, maybe you could help me. Come with me.” He crossed back into the room with his keys.

Rachel stood. “We’ll all go.” She checked her watch. “Oh. No, we can’t all go. The six o’clock class will be here soon.”

“I’ll stay.” Connie bent and looked under the front counter. “Which purse is yours, Mira?”

“Little white one.” She let Mel carry her to the front seating area and set her down in one of the chairs.

Cruz left for his car.

Mel gingerly lifted Mira’s leg to rest it on another chair, and Rachel arranged the ice-filled towel under the injured ankle while she addressed Connie. “Are you sure you can handle the class all by yourself?”

"They'll have to understand, won't they?" Connie's voice held steady, without a hint of concern. "It's not like they've never attended a one-teacher class before. And it's not like I've never taught one. Don't you worry about the studio."

*****

But that's exactly what Rachel did. She didn't worry so much about the class Connie taught without Mel's or her own help. Her concern was more, well, selfish. She saw so much promise in Cruz and Mira, and she considered this upcoming series of competitions as an important part of her plan for making her business grow.

And as Mira's comment had brought to mind, Mr. Longworth's reaction to this development could affect the business as well.

Not that she wasn't concerned for Mira's well-being. The poor girl was obviously hurting. She considered it a blessing that, nearly as soon as they arrived at the emergency room, they gave Mira something to relieve her pain.

In fact, Mira's pain became so alleviated, the medication so effective, that she grew to be more frank than she probably would have been otherwise.

She sighed like a satisfied child and made big teary eyes at Cruz. Her voice was slightly tipsy. "You're *so* strong, with that carrying-me thing you did." She attempted to raise her arms in a strongman gesture, as he did before she fell, but she wasn't up to the effort. So she only lifted her hands as far as her shoulders before letting them drop again. She pushed out her lips and attempted to speak like a tough guy. She sounded more like a very young Shirley Temple. "Big. Strong. *Man.*"

"Okay." Rachel thought she'd better interrupt before Mira delivered more information than she could ever retrieve, poor thing. "Cruz, maybe you could go ask the nurse when the doctor will be available?"

Cruz stood. "Sure." He studied Mira for a moment before he left. Rachel couldn't quite read his expression.

He and the brisk young doctor nearly walked into each other at the door to Mira's examination room.

"You the doctor?" Cruz asked.

The doctor nodded. "I am."

Cruz smiled at Rachel and gestured toward the doctor as if he were presenting him on stage. "As you ordered, ma'am. The doctor."

"See?" Mira's voice floated like fairy dust across the room to Cruz. "You're cute *and* ee-fish…ee-fish…"

"Efficient?" Cruz asked.

Mira squinted one eye at him and barely raised her hand from her lap to point at him. "You got it, buster."

"Ah." The doctor looked at Rachel. "They gave her painkillers."

Rachel nodded. "A *lot,* apparently."

"I would have rather examined her beforehand, to be honest, to get a better diagnosis." He gently probed her ankle and stared at the wall as he considered what he felt.

Rachel understood his point. No doubt Mira's reaction to his prodding would have added to his information, showing where she hurt the most. But he didn't seem terribly challenged in reading her, based strictly on what he felt.

He nodded when he finished. "Right. Well, there's no break."

Everyone released their breath. Everyone except Mira, who took hold of the doctor's stethoscope and pressed the diaphragm against her eye like a monocle. She spoke with a stuffy British accent.

"I do *so* love the opera."

Cruz laughed. "She's crazy."

Rachel cast a quick smile at Mel before addressing the doctor. "So, it's just a sprain?"

The doctor gently pulled the stethoscope free from Mira's hand so he could stand straight again. "Just a sprain. She needs to stay off of it for a little while and she'll be fine. I'm going to wrap it to reduce the swelling, and she'll need to apply ice several times daily and rewrap it. And we'll give her some crutches. She'll be fine to use them tomorrow, just to keep her weight off the ankle."

Rachel frowned. In Mira's condition, she couldn't be alone tonight. "All right. Mel? Do you think you could help me get her to my apartment tonight?"

"Anything you need, Rachel."

"She'll probably be okay to tend to this herself tomorrow," Rachel said. "Right, Doctor?"

"Yes, we'll give her something to take for the pain, but I don't think she'll even need to use it after the first day or so. She's going to be up and about in no time."

Now that was what she wanted to hear. The competition took place in two weeks. She had feared a break and Mira's inability to compete.

"So, how long is 'no time'? I mean, how long before she can dance again?"

The doctor gave Rachel a pleasant smile. "She'll be fine to walk on it within a week. And I think I can confidently say she'll be dancing again in a month. By then she should be right as rain."

Rain. Yes, that was how this felt. Rain, thunder, lightning, an entire hurricane of distress. Rachel met eyes with Mel and felt as numb as she figured Mira did. And as much as she loved Mel, he said the one thing she had feared ever considering again.

"I'm sorry, Rachel. It looks like you're going to have to dance."

CHAPTER TWENTY-SIX

Reminiscent of Mae West, the hairdresser patted her bleached-blond pageboy a few times. She propped her hand on her plump hip and gave Josh a frown of confusion. Despite her buxom size she had the tiny voice of a young girl.

"*You're* my ten thirty? I think you want Gino's barbershop down the street, mister."

Josh stood, his hat in his hands. He gave her the most charming smile he could muster. "Actually, Doris, I just wanted to ask you a few questions, and I thought I'd pay you for your time."

"You a cop?" She didn't sound the slightest bit intimidated.

"No." He pulled one of his cards from his suit pocket and extended it to her. "My name is Josh Reegan. I'm with the *Washington Tribune*."

Another frown while she studied the card. "A reporter?" She cast a guarded glance at him. "We're not doing anything newsworthy here, Mr. Reegan. Everything is on the up-and-up here."

Man, she was a suspicious one. Too bad Candy hadn't been more like her when she got tangled with Wiley.

"I'm not here in connection with the beauty parlor. I want to talk with you about Candy Friskin."

Doris straightened at that. She glanced around as if she were concerned someone might overhear their conversation. She kept her beautician's jacket on but headed for the front door. "Let's talk outside."

She tossed a comment at the receptionist as Josh followed her out. "I'll be outside if you need me, Linda."

She lit a cigarette almost before Josh closed the front door behind himself. She held up the pack to Josh, her nails long, red talons that poked the air around her.

He shook his head. "No thanks."

Doris sank down onto the brick ledge of the salon's picture window and tucked the pack away. "What do you know about Candy?"

"I know she dated Ted Wiley for a while."

Doris immediately blew more than smoke from her mouth. "That creep."

Ah, good. Like-minded.

"Yes. Wiley's the creep that brings me here."

She crossed her arms. "What do you mean? What do you have to do with him? And what do I have to do with this?"

"I wrote an article exposing some of his illegal practices not too long ago. I had to retract it—to, to withdraw it—"

"I *know* what retract means."

"Sorry. I had to retract the story because I lost one of my sources. Candy."

Doris blew out more smoke, apparently unmoved. He continued.

"I visited with Candy's parents the other day. They had some of her photographs there at the house, and you were in a few of them. They're really worried about her."

"Why?"

"They don't know where—we wondered if you had any idea where she might be."

She jerked her head toward Josh. "Where she might be? She's missing? Her parents don't know where she is?"

"Do you?"

Doris stood from the ledge. "Are you telling me she's been kidnapped or something? Is that what you're saying?"

"No, hang on." He put up his hands and shook his head. "She hasn't been kidnapped. She's called her parents, and she says she's all right."

Doris released an angry huff. "Well, why didn't you say so?" She tsked and muttered under her breath. "Get me all worked up." She patted her forehead with the back of her hand and sat back down.

"Okay, so if she's all right, whose business is it where she is? She's a grown woman. She's entitled to be where she wants to be. Her parents were always a little overbearing, if you ask me."

"I said she wasn't kidnapped, Doris. I didn't say she was necessarily somewhere she wants to be."

Her expression softened. "Why do you say that?"

Josh settled down next to her on the ledge. "You mind?"

She scooted over to give him a little more room.

"Candy was one of two important sources for my article, which could have nailed Ted Wiley for skimming from the county treasury."

"I *knew* that guy was trouble."

"When Candy found out about his new girlfriend—"

"Yeah, that stupid so-called society dame," Doris said.

"Uh, yeah, when Candy found out about her, she was angry enough that she talked with me about his shady dealings. She told me the same things my other source did, so her testimony corroborated..." He nearly translated, but he glanced at Doris first.

She rolled her eyes at him. "Context, Josh. I get it. Went along with. Agreed with, right?"

Josh chuckled. "Clearly I'm the ignorant one here. Sorry."

She almost cracked a smile.

"Anyway," he said. "Yes. Candy's testimony corroborated my other source's statement. But Wiley got wise as soon as the article was printed. I didn't think he'd be able to convince her to withdraw her comments. She was livid with him when she talked with me before. And she didn't exactly withdraw her comments. But somehow he managed to get her to go into hiding to keep her from being available if we went to court."

"She has a weak spot for him." Doris stubbed out her cigarette. "Beats me *why*. I never liked the skinny little cuss. The longer Candy was with him, the less she was willing to hang out with me and our other friends. Stopped returning my calls. Didn't go the same places she used to. It's like he wanted her all for himself, and she let him do that." She looked out into the street. "I hate it when girls do that."

"Well, soft spot or not, from what I hear, he hasn't taken a single step to end his relationship with the woman—the so-called society dame—that prompted Candy to inform on him in the first place. Wherever she is, I have a feeling she doesn't know that."

Doris nodded. "You have a good point there. I'll bet that's exactly what he's done. He's got her fooled and in the dark. That was how he treated her in the first place." She sighed. "Poor Candy doesn't have much of a backbone. And don't he know it."

Josh stood and brushed off his trousers. "So you have no idea where she might have gone? You don't know of any places she liked to go to, to be alone? Or away from things?"

A derisive laugh. "It's not like she's the queen of Sheba. She barely made enough to pay her rent. Where would she go to be alone?" She gasped. "Hey! Maybe Mitzy knows something! Her roommate. Did you—"

"Yeah, Mitzy and I have talked quite a lot. She doesn't have any ideas, either. And Candy left three months' rent for Mitzy when she took off, so she obviously doesn't plan to return or correspond for a while."

"Well, it's my guess she's staying someplace *he* set up, not someplace she knew about."

Josh nodded. He leaned against the wall and rubbed his jaw. An idea struck.

"Uh, Doris, would you be willing to contact Wiley and ask if he knows where you could reach her? Maybe see if he'd give you a phone number? You don't have to let on that you know they've broken up."

She stood too. "I don't have a problem with that. But I doubt he'll roll over so easy."

"Probably not. But it's worth a shot. Let me go back to my office and see if I can get his direct line at the treasury. I'll call the salon to give you the number."

"I'll be here." Doris shook the hand he offered. "I know you're doing this for your story, but I still appreciate your trying to find her."

He looked at the ground for a moment before answering. "To be honest, you're right. I have been chasing this lead for my story. For my job. But I like Candy. I could tell when we talked that she was a good gal. And she was really hurt by that crumb. She deserves better than Wiley. So I want to help her get away from him too."

Doris opened the salon door, and the muffled sounds of the radio and hairdryers filtered out more clearly. "I'll call him as soon as you get me the number. I can act like I just haven't talked with her for ages and want to track her down. We'll see what happens."

Josh had parked his Chevy in front of an ice cream parlor down the block. When he neared the car, he crossed paths with a woman and her little red-haired girl, both holding ice cream cones. The mother said something that made her daughter giggle. The girl was the picture of trust and innocence.

He had only met with Candy a few times, and maybe his conversation with Doris had simply put her at the forefront of his thoughts. But he figured Candy probably looked very much like that little girl when she was her age. She had probably shared just such a moment with her mother when she was still young and protected.

He realized he was frowning as he got in his car. He wanted to put Wiley away for what he was doing to the county treasury. But now he realized what he told Doris was even more true than he knew. Candy didn't deserve whatever was happening to her right now. Getting her away from Wiley was reason enough to follow this story through.

CHAPTER TWENTY-SEVEN

That evening Rachel said good night to Mel and Connie and prepared to lock up the studio. She had turned out all but the front desk light. When the telephone rang she almost let it go. But business is business. As far as she knew, a new customer was on the other end of that line.

"Good evening. Arlington Ballroom."

Josh's warm voice put a smile on her face. "I don't suppose you have late-night grocery shopping to do, do you?"

She laughed. "Not really. Why?"

"I thought we might shop together."

Was this guy ever going to ask her out on a real date?

"Sorry. I have plenty of bread and eggs." Let him stew on that.

He sighed. "Actually, I wanted to see if I could take you out to dinner, but I left it too late."

"Too late for what?"

"Well, you know. It's rude to ask a woman out at the last minute. Makes it seem like she hasn't been on your mind."

She smiled. "And what do you have to say for yourself?"

He didn't answer right away.

"I'd like to refer you back to my sister's comment. The one about my being an ox?"

She laughed. "Listen. I'm going to write it down right now. Josh. Is. An ox. There. Now you never need to do anything to remind me of that again. How does that sound?"

"That sounds…unlikely."

"So are you going to take me to dinner or what?"

"I am."

"All right. Let me get myself home and tidied up a little. Give me forty-five minutes?"

"I'll be there."

*****

A few hours later they left Lorenzo's Italian Restaurant, full and as happy as they could be, given their respective professional concerns. The nearly full moon lit their way to Josh's car.

"You want to walk some before I drive you home?" Josh asked.

"Sure." Rachel wasn't eager to be home, even though she needed to get some rest before a full day of teaching and practicing for the competition. The very thought of competing in the contest made her shiver.

He noticed. "You cold?"

Hmm. Perhaps he planned to put a nice warm arm around her.

"What if I am? What will you do?"

He shrugged and started to remove his suit coat. "I'll let this swallow you up. I'm pretty warm."

"Oh. Well, no. I'm not cold." He did smell awfully good. No doubt his jacket did too. And she wouldn't have minded letting it swallow her up, but it wasn't cold out at all. On the contrary, the air was typically warm and moist for a July evening. She didn't want to get all sweaty around him.

"You shivered, though," he said.

She had avoided talking about the topic during dinner, but now she confessed. "I'm thinking about the competition."

"You're nervous? I would think you'd be even more confident, now that you're the one who will be dancing. Aren't you a stronger dancer than Mira?"

She sighed. "It's not nervousness. And yes, I'm probably a stronger dancer. But I just never thought I'd have to compete again."

"Have to?" They stopped at a crosswalk and waited for traffic to pass before they stepped into the street. "I thought you loved dancing. Why would you put so much of yourself into the business if you—"

"I do love dancing."

He put his hand against her back to prompt her to cross the street with him, but he removed it once they walked a few steps. "So?"

She frowned, but he couldn't see that. "I don't really like to talk about it."

He didn't say a word in response. She waited for him to dismiss the subject, but he kept his mouth shut. The silence began to feel awkward, so she tried to change course.

"So I read your A&W article—"

"You're honestly not going to talk about the dancing problem?" He smiled, but there was something behind the smile. Annoyance? Hurt?

She answered with a huge sigh, and his tone softened.

"Come on, Rachel." When she hesitated, he teased her. "How bad could it be? Did you have a fatal dancing accident, take out one of your partners, vow to never dance again?"

"It's not funny."

"Well what *is* it, then? I'd think we're good enough friends that you could trust me with your story. Aren't we pretty good friends? I already think you're terrific. That's not going to change, unless you kicked a puppy or something."

"That's all it would take to shatter your good impression of me? Kicking a puppy?"

"What? Did you have *plans* along those lines? No, actually, I'd probably still think you were pretty terrific, even after the puppy incident." Now he leaned toward her and put his arm around her, protectively drawing her toward him. "So let me hear it."

"It's not even something bad I did. It was something that happened to me."

No response.

"Okay," she said. "So you remember I mentioned I dated a guy—"

"Billy."

Whew, *that* was a fast response. He had that name right at the front of his mind. "Right. Billy."

"And he was more than a date, right? Your boyfriend? Of three years?"

She looked at him to see if there was a jealousy problem, but he looked more like he wanted to coax her, to encourage her to be frank with him.

"We were pretty serious, Josh."

"I figured."

"And we danced in some competitions together. I think I mentioned that."

"Mm-hmm." He gently squeezed her shoulder to make her stop at the corner. They had reached a picnic area, over which several street lamps flooded soft light. The fragrance of honeysuckle suggested the vine had grown throughout the chain-link fence that separated one side of the park from the sidewalk. "Let's sit."

He waited for her to sit on the bench first, and when he settled in next to her, she waited for him to replace his arm over her shoulders. Instead, he draped it across the back of the bench so he could face her better. "All right. The competitions?"

"Yeah. We danced well the first couple of times, but we didn't win at the first level. Not until the third year. The third year we won the local competition, and we qualified to dance at the state level. So we went to Richmond for that."

"Sounds like you were similar to Cruz and Mira. A good fit."

Well, that was certainly a gracious thing for him to say. Her concern about jealousy abated even further.

"We were. But Billy had a… Well, he was kind of possessive, I guess you could say."

"Possessive of you?"

"Yes. He couldn't accept my dancing with other men, unless they were really old or unattractive. It made it pretty uncomfortable if he was around while I taught classes."

Josh scratched the back of his head, a slight grimace in his expression. She could see he held back a comment.

"What?" She felt he should be as frank with her as she was being with him now.

He tilted his head and clearly didn't want to say anything.

"What is it, Josh?"

"No, you should tell me the rest. It's just… Well, I shouldn't jump to conclusions. But so far the guy sounds like a bit of a jerk."

"He didn't mean to be." She couldn't believe she said that. She still defended him, even after what happened. "But you know what? He *was* a jerk."

"Okay." Josh chuckled. "I'm glad we established that. Now I'm ready to hear the rest."

"Well, when we went down to Richmond, oh, it was so crowded! It was close enough to home that lots of our friends and family were there, and it was like that with most of the competitors. It was in a huge ballroom, filled to capacity. But we had all—all of us competitors and teachers—we had been there together since the day before, practicing and breaking for meals and stuff, and we…mingled, you know?"

"Ah. I see. Mingling probably didn't go over well, considering the other dancers probably weren't all old and unattractive."

She smiled. He caught on well.

"There was this guy from Williamsburg. Daniel. Very good-looking. Very friendly. Not just with me. Not just with the women. With everyone."

"And Billy was jealous."

"He let it bother him so much. I could see he was bothered, but I didn't realize how bad. During the competition the next evening, he started to get kind of snippy with me, and then he actually got mean, but everything he said, he said to me under his breath. Still, I didn't realize that he had worked up this entire fantasy about Daniel and me being involved with each other."

"Oh, brother."

"Josh, I had barely been out of Billy's sight the whole time we were there. But he suspected me of… Well, it was awful. Right in the middle of the competition, after Daniel just happened to smile at me when Billy was looking, Billy lost his temper. He broke away from me right in the middle of the dance, and his shouting was so disruptive, they stopped the music. Everyone stopped dancing just in time for Billy to accuse me and Daniel…"

She was embarrassed all over again. The wave of humiliation flooded her as if she were right there on that dance floor again.

"I can't even tell you what he called me."

Josh's brows furrowed so deeply, he looked as if he would have decked Billy, unprovoked, if he just happened to pass by their bench at the moment. Neither Josh nor she spoke for a moment, and then he seemed to will himself to a neutral expression before he spoke to her gently.

"But *he's* the one who has a reason to avoid competitions now. You didn't do anything wrong."

"Very few people really knew me, Josh. Only my friends and family. For all everyone knew, the accusation was true. And of course I was disqualified. Right in front of everyone. I couldn't exactly compete on my own, after all. I mean, they did it gently. They treated me as kindly as they could. But I had to walk off the dance floor in front of a million pairs of eyes. I felt naked."

Now he enveloped her with his arm. "And how long ago did this happen?"

She shrugged. "Like I said. A few months ago."

"Well no *wonder* you're gun shy, Rachel! Man!"

She heard him exhale deeply.

"And is this nut running around now? Anywhere where I might happen to find myself? Maybe while I'm behind the wheel of a very large truck?"

She laughed. "Thank you for your chivalrous nature. I haven't talked with him since then, but last month my brother mentioned he saw him somewhere, so he's still around."

"And this is why you don't want to dance in a public competition? Because of that lunatic?"

"You don't know how humiliating it was, Josh. A lot of the same people will be at this competition. Probably *most* of them. And I'm sure they'll remember, as soon as they see me."

He stood and offered his arm for her to join him. She stood, dusted off the back of her skirt, and they walked again.

"I think I want to go to this competition of yours," he said.

She smiled at him. "Why?"

"To give you moral support, of course."

She sighed. She had to look away so he wouldn't see how moved she was.

He continued. "And to make a scene of my own if anyone gives you a hard time."

She laughed. "Somehow that doesn't fill me with eagerness about either *one* of us being there."

He patted her hand. All of this touching was quite all right.

"Rachel, you're a sweet, hardworking woman, and you shouldn't let anyone intimidate you, especially in your own field of expertise. I don't know a thing about dance, but I do know about jealous idiots like that Billy character. I've come across plenty of them. I've even *been* one of them."

She gasped. "You're kidding, right?"

He tilted his head. "Well, I've been jealous, I'll say that. But I've never acted on it, I've always kept my head on straight, and I would *never* call a woman a filthy name. Or deliberately embarrass her in public."

They walked a few steps more.

"Not deliberately." Rachel grinned up at him, and he grinned back.

"The girl knows how to listen."

CHAPTER TWENTY-EIGHT

When they arrived at Rachel's apartment, she turned the conversation back around to Josh's writing. She spoke before he got out of the car to open her door.

"I wanted to tell you I enjoyed your A&W article."

He chuckled, as if the piece were no big deal. "At least someone did." He got out before she could react, but the moment he opened her door, she picked the topic back up.

"What do you mean? Have there been complaints?"

"No. Not that I've heard, anyway, and I'm pretty sure Lou would have said something if that were the case so far."

He took her hand and helped her out of the car. They walked to her door, and she kept talking to avoid thinking about the big question: kiss or no kiss?

"So why do you make it sound like I'm the only reader who liked it?"

Josh shrugged. "Oh, well. You know. It's just an article about root beer. No one's life is going to be changed by root beer."

"Ah. So *you* didn't like the article."

"It was all right, for what it was. A fluff piece." They reached her door, but she felt tension between them on this topic for some reason.

"I don't agree. It *could* have been a fluff piece, if you had just written about how tasty vanilla ice cream is in an icy mug of root beer. Or if you had *only* talked about the history of the chain."

"I did talk about those things."

"But you covered much more than that."

"Oh." He nearly rolled his eyes. "Lou's human element, you mean."

"*Lou's* human element? Are you saying Lou wrote the part about that franchise owner—"

"Frank Bowry."

Rachel fought a smile. Oh no, Josh wasn't involved with the so-called human element, but he had that man's name right on the tip of his tongue.

"No," Josh said. "Lou didn't write that part. I wrote the whole thing."

"So you wrote about Frank's GI service and how he parlayed that into getting a loan. And how he built up his share of the franchise by focusing on the importance of service to the customer above everything else—"

"Man, you really *did* read it, didn't you?"

He could tease all he wanted. She could tell he was pleased.

She pulled her keys out of her purse. "Yes, I read it. And I know you don't like to accept it, but you're very good at this kind of writing."

"A chimp could write this stuff. But squishy sells papers, I guess."

"Squishy."

"Yeah, squishy. I'm sorry, Rachel, but this just isn't what I became a reporter for. I'm never going to—to make a mark in life—not the mark I want to make, anyway—by chasing after meaningless stories about jukeboxes and hamburgers. And although I want to do my best at any job I do, it kind of gives me the heebie-jeebies when you praise these articles as if I've written the Declaration of Independence."

"That's not what I'm doing at all. I simply said—"

"The absolutely worst thing that could happen, in my book, would be if the Powers That Be at the *Tribune* decided I was better at writing *this* junk than at what I wrote for the city desk."

Ah. She watched him clench his jaw. She glanced at the ground before she spoke again.

"That's what this is about, then. You're afraid—"

"It's not fear. It's frustration."

"Sorry. Wrong word choice. You're frustrated over the fact that you might never make it back to the city desk. Especially if your Style pieces keep doing well."

He ran his hand through his hair. "They're getting good feedback. Better than anything I ever wrote for the city desk. And since my last job for Sal—"

"Sal?"

"The city editor. Since my last job for him was such a bust, my chances aren't leaning in the right direction."

"Kind of puts you in a bad spot, doesn't it?" She tried to look him in the eye, but he didn't seem to want to meet her gaze at the moment. "I see that. You need to write your best to stay with the *Tribune,* but if you're too good where you are, you could get stuck."

He leaned against the door jamb. "Exactly."

She wished she could brighten up the outlook for him. "But, Josh, I'll bet there are all kinds of journalists who would be thrilled to get *any* job on the paper. Would it really be the end of the world if you never got back to the city desk?"

"Yes! It would!" He pushed away from the wall, his hands held open as if her ability to empathize rested in them. "I want to uncover evil in the world and be a part of fighting it. I want to write about things that matter."

"But you *are* writing about things that matter. You're writing about people."

"I don't care about people!"

He said this last rather loudly, and she straightened, shutting her mouth.

They looked at each other. Neither spoke, and she became aware that her neighbor's dog was barking. Probably about them.

Josh released his breath and shook his head. "I didn't mean that."

"No. I know you didn't." She turned her key in the lock. "I understand."

He tsked and sighed again. "I'm sorry. I don't know how I managed to ruin the evening so quickly."

"You didn't ruin it, Josh. Don't worry about it. You care about your work. I know what that feels like."

But a somber note lingered there on the doorstep with them, and they couldn't simply ignore it.

Josh checked his watch. "It's late. I should let you go."

"Yeah. We both have a lot of work in the morning." She smiled at him, and she knew it wasn't the brightest smile in her arsenal. But it was the brightest one she could retrieve at the moment.

Certainly the kiss-or-no-kiss question had been answered for the evening. Still, Josh looked as if he were going to give *something* a try. He leaned in awkwardly but ended up giving her a kiss on the top of her head.

Rachel frowned.

Terrific. Be still my heart.

It was like getting a send-off from her grandpa. She opened her door. "Good night, Josh."

"Yes, good night. Sorry."

She turned to assure him the apology was unnecessary, but he had already turned to walk away. Better to just let him go. Up until this discussion, the evening had been lovely. She had hated the idea of its coming to an end, and she thought he felt the same. Now, apparently, it couldn't end soon enough.

CHAPTER TWENTY-NINE

If anyone had wanted to pour salt into Josh's minor wound from his talk with Rachel, they might have encouraged Frank Bowry to give him a call. The A&W franchise owner called shortly after Josh got into the office the next morning.

"I have to tell you, Josh, your article has been a big hit here. My wife has gone to the five and dime to buy a frame. We're going to put it up on the wall here, right next to the first buck the business made."

"Yeah, that's great, Frank."

"You all right there, Josh? Something wrong with the article? Your paper didn't like it?"

"No, no. I'm sorry. Had a rough night last night. No, the paper loved the article. We've gotten good feedback on it."

"Same here! Had a lot of customers mention it. And I swear we've already seen an increase in business from it. I don't think it's my imagination. We're getting plenty of people here we've never served before. You did a good thing there."

A smile managed to tug at the far corners of Josh's mouth. "I'm glad to hear it, Frank. But, hey, I've got to get to work on the next article, okay?"

"Oh, sure. I'll let you go. So what's the next one about?"

"Don't know yet. I'm thinking on it. I'll talk with you later."

He hung up and sighed. The next one. And the one after that. Dog shows. The Hokey Pokey. Drive-in theaters. All earth-changing stuff.

He took a long drink of his coffee. He needed to get out of this frame of mind or he wouldn't even have *this* job for long. Rachel was right. There were plenty of journalists out there hoping to catch a break anywhere on the *Tribune.* He didn't want God teaching him the hard way that he needed to appreciate what he had.

His phone rang. He hoped it wasn't someone else telling him how well suited he was to the fluff desk.

"Yes, hello. I mean, Style and Leisure. Josh Reegan."

"Josh, oh good, it's you."

That little-girl voice perked him up before his mind clicked on who it was.

"It's Doris. From the beauty parlor?"

"Oh! Yeah, Doris."

"Candy's friend?"

"Yes, yes. I remember." He had come fully alive once he realized who she was.

She said, "I talked with your friend Wiley last night."

He grabbed a pad of paper and a pen. One glance toward Lou's office told him Lou wasn't likely to walk out anytime soon. He had the door closed, and it sounded like he was on the phone himself.

"Terrific. How did it go?"

"You would have been proud of me, Josh. I oughta be in pictures, I'm such a good actress."

He smiled. "Tell me."

"Okay, so I said, 'Hey, Teddy, I'm not sure if you remember me, but I'm a friend of Candy's.' And right away he gets kinda quiet, ya know? Then he just goes, 'Yes?' Real careful-like. I acted like I didn't notice. I said, 'I was hoping you two didn't have anything planned next weekend, cuz I was hoping to steal Candy away for a baby shower. For

Maybelle Arnstein. From the old gang. Maybelle would *love* it if Candy was there.' And, Josh, I'm telling you now. None of that is a lie. I'm a good girl, and I don't lie, not if I can absolutely help it."

He chuckled. "I understand—"

"I *do* hope to steal her away. From that crumb-bum, that is. And we *are* having a baby shower next week, and Maybelle truly would love it if Candy could be there."

"I appreciate your wanting to be honest, Doris," Josh said. "I'm not comfortable with lying either."

"Okay. And he takes the bait. At least as far as believing that I don't know about him dumping her. Josh, I could just see the wheels turning in his sneaky little mind. He goes, 'Have you called the apartment?' And I know right away, he's checking to see if I've talked with Mitzy. Checking to make sure Mitzy didn't fill me in. And since I *have* called the apartment in the past and there was no answer, I very honestly said that. I said, 'Yeah, I tried calling, but no one answers, and we're running out of time, so I thought I'd try to catch her through you.'"

Josh nodded. "Nicely done."

"Didn't I tell you? A natural-born actress." She sighed. "Unfortunately, I don't think I helped you much in the long run."

"Why? What did he tell you?"

"I could tell he was deciding what the best thing was to say. You know, he took his time before coming to the point? But eventually he told me he and Candy had broken up, and he didn't know where she was or what she was doing these days."

Josh slumped back in his chair. "Shoot."

"Yeah. I'm sorry. I wish I had more for you."

"No, I appreciate your trying." He felt the city desk fading farther away from his future.

"But I'll tell you what," she said. "I can ask around. Talk with any of our mutual friends. Maybe she's been in touch with someone."

"Would you? That would be great, yeah. You're kind to help me out."

"Hey, I'm happy to help you, but to tell you the truth, I'm mostly concerned with Candy. It's just not right, no one knowing where she is. Her not being able to talk with people who love her. We gotta find her."

"Candy's blessed to have you in her corner. So am I."

"Blessed?" He heard her smile when she spoke. "Well, isn't that something? I can't say I've had anything to do with anyone being blessed in the past."

"Don't be so sure. I'll talk with you later, Doris. Call me anytime."

He didn't have much time to wallow in his disappointment. Moments after he hung up the phone, Lou walked out of his office, a pad of paper in his hand.

"What are you working on, Reegan?"

"Uh, just looking into ideas for a story, Lou." Josh squirmed in his chair. He and Candy both had been walking on the edge of honesty in their statements lately.

"Perfect. I've got one for you here. You did so well with the last two, I'm going to send you on this one." Lou ripped the top sheet from the pad and tossed it on Josh's desk.

Josh scanned the sheet, reading aloud. "Peek into Fall. Lord and Taylor. July's advance look at..." He jerked his head up. "Oh, come on, Lou. Ladies' fashions? You're making me cover a fashion show?"

Lou shrugged. "You can do it, Reegan. Normally I'd have Babs cover it, but she's got her hands full."

"With what? I'll take over whatever she's working on."

"That's not your call. Cover the show. Freddie will go with you to take a few snapshots. He'll give you some pointers about what to look for. He's a seasoned pro."

Josh pressed his palm against his forehead. "This is *not* why I became a journalist, Lou."

"Well, it's how you're staying one. You might as well get used to it."

Lou left him to simmer. How much worse could this job get? He could feel his masculinity being wrenched away from him, and he didn't know how to pull it back. His family and friends were going to see his byline on this piece. He would never hear the end of it.

At once his father came to mind. He had never seen a blessing in his father's early passing. Not even a remote one. But he had to admit he found a moment's comfort in knowing that his dad—such a man's man, a tough bastion of strength—wasn't around to see how far his son had fallen.

CHAPTER THIRTY

"Cruz, stop adjusting that tie." Rachel brushed off his shoulders—strong and broad in his tuxedo—and gave his arms a reassuring squeeze. "You look very handsome, but you're going to get the tie dirty if you keep playing with it." She straightened the white bow tie that accented his crisp white shirt and stepped back to give him a final once-over. "Perfect." Even if he *had* gone a little overboard with the aftershave.

"I never wore tails before." He jockeyed for a chance to see himself again in one of the backstage mirrors. "My mother will be in tears."

Rachel smiled. "I'm so glad your family came to cheer you on."

"Is your family here?"

She tilted her head. "Some of them. One of my brothers and his family are at the beach on vacation this week. They didn't realize I would be dancing, and I certainly wouldn't expect them to cancel their plans for this. But my parents are here. And my other brother and his wife are out there too." She tried not to think of who else might be. Surely people who had witnessed her shame in the spring. Maybe even Billy.

Connie and Mel rejoined them from out front. Connie said, "It's quite a large crowd out there, kids. Mira's there, off her crutches, little trooper that she is. She's putting a brave face on it, as much as she hoped to dance. She's with her folks."

Rachel grimaced. Mr. Stanhope had promised to remain true to his word, despite Mira's injury. Even though she was unable to compete at this level, there was still a chance for her to compete at the state level, if Cruz and she won today. And Mira had continued coming to work—

even if a little more sporadically—and watching the practices, while she healed. Rachel would be glad when this round of the competition was over. If she and Cruz won, the doctor said Mira would be fully healed by the next level of competition, scheduled in Virginia Beach in two weeks. It would be a tight squeeze getting her prepared, but Mira would be up to it. She was sure.

"And lots of the studio's customers are out there, rooting for you." Connie studied them and brought her hands to her face. "You look so gorgeous, the two of you."

"You're the picture of the perfect gent, Cruz." Mel patted Cruz's arm. "Just remember out there. Elegant. Strong." Mel stood tall, as if he were about to dance himself. "Long lines."

Connie took her by the hand and pulled her away to speak privately. "How are you feeling, sweetie?"

"Only slightly terrified." She smoothed down the lines of her pale aqua dress, which dramatically flared out from a snug waist over numerous layers of petticoats.

Connie took her by the arms and peered into her eyes. "I understand why you're hesitant, Rachel, but this is an entirely different event. You're dressed differently, and your hair is down, so you don't look the same as you did in Richmond. Many people aren't going to remember—"

"You're wonderful to say that, Connie, but I can tell plenty of these competitors recognize me. I know *I'd* remember if any of the regular competitors were part of a scene like Richmond. My heart would break for them, but I'd remember."

"Well, there, you see? Just know if anyone recognizes you, their hearts are broken for you—that's better than laughing at you, right? And that's really what you're afraid of. That they're getting some kind of pleasure out of your past embarrassment?"

"Or they believe what Billy said about me." She frowned. "Maybe this dress is too…va-va-va-voom—"

"Now stop. You look beautiful, not trashy. What do you want to do, wear sackcloth for this thing? You are a total class act, and don't you forget it."

Rachel sighed. "I shouldn't even be talking about this right now, Connie. It's making me perspire."

"Oh, honey, I'm sorry. I just wanted to comfort you."

Rachel nodded. "I know. I—I think I need to find someplace to say a quick, private prayer."

Both women surveyed the room, but it was bustling with people.

"The bathroom." Connie pointed deeper backstage. "It's a one-person room. Hurry. If no one else is in there—"

"Yeah. I'll be right back." Rachel hurried toward the restroom, starting her prayer before she even got there.

I'm scared, Lord. My heart's beating so fast I feel like I could faint. I know I shouldn't care what others think—

A young woman in layered, frilly chiffon exited the bathroom just as Rachel got there. Rachel simply shut the door and stood there, her eyes clamped shut, and collected her thoughts again.

Lord. I shouldn't care about the crowd. I know that. I should rest my confidence in Your love and acceptance. Should should should. But You know what's going on in my heart. I'm weak and full of pride, and I really need You to make me stop noticing the crowd and focus on dancing beautifully. Please, Lord?

A knock at the door jolted her out of her prayer. "Anyone in there?"

"Hold on just a moment, I'll be right out."

She quickly closed her eyes again.

Thank You, Jesus. Amen.

That was going to have to do. She could keep praying little requests right up to when the dancing began, but after that she needed to focus completely on the steps and her posture and following Cruz as best as she could.

She returned to her group, and the competition organizer, a full-back of a woman, with upswept blond hair and elaborate makeup, took control of the room. She clapped her hands and called out above the din, "All right, dancers, listen up!"

The room quieted quickly, and all eyes turned to her.

"Gentlemen? Are your numbers securely fastened on your backs? We don't want anything flying off during the competition. Yes? I want all couples to line up right where I'm standing, and we'll bring you out in a moment."

Mel draped his arms around both her and Cruz. "You've both been stellar in practice. Just do what you've been doing. We're pulling for you."

Connie gave them each a quick hug and left with Mel.

As soon as they left, she once again felt responsible for Cruz. In a somewhat maternal fashion, she gained strength, knowing he needed encouragement from her. Of course, she didn't discount the effect of that prayer in the bathroom, either.

She took a deep breath, let it go, and flashed him as relaxed a smile as she could gather.

"We're going to dance beautifully out there, Cruz."

He smiled back, his nerves barely hidden. He gave her a quick nod before the big blond organizer returned backstage, barking out her orders.

Before she could think further, they all paraded, hand in hand with their partners, onto the dance floor.

The cheers and applause melted away much of her concern, and she saw Cruz undergo the same change. Their first dance was the waltz, and no one would have guessed Cruz claimed a certain failing with the Modern dances one short month ago. His confidence broke through as soon as they successfully executed their first turn, and he led her around the crowded dance floor as if they were the only couple there. Rachel heard both their names called out from supporters in the crowd, and her smile became genuine.

"That was absolutely perfect." She quietly spoke to Cruz between dances.

He looked away from the crowd and back at her. "What did I tell you? My mama's crying."

They both laughed, and the relief spurred them on. They had worked on the dreaded quickstep as soon as they knew they'd have to perform it today. Their hard work had paid off. And by the time they finished the foxtrot, she felt as much confidence as she had with Billy when they won at this level. She still clung to the comfort of knowing this was a one-day event for her, but she knew she would survive unscathed at this rate. They would handle the tango just fine. And they'd perform the Latin dances at least as well as the Moderns, since the Latin dances were Cruz's strongest styles.

Just as they were about to leave the stage to change clothes for the tango and the Latin dances, Rachel caught sight of Billy in the crowd. He stared at her with an expression she couldn't read. She gasped and looked away as if he were Medusa, but the damage to her self-confidence was already done.

"What's the matter?" Cruz spoke softly to her as they walked backstage.

She shook her head. "Nothing. Just a little catch in my throat."

While changing with the other female dancers, she kept looking at the more familiar faces to see if anyone seemed to pass judgment on her. A couple of them smiled uncomfortably at her, but she didn't know if that was because they remembered the incident with Billy or because she was staring at them now.

Connie came in to help her zip up the slinkier dress and fix her hair. "You two are like heaven out there, Rachel."

"Oh my goodness." Rachel spoke as quietly as she could. "Billy's out there."

She saw that Connie already knew. "Oh, honey, I was hoping you wouldn't see him. Look, you just ignore him. He probably feels like a complete fool for how he treated you, and well he should. I'm surprised they even let him in here."

"Well, maybe that's a good sign." Rachel sighed and turned so Connie could zip her up. "If the organizers don't remember how disruptive he was, maybe no one else does, either."

"That's the spirit. Regardless, Mel has positioned himself in Billy's proximity. If he gets any funny ideas, Mel will put a stop to him faster than you can smash your shoe on a cockroach."

Rachel felt a tug on her skirt and turned to see a young girl around Mary's age who handed her a note. "Are you Miss Stanhope, ma'am? He said to give this to the one with the reddish-blond hair, and that seems to be you."

"Yes. Thank you." Rachel took the note and glanced at Connie. The girl ran out, and Connie took the note from Rachel's hand.

"You don't need to read this before you go out there."

"It's from Billy, don't you think?" Rachel bit on her thumbnail. She shouldn't allow him to affect her confidence so seriously, but she knew just a few bitter words would hurt her concentration out there even worse than it was already hurt.

Connie pulled Rachel's hand away from her face. "You're going to ruin your pretty polish, honey. You want me to read it first?"

Rachel nodded. "Okay. If it's bad, just save it for later."

Connie opened the note and Rachel watched her read. Connie's hesitant eyes suddenly sparkled. With a broad smile she turned it around for her to see.

You dance like an angel.
Josh

Rachel's smile matched Connie's. "Josh is out there?"

Connie shrugged. "I didn't see him, but obviously so."

She and Josh hadn't spoken since their awkward good-bye at her apartment door last week. He was the last person she expected to show up today, even though he said he would. That plan had been before they clashed. But his coming to support her, as well as his going to the trouble to get this note to her, made all the difference in how she felt about going back out on that floor. If nothing else, Josh Reegan was a true friend.

The organizer stuck her bouffant hairdo through the curtains. "Let's go, ladies. Five minutes. You all need to be out here with your partners."

Rachel's renewed confidence spilled over onto Cruz, who was already excited to show off his favored styles of dance. They breezed from the tango to the cha-cha, to the rumba, and finally the samba.

They were worn out from both the dancing and the suspense by the time the judges made their decision. Relief finally came when the master of ceremonies made the announcement. They didn't win second runner-up. They didn't win first runner-up.

"And the winners of the Summer Northern Virginia Ballroom Dance Competition, representing Arlington Ballroom, Rachel Stanhope and Cruz Vergara."

CHAPTER THIRTY-ONE

Rachel and Cruz screamed at each other in the middle of the noisy room, laughing in disbelief. He grabbed her and lifted her from the ground as he had done when she first hired him. By the time he set her back on the ground, the rest of the competitors—other than the first and second runners-up—headed off the floor. The master of ceremonies was at their side, a trophy in one hand and his microphone in the other.

"For the second time in a row, the Arlington Ballroom Studio has won the Northern Virginia Ballroom Dance Competition." He turned to her. "We look forward to seeing you—" He looked back out at the audience. "We look forward to seeing *all* of you at the state competition at the luxurious Cavalier Hotel in Virginia Beach on August 11." He turned back to her and Cruz and handed her the trophy—a golden couple dancing atop a thick slab of marble. "Congratulations."

The rest of the announcements were drowned out as people seeped onto the dance floor or made their way to the exits.

"Rachel." Cruz spoke to her as he scanned the jumble of people. "I don't see my family."

Rachel laughed. "I can't see mine, either. But something tells me your mother is going to find you."

The MC rested his hand on Rachel's arm. "When you can, please come over to the judges' table to fill out the required forms and get your certificate."

"Okay. Thank you."

Connie and Mel reached them right after the MC turned away.

Connie grabbed Rachel almost as energetically as Cruz had. "My darling, didn't I tell you this would happen? You both looked fabulous out there!"

Within moments, they were surrounded by studio clients, family members, and people who had questions about the studio. Although busy responding to everyone, Rachel scanned the crowd. She was unable to spot Josh at all. She made her way back over to Connie.

"Did you see Josh?"

Mel, who stood with his back to them, turned around. "I saw him, Rachel. He passed me on his way out. He had to leave early, so he doesn't know yet that you won. He asked me to let you know he was sorry he had to go. Something about his current news assignment."

She nodded. She refused to be disappointed that he wasn't still there. How thoughtful that he had come, even though he was under a deadline.

With delight she saw Mr. and Mrs. Chambers approach.

"I can't believe you two came!" She left the crowd to shorten their walk. She gave a quick hug to each of them.

"Rachel, you two were wonderful out there," Mr. Chambers said.

Mrs. Chambers drew her hands together near her chest. "Perfect together. Like two early birds of a feather!"

Rachel skipped only a second's beat before responding. Was any cliché safe from sweet Mrs. Chambers's jumbling? "Oh, thank you, Mrs. Chambers. You two are so kind to have come. But how did you get here?"

"Our daughter is in town. Our grandkids, too." Mr. Chambers put a protective arm around his wife as several teens ran past them. "She went to get her car and she's probably waiting for us out front, so we have to get on. But we couldn't leave without congratulating you."

Rachel felt a slight sting of tears in her eyes. Their coming touched her. But she also appreciated their getting attention from their daughter and grandchildren. She hated thinking of them being alone so often.

When she rejoined her group, Mel raised a brow. "That troublemaker left early."

"Billy?"

"Yeah. I don't think he had any mischief in mind. He looked pretty... Well, he was quite the sad sack."

Better a sad sack than a raging bull.

Rachel noticed Mira and her parents entering the fray. Mira's father had his arm around her shoulders and his other arm protectively extended in front of them so no one could step on her feet. She barely favored one side, and Rachel could see she was assuring her father that she was fine without his protection. She approached them so they wouldn't have to come deeper into the crowd.

Mira gave her a hug. "You look beautiful, Rachel."

Rachel nodded at Mr. Longworth, who shook her hand wordlessly. She looked back at Mira.

"It should have been you. It *will* be you in a couple of weeks, assuming you're up for it."

"The doctor says I'll be ready to dance within the week. Will that be enough time?"

She saw Mira glance over the crowd as she spoke. When Rachel turned to follow her gaze, her eyes landed on Cruz.

"Yeah, plenty of time."

Cruz happened to turn at the same time, and he grinned at Rachel.

Rachel smiled and energetically pointed at Mira, hoping the boy would get the hint.

His smile did brighten, and he waved at Mira. He made his way over to them, getting congratulatory slaps on the back on his way.

He gave Mira a little peck on the cheek. "You look better. That was nice of you to come."

"Of course I came, silly!"

Rachel ached for Mira. Just her using that name, *silly*, made her sound like a giddy young girl. She was smitten.

Rachel tried to address them as a couple. "Hey, you two, come with me to the judge's table. We have to fill out forms for today's win and probably the Virginia Beach competition, too. I might need your personal information, Mira, to sign you up as Cruz's partner."

The three of them broke away from the slowly dwindling crowd and were greeted by several of the competition organizers at the judges' table.

As soon as they determined who they needed to see, Rachel explained the switch in dance partners they planned.

"I only filled in for Mira here because she got injured right before the competition. But she's the one I want representing Arlington Ballroom in Virginia Beach."

The woman tilted her head and lifted her brows.

"How's that, now?" Unlike the big, overdone organizer who corralled them during the competition, this lady didn't seem like the dance world type. She looked like she should be home serving cocktails to her guests or presiding over the bridge club.

Rachel tried again. "I said, Mira, here, will be dancing with Cruz in the state competition in Virginia Beach. I only danced today because—"

"Oh, no dear. That won't do."

Rachel thought she heard incorrectly. "Won't do?"

"Well, I'm pretty certain that the same dancers are required to compete at all levels or forfeit their place in the competition." The woman smiled politely, as if that settled that.

"No, we can't do that. I didn't want to compete in the first place."

"But you did, dear." Another smile. This one had a little eye blink that went with it.

Rachel looked at Cruz and Mira. Mira turned a shade paler than she had been a moment before.

Rachel hated to make waves, but she didn't know what else to do. She smiled at the woman. "Um, I don't mean to be a problem, but is your… Is there someone here who is, um, of a higher rank than you are?"

A little release of breath, a hint of insulted disbelief, escaped from the woman's mouth. Still, she spoke calmly. "This isn't the military, dear. But if you'll wait here a moment, I'll get Mr. Sperling over here to chat. That should settle things."

Rachel turned back to Mira and Cruz. "I'm going to try to get this straightened out."

Cruz shrugged. "Hey, whatever works, Rachel. I'm fine with your dancing at the next one." He frowned, as if he had just heard what he said, and looked at Mira. "I mean, I'd love to dance with you, of course, Mira. But we can't forfeit, right?"

"Right." Mira's voice was so small. She glanced at the floor.

Rachel widened her eyes at Cruz, who frowned and mouthed *What?* Completely oblivious. She shook her head and turned back to see Mr. Sperling approach. She had seen him at past competitions. Dressed in a handsome tuxedo, he was balding, paunchy, and usually very gracious.

In fact, he wore a far more friendly expression than had the woman. He reached out and shook her hand and then Cruz's. "Congratulations to both of you. Fine performances, all."

"Thank you so much, Mr. Sperling. But we have a little request."

"Yes, Mrs. Steffan explained to me." He gestured toward Mira. "Why didn't this lovely young lady compete today?"

"She was injured, so I had to step in. But she's our competitor."

He stood straight and rested his chin in his hand. "Right right right. Ah, well, that *is* a shame. But I'm afraid Mrs. Steffan told you right. We're not allowed to make personnel changes in the middle of the process. That's stated in the competition rules. I would have thought you would know that, being a studio owner and former competitor."

"I've never been in this kind of situation before. I was always the one to compete before."

"Well, there, you see. Then it worked out nicely." He gave a fatherly smile to Mira. "Not so nicely for you. I understand that. But there will be other competitions." He looked back at Rachel. "I'm very sorry we can't accommodate you."

Rachel nodded as he walked away.

Mrs. Steffan returned, kept her *I told you so* to herself, and presented the forms for Rachel to complete.

"I'll be back." Mira walked toward her parents, and Rachel cringed. This wasn't just sad for Mira and nerve-racking for Rachel. This was a bad turn of events business-wise, as well. Now that there was no way Mira could compete at any level, Rachel would definitely lose three months' coverage on her mortgage. And if Mira couldn't compete, she certainly couldn't win. That meant the loss of another six months. That was one expensive ankle sprain.

Rachel had meant for the studio to compete to win, right from the start, even before she received the mortgage offer from Mr. Longworth. Now that she would lose some of his financial support, the possible win in two weeks meant even more. If she hoped to achieve the growth she had planned for the studio, she was going to have to find funding through ways other than Mr. Longworth's generous pockets. She needed the relative fame that accompanied a win at the state level in order to attract a larger clientele.

She sighed. She would have to dance in at least one more competition. It was a good thing she felt stronger after dancing in front of everyone tonight, despite her earlier trepidation. She still felt immediate fear in her gut whenever she thought about Billy, but she chose to push that concern to the back of her mind. She'd consider what that was all about later.

In the meantime, the shame of last spring's debacle had diminished noticeably. She much preferred the former security of Mr. Longworth's funding, but maybe the Lord thought it was more important for her to work through her insecurities and find success for the studio another way.

If that was the case, she was going to have to avoid looking at her bank account in order to avoid a weakening of faith. She prayed she would be receptive to what might very well be a lesson of divine proportion.

CHAPTER THIRTY-TWO

Rachel looked twice when Mark and Mary came in for Monday morning's junior high class. Josh was with them. Her quick heartbeats annoyed her. She and Josh hadn't crossed paths—hadn't even spoken—in more than a week. Her last contact from him had been that wonderful note at the competition.

But since then, nothing. Not a phone call. Not a visit to the studio. To her own private chagrin she had even made a couple of extra trips to the grocery store, on the off-chance she might run into him. But no.

And the moment she sees him, her heart pitter-pats as if she were a schoolgirl. It was downright embarrassing.

Jerry, one of the other junior high students, tried to get her attention while the students mingled and waited for class to begin. "Miss Stanhope? Can we go over the reverse turns in the tango today? I'm stuck on that and can't figure it out."

She looked at Jerry, but she wasn't really listening. Her attention was focused on the fact that Josh had greeted Mira, who was at the front desk, as if they were old friends. He hadn't been here often enough for them to chat all that much. So how did that happen?

"Miss Stanhope?" Jerry actually tugged on the sleeve of her blouse. Until he did, she hadn't realized she had looked away from him and was staring at the front desk.

"What? Oh, yes, Jerry, I'm sorry. We'll start class in just a few minutes."

"But the reverse turns? In the tango?"

"Yes, there are reverse turns in the tango."

"I know *that*." Jerry's frown alerted her to her rudeness.

She forced herself to listen to him. "Uh, what was it you wanted, sweetie?"

"Can we work on them today?"

"Work on what, now?" Josh turned to look at her, at which point she realized she had looked away from Jerry again. She quickly turned back to Jerry, who drooped his shoulders and walked away. "Oh, Jerry, I'm so sorry. We'll work on whatever you—"

"Hey there, winner."

She turned at Josh's voice. "Oh! Josh. Hello." He looked wonderful. Why hadn't he been in touch?

He spoke as if his dropping out of sight was completely unimportant. "I didn't get a chance to congratulate you last week at the competition. I had to run out and get a story turned in, so I missed the announcement. But I wanted to tell you I really enjoyed what I was able to watch. Congratulations."

She nodded. Did he have to smell so good? "Thanks." Her nostrils actually flared—she felt it happen, as if she were part bloodhound. "And thanks for your note. It's—it's nice to see you. Pete's out of town again?" She glanced at Mark and Mary, who were playing some type of hand-play game with a couple of other students in the corner.

"Yeah, just for a few days. Say, I'm sorry I haven't called or anything."

Finally. An explanation. "Oh, that doesn't matter. I've been swamped by work. Has it been that long?"

"Seemed like it to me." He shrugged. "Maybe not. Lou's been giving me quite a few assignments."

"Yes, I've noticed your articles." Surely he had time to pick up the phone, despite his busy schedule. "Very well done."

"Thanks. And I know you've been busy getting ready for the competition this weekend. Mira—"

His mentioning Mira and then stopping so abruptly brought her up short. What in the world?

"What about Mira?"

Josh checked his watch and shook his head. "Nothing important. Hey, I'm cutting into your class time. Hi, Cruz." He smiled at Cruz, who had just walked out onto the dance floor. She could swear Josh had turned his attention to Cruz simply so he could look somewhere other than her eyes. He backed away from her and barely met her gaze. "I'll see you at the end of class, okay?" He lifted his hand in a wave.

On top of his odd behavior, he stopped at the front desk again and chatted for a moment with Mira. She nodded in response to whatever he said, and she gave him a sweet, yet coquettish, wave as he headed for the door.

Rachel restrained herself from gasping. For goodness' sake, he had to be… Well, didn't he say he was thirty-five? And she knew for a fact that Mira was in her early twenties. That *couldn't* have been what she just witnessed.

But she wasn't the only one perplexed. When she forced her attention to the class, she realized Cruz had watched the same exchange. And as he watched Mira come out from behind the desk to join them in teaching the class, he didn't work as hard as Rachel did to hide his disapproval.

* * * * *

Still, the three of them taught the junior high class as if everything were fine.

Mira, in particular, seemed in fine spirits. She had pouted quite a bit last week, as she struggled to adjust to the idea that she wouldn't get to compete this season. But Rachel had encouraged her at every turn, promising that the next competition was all hers. She had even invited her to come with her, Cruz, Connie, and Mel to the competition this weekend in Virginia Beach. She decided to close the studio for two days so they could all drive down together the day before in Connie and Mel's station wagon.

"That way you'll be good and familiar with these competitions by the time you get to dance," Rachel had said.

But now Mira didn't seem to need any encouragement in order to enjoy teaching.

When Rachel gave the children a bathroom break she smiled and put her hand on Mira's back. "That's what I like to see. You seem to have bounced right back from your injury and your disappointment and everything."

Mira's expression was as innocent as ever. "My parents helped a lot with that. My father hadn't ever gone to a competition before. But after watching you two and realizing I would have been competing at that level if I hadn't hurt myself? He told me he was proud of me."

"Oh. My." Rachel hadn't thought of that before. Mr. Longworth had sounded so uninvolved with Mira's dancing when he made his deal with Rachel. He had been willing to back his daughter's success financially, but he had never actually gone to see her dance. And when does he finally go to a competition? When someone *else* is competing. No wonder Mira had been upset. There was so much that seemed unfair about the way things had worked out.

"I'm sure he's always been proud of you, Mira. You're a hardworking girl, and you're wonderfully talented."

The kids filtered back from their break. "All right, kids, let's get back in place, please." Rachel clapped her hands a couple of times and then heard Cruz talking to Mira.

"So what's going on with you and Miss Stanhope's friend? The old guy?"

Rachel didn't look around at first. The *old* guy? Josh was a mere three years older than Rachel. She didn't want Cruz to carry on his crush on her, but she wasn't quite ready to be considered *old*.

When Mira didn't answer Cruz right away, Rachel couldn't resist turning to see what she would say.

Mira had been watching her, possibly to see if she heard Cruz's question. Now she looked down and shot a swift glance at Cruz. "I'd rather not talk about that, if you don't mind."

Cruz straightened, raised his eyebrows, and nodded. "No, that's fine. That's just fine." And then *he* clapped his hands at the students as he walked briskly away from her.

Rachel sighed and walked toward the phonograph. "Kids, let's take up from where we left off. Jerry, you'll be happy to know we're going to work on those reverse turns you keep asking me about." She had finally heard the poor boy's request.

What she hadn't heard yet was the real story. She knew she hadn't made things easy for Josh in the courting department. And surely Cruz could have been more attentive to the lovely young Mira. But Mira and Josh?

Something just wasn't right.

CHAPTER THIRTY-THREE

Across the street in the diner, the smell of breakfast was just what Josh needed. Bacon and eggs, toast, hash browns, fresh coffee. Like heaven on earth. He had meant to be a more frequent customer once he discovered Fran and the comfy dining spot, but since he hadn't driven Mark and Mary to class for a while, the place had simply slipped his mind.

"Well there's that handsome stranger." Fran put her hand on her hip. "Where have you been keeping yourself, Josh?"

He grinned. "I'm flattered you remember my name, Fran."

"I never forget a rugged jaw or a pair of blue eyes, honey." She flashed him a friendly smile and turned over a cup on the counter. "Coffee?"

"You bet. Thanks." He slid onto the stool and placed an order for a big hearty breakfast.

Fran set a small pitcher of cream next to his cup. "Are the kids at Rachel's class?"

"Yeah. My sis tells me there aren't that many more classes before the session ends. School starts in less than a month."

Fran replaced the coffeepot on its burner and rested her arms on the counter. Her Jean Naté gave a momentary sucker punch to the tasty food smells he preferred. "So what are you going to use for your excuse after that happens?"

He smiled. "My excuse?"

"Have you asked that girl out yet?"

"Which one?"

Fran feigned anger and smacked his arm. "Which one! I know you're not dating her, because she's in here plenty, and I know she would have mentioned it. Didn't you two hit it off? I was sure you were going to."

He shrugged. "We've gotten together a few times. She's a great girl."

"Yes, she is. And she deserves a great guy."

He looked Fran in the eye for a moment. "Uh, yeah. I think that might be the problem." He studied his coffee cup with a frown.

Fran straightened up. "Josh, let me ask you something."

He looked up at her and waited.

"You served in the war, right?"

"Yep."

"A fighter pilot, I think you said?"

"Right."

"Worked hard to get a college education? Got your nose out there to find a job with one of the most important newspapers in the country?"

He had a feeling she didn't need him to keep answering in the affirmative, and it was starting to get a little embarrassing.

"And you drive your sister's kids to class pretty often. Why do you do that, again?"

"I only do that when Pete, my brother-in-law, is out of town."

"But why do you do it?"

Another shrug. "Just to help out. We're family."

"You ever visit your sainted mother?" Fran slipped her hand back onto her hip.

He laughed. "What makes you so sure she's sainted?"

"Order up!" Eggie called out from the pick-up window.

Fran answered him while she retrieved his order. "Let's just say I have a hunch about your mom."

"Well, you happen to be right. And yes, I visit her fairly regularly. She doesn't live too far away."

Fran put a plate, heavy with eggs, bacon, and several versions of starch, on the counter before him. "And you work hard at the newspaper, writing your articles?"

That comment prompted a derisive, bitter laugh. "My articles." He yanked several paper napkins from the dispenser on the counter.

Fran stopped to cross her arms across her chest. "Your article yesterday? The first anniversary of the establishment of Arlington County's Fire Department?"

He looked up at her as he scooped eggs and hash browns into his mouth. He nodded rather than attempting to speak.

Fran cocked her head toward the kitchen. "Practically had Eggie back there in tears."

Josh swallowed. "My writing was that bad, huh?"

She leaned forward and lowered her voice. "The part you put in there about the nobility and sacrifices of the men? Eggie and Artie lost their big brother through his service to the department."

Josh put down his fork. "Oh, man. I didn't know."

Fran tapped her fingernail on the counter. "You touched him." She patted her heart. "Right here."

He stared at her, unsure of how to respond.

"Eat." She pointed at his food.

He went back to work on his breakfast.

After a quick scan of the diner, Fran resumed her questions. "And what are you writing about now?"

He washed down a bite with his coffee, and Fran got the pot to warm up his cup.

"I'm not sure if they'll go for it yet," he said, "but we didn't cover the graduation of the first sixth-grade class to graduate from the Kemper Annex a couple months ago."

"The Negro school?"

"Mm-hmm. I think that was a milestone we should have noted."

Fran nodded. "Rita's girl was in that graduating class. You know Rita? Works in the kitchen on weekends?"

"No, but if they let me write the story, I'd love to talk with her. And her daughter." He took another sip of coffee.

Fran gave him a crooked smile.

He set down his cup and smiled back. "What?"

"Do you remember what we were discussing before I asked you all of those questions?"

He chuckled. "I can't honestly say I do, Fran. You do go off on tangents."

She lifted her chin. "Not at all. It simply sounded like someone needed reminding of what made a man a great guy. I said our Miss Rachel deserved a great guy, and you seemed to think that didn't describe you. The man we just discussed served in the war, loves and helps his family, and is hardworking as all get out. *Plus* he manages to write articles that touch people's hearts."

"Yeah, I'm sure the fashion show coverage touched lots of hearts."

Fran raised an eyebrow and spoke sternly. "I *like* fashion shows. It touched *me*. Okay?"

He laughed and wiped his napkin across his mouth. "Thanks, Fran. You're a real cheerleader. But you don't understand how important that city desk job was to me. Rachel didn't, either. I guess I'm just having a hard time letting go of the job. I mean, I haven't let go of it. I'm trying to work my way back to the city desk again."

"That's the spirit." She spoke more softly to him. Shoot, the last thing he meant to do was elicit pity.

"I'm letting the whole thing bother me too much, I know. But knowing that doesn't seem to make it stop bothering me."

"All right. I understand that. But why should any of that keep you from dating my girl Rachel?"

He shook his head. "It shouldn't. But I kind of flared up at her the last time we got together. Over the job."

"She won't forgive you? That doesn't sound like her."

"Oh, I think she's forgiven me. I just don't want to do it again."

"Well, honey, you can't go through life avoiding people who are important to you just to make sure you never wrangle with them. That's just life, that's all."

He wished Fran would stop making so much sense.

She said, "You know she's headed to that dance competition in Virginia Beach this weekend."

"Yeah, I heard. That's terrific."

"You should go. A gesture like that would carry a lot of weight."

He stood and took out his wallet. "I can't, Franny. I have to work."

And he had that other thing to take care of too. But he wasn't about to tell Fran about that.

CHAPTER THIRTY-FOUR

Days later, Mira surprised Rachel when she suddenly took her by the hands and spoke in a hushed voice. They stood together in a room off the Cavalier ballroom, moments before the Virginia State dance competition began. Rachel was dressed to the nines, hair sprayed within an inch of her life, and fighting a colossal case of frayed nerves. "I have to confess something to you, Rachel."

Oh no. Rachel hesitated in encouraging Mira in her confession. Was this something better left unsaid? She wasn't convinced she wanted to know what Mira planned to tell her. "Um, are you sure? Now?"

Mira nodded. "I know I've been like a sullen child for the past two weeks. I got my hopes up about these competitions, and it's been hard for me to accept what happened because of my stupid sprained ankle."

Well, this wasn't what Rachel expected. She breathed with relief. She didn't want an admission about Mira and Josh right before she and Cruz were about to enter this intense competition. She was tense enough as it was.

"No, that's all right, Mira." Rachel smiled at her. "I would have been just as upset. I *was* upset! I didn't want to do this myself."

Mira's eyes grew wide. "But that's just it! Now that we're here—I mean, the state finals! I'm scared to death about them, and I'm not even dancing. I didn't want to say this in front of Cruz, but I'm *so* glad I'm not representing the studio tonight. I wasn't ready for this, Rachel.

I know it now. God protected me from my own haughty self. I would have failed miserably here."

Rachel laughed. "You would not have. We're going to have to work on your confidence. This is just another contest tonight. Just because it's in a far more beautiful place doesn't mean it has to be more frightening."

Rachel was glad her full skirt and petticoats hid the fact that her thighs were twitching with fear.

Above the noise in the staging room and the ballroom next door, they heard an announcer's voice address the crowd of judges and spectators. Mira gave her a quick kiss on the cheek. "Go get 'em, Rachel."

Connie motioned for Rachel and Mira to join her where she stood. Cruz and Mel were already there, waiting.

The five of them had taken the four-hour drive down to Virginia Beach the day before. The drive had done them all good. Mel, Connie, and Rachel all knew each other well, but during the drive Cruz and Mira talked more about themselves and their lives than they normally did. The romantic in Rachel still thought they'd make a cute pair. But that didn't seem to be in either of their minds. They behaved more like brother and sister toward each other than anything else.

She decided that was probably for the best. She shouldn't really encourage anything that might lead to melodrama at the studio.

The hotel, built during the 1920s, featured dramatic architecture, elegant dining, and sunken gardens. Once they had arrived and freshened up, they had dined at the hotel's Beach Club, down by the water. Many competitors had arrived early, as her own group had, so the Beach Club's outdoor dance floor was filled with some of the finest dancers in the state. Their evening had been festive and wonderful.

But tonight's atmosphere was totally different. The tension crackled in the staging room, and she had come to the point that she just wanted to get the whole thing over with.

Consequently, Mira's "confession," while not about some clandestine romance with a man twelve years her senior, still wasn't the best thing for her to hear right before the competition began.

She tried to seek assurance from Connie, but the announcer's voice was revving up the crowd. The rising noise in the ballroom, coupled with the nervous chatter backstage amid the dancers, distorted what Rachel said. "Connie, my nerves are getting the better of me."

Connie frowned with the effort to hear her. But then she nodded and answered. She thought what Connie replied was, "No, I doubt anyone here is better than you, sweetie. You and Cruz are going to be fabulous out there."

Rachel sighed. This wasn't the place to have this conversation. She remembered what she did at this point two weeks ago, but she didn't have time to hunt down a restroom for a quiet prayer. So she lowered her head right there, closed her eyes, and tried her level best to shut everyone out but God.

By the time she and Cruz walked onto the dance floor, hand in hand, the fluttering in her stomach remained but had quieted down to a tolerable hum. She knew the same thing would happen that occurred back home. She and Cruz would lose the fear the moment their dancing began.

And so it was.

She and Cruz had further refined their choreography. Connie and Mel had added nuanced touches to the way they finished off steps, the way they moved their heads, even the way they looked at each other to add drama to their performance.

When they broke to change for the Latin-dance portion of the competition, Connie looked as if she were fighting back tears. The dressing room was raucous but not as noisy as the staging room had been, so they could actually hear each other now.

Still, Connie clearly tried not to shout as she spoke to Rachel. "I swear, honey, you two are head and shoulders above any other couple out there. Barring some kind of prejudice on the part of the judges, I can't see how anyone else is going to win this thing."

Rachel laughed and fanned herself. "Oh my goodness, Connie, I'm already trying to hold down the perspiring. Don't go getting me too excited, or I'll mess up the Latins! Cruz will kill me."

"Nonsense. The boy is completely in his element. You're not going to get away with any mistakes while he's leading." She forced Rachel's hair flat against one side of her head and pinned it. Rachel looked slightly more Spanish, aside from the strawberry-blond hair.

Rachel looked around the room. "Where's Mira?"

"She stayed where we were standing. Didn't want to get in the way."

"I think she's going to be a real shining star in future competitions, Connie."

Connie patted Rachel's shoulders and nudged her toward the staging room. "I'm sure you're right, honey. But let's focus on you and Cruz for now. We'll give Mira plenty of attention after you and Cruz win the East Coast competition in New York in two weeks."

Rachel spun around and met eyes with Connie. They both laughed. "You *are* confident about tonight, aren't you?"

Connie tilted her head. "That's what I've been trying to tell you! The big win. I see it in your future. Now get over there. Cruz is waiting."

Cruz impressed her with the cool composure he showed. "You ready to win this thing?"

She laughed. "I am, yes. We're doing well."

"We're doing the best. I can feel it." He flashed her an adorable grin.

"Then let's keep our wits about us and have fun. Other than that, it's in God's hands now." She figured she might as well throw that little reminder in there, while they were getting all cocky and sure of themselves.

Cruz gave her a comfortable nod about her comment just before they marched back out to the ballroom.

Throughout the second half of the competition, she felt that confidence persist. She embraced the applause and cheers of encouragement from the crowd, which only helped Cruz and her to perform better. And she felt God's blessing when the dancing was over and the master of ceremonies announced the judges' decisions.

"Ladies and gentlemen, on behalf of the Virginia State Ballroom Dance Federation, the winners of the Summer Ballroom Dance Competition, representing Arlington Ballroom dance studio—"

He finished his announcement, but he was drowned out by the crowd's thunderous reaction. She and Cruz were the most thunderous of them all. In a moment similar to what they experienced back home, but amplified by sheer numbers, the crowd surrounded them in congratulations.

Moments after the din died down to a less frenetic level, she and Mira met eyes. Not only did the girl look thrilled with the outcome, she looked completely content. And not terribly focused on Cruz.

Despite everything going on around her, Josh's image sprang to mind. It was all she could do to dub her suspicions as foolish and shove them out of the way.

CHAPTER THIRTY-FIVE

Later that week Josh worked at his desk at the *Tribune*. The noisy office bustled with reporters scrambling to get their stories completed in time for that evening's deadline. Josh glanced up from his article when he sensed someone in front of him. Sheila, his old secretary from the city desk, had stopped by.

"Sheila! What are you doing slumming down here, young lady?" He leaned back in his chair and stretched.

"How you doing, Josh?" She had her arms full of folders. "I just had to get some research material for a couple of the guys up there."

He tried not to clench his jaw. He used to be one of the "guys up there."

Sheila smiled. "I've been reading all your articles. You're just as excellent a writer for this section as you were for Sal's."

He exhaled audibly. "I wish I could say that was enough. But I'm having a hard time accepting this as a permanent thing."

"Well, I think that's a good attitude, frankly." She leaned in slightly and lowered her voice. "They need you up there, and Sal knows it."

Josh sat up. "You think so?"

"I know so. Sal's never worked so hard. You were always the most thorough young writer he had. He's keeping the red ink industry flush with all the cutting and slashing he's been doing. The other day I heard him yell at one of the guys—I won't say who—that he might as well write the articles himself at this rate."

Now Josh had no trouble keeping his jaw unclenched. His broad smile took care of that. "Sheila, that's the kind of information that keeps my blood pumping."

"Yeah, well, I think you should just keep doing what you're doing. Write the best articles you can and keep your ears open. I'll let you know if I hear anything more."

"You're a great gal. Thanks."

Lou's door opened, and Sheila turned away with a wink.

"Reegan, how's the Kemper Annex article coming?" Lou had a section of newspaper in his hand.

Josh held up his work. "Doing some final editing now. I'll have it to you within the hour."

Lou nodded. "Good." He opened the newspaper to an inside story and set it on the desk. He realized it was one of the small community papers.

"This would have been a good one for us to cover," Lou said.

Josh lifted his eyebrows when he saw a photo of Rachel and Cruz, all decked out in their ballroom attire. Man, she was pretty. The article covered their win in Virginia Beach, with the headline, "Local Dance Studio wins State Competition."

He looked up at Lou with a smile. "I actually know these people."

"That's good, 'cause you're going to cover their participation in the big one in New York."

"The big one?"

"Yeah." Lou flicked his hand in the air as if swatting away the actual title of the competition. "Whatever it's called. It's the big win on the East Coast or something like that. Competition at the Waldorf Astoria. I want you there to cover it. Midge has already reserved a flight and a room for you. Next week."

"But—" He actually liked the idea of crossing paths with Rachel more than he had done. He liked having a good excuse to do so without interfering with her work for the studio. But Doris the hairdresser was talking with a lot of her friends who knew his source Candy. She was going to report back to him this weekend after some party she planned to attend.

"No buts." Lou walked away. "Just keep up the good work, Reegan. And don't think I'll accept any less from you."

Josh stared at Lou's shut door and wondered whether he had just been complimented or been given a talking to.

He tried to go back to polishing his work, but an idea struck him in the middle of it. He walked around to Midge's desk.

"Hey, Midge, what size room did you book for me in New York for next week?"

She pushed her glasses up on her nose. "A double. Lou hasn't decided yet whether he's going to send Freddie up with you that Friday or just have him fly up Saturday to take photos."

Josh nodded. "I think Saturday's going to be plenty of time for Freddie. I'll get more work done on this project if I don't have him hanging around with me overnight. It would save the paper some money on meals too. But I guess you should keep the double reserved just in case."

Midge was perfectly happy to take his suggestion at face value.

He went back to his desk and called Rachel at the studio. He heard surprise in her voice when he first spoke.

"Oh! Josh. Is something wrong?"

He chuckled. "Have I been that bad, that you think I'd only call you if something were wrong?"

"Uh, frankly, yes."

He grimaced. "I'm sorry. I've been… Well, I've been preoccupied, Rachel. I'm kind of trying to work both ends at once here. Between researching and writing my stories for the Style section and trying to fix what I messed up on my old job, I've let a lot of other things falter, I guess."

"I suppose."

She didn't say it angrily, but there was no denying she was disappointed in him. He sighed.

"Anyway. I have a little proposition for you."

"The man completely ignores me for weeks and then calls to proposition me. Did you learn this stuff at charm school?"

This time he heard the smile in her voice. He loved how easily she fell into that spunky, forgiving banter with him.

"The charisma just comes to me naturally, if you can believe it."

"If you say so."

"So, here's my idea. First of all, congratulations on your win in Virginia Beach. I'm really proud of you."

He wasn't sure why she hesitated, but her tone was more serious when she answered. "Well, thanks, Josh. That—that actually means a lot to me."

He grinned. Finally he was saying the right things to her. "Despite my editor's better judgment, I've been assigned to cover your competition in New York next week."

He heard a soft laugh. "And what's bad about that judgment? The journalist? Or the subject matter?"

He laughed. "The journalist. And here I thought I was on a roll, phrasing everything in keeping with my charm-school training. I meant that in the most delightfully self-deprecating manner possible."

"All right, so taken. I think you'll do a fine job. I really have enjoyed your articles. I know you don't like hearing that while you're writing for the Style pages—"

"No, no. I appreciate your opinion. At least I have a job." Sheila's encouragement had gone far in boosting his positive attitude about the Style section. "When are you and Cruz heading up to New York? Are you just flying up on the day of the event?"

"Oh. No, we'll go at least the day before. Friday. I want us both to be refreshed when we compete, not feeling tired and grimy from travel. Why?"

"The paper's sending me up the day before too. I thought maybe I could take you and Cruz to dinner and interview you some for my article."

"I like that idea. Sure."

"And if it would help you out financially, the paper has already reserved a double room for me, but chances are fairly good one of the beds will be free, especially if I convince them to wait until Saturday for my photographer to come up. I could put Cruz up for the night and save you the cost of his room."

She didn't immediately respond. "Yes. Thanks. If they haven't booked you too far away from the Waldorf. I mean, I won't be staying in the Waldorf. Too pricey. But I'm probably going to stay in a smaller hotel nearby. You know the competition is being held there, at the Waldorf, right?"

"Right. I knew that. Great. I'll look into the hotel Midge booked and get back to you."

After they hung up he sat at his desk, staring into space. Something hung there between them, but he wasn't sure what it was. Certainly he had let too much time pass between chats or visits with Rachel, but he had every hope of rectifying that situation soon. Maybe that was all he sensed, the uncertainty caused by a man who fails to pursue a woman the way he should. Maybe it was something completely unrelated to him. He was terrible at reading women's moods.

Still, he couldn't shake the feeling that, right there at the end of their phone call, there was something Rachel wanted to ask him about but chose to keep to herself.

CHAPTER THIRTY-SIX

"Rachel, what I'm trying to say is I think I'm in love with you."

Cruz happened to be a foot away from Rachel when he made his announcement. He had interrupted their tango practice and announced his need to discuss something with her. He had stammered and fumbled with his words, and she began to piece them together. She kept expecting him to mention Mira at some point.

But once he released his melodramatic proclamation into the studio, empty of everyone but the two of them, he lunged for her as if he had rehearsed this moment repeatedly in his mind.

"Cruz!" Rachel gasped and pushed him away. "What in the *world*?" She stepped back from him and straightened her blouse and skirt. "You are *not* in love with me."

"I am. I can't help it. How can I be expected to dance with a woman, create such beauty on the dance floor over and over, and not feel something for her?"

She frowned. "Well, then I can't have you teaching my students, can I? You can't go making passes at women just because you're dancing repeatedly with them, Cruz! That's your job here. That's what dance teachers do!"

"No, this isn't about other women. Only you."

Rachel rested her hands on her hips and sighed. "Look. You're young—"

"Not that young. I'm twenty-one, remember, and I've dated plenty of girls."

"Okay, fine. But I'm twelve years older than you...." At once she thought of Josh and Mira chatting last week. Twelve years. That was *their* age difference. There just had to be an explanation for that. As ridiculous as this issue with Cruz was, Josh had to feel the same with regard to Mira.

Cruz misread her hesitation. He smiled and pointed his finger at her. "There, you see. Even you don't think twelve years is so bad." He pressed his hand to his chest and lifted his eyebrows as if he were acting on stage. "Not so wide a chasm that our love can't bridge it."

"Oh, for goodness' sake, Cruz, snap out of it!" Like she needed this complication right before they were due to compete in New York. "Look. You're obviously experiencing a little crush. That kind of thing can happen when people work closely together for a while—"

"Is it happening to you too?" Hope sprang to his eyes.

"No! You're like a little brother to me, Cruz. That's all. Frankly, I half-expected you to develop an interest in Mira."

Despite his claims of love for her, she saw a moment's twinge in his expression. But he swiftly shook his head as if dispelling whatever thought went through his mind. "There's nothing between me and Mira. Anyway, she's involved with that old guy."

Rachel gasped again. "You don't know that! Do you?"

He shrugged. "I don't want to talk about Mira."

The phone rang, and she was glad for a reason to walk away from Cruz. She called over her shoulder to him, "We're going back to practicing as soon as I'm done here. We leave in one week, Cruz. Get your thoughts straight, please."

She practically scowled into the phone. "Hello."

"Uh, who's this?" The man's question brought her back to her senses.

"Oh, I'm sorry. Arlington Ballroom. May I help you?"

"Is this Miss Stanhope?"

"It is."

"It's Harper Longworth, Miss Stanhope, from the bank."

"Mr. Longworth, yes! Please, call me Rachel." Oh no, here it came. She had been dreading this call ever since the local competition, when they learned Mira wouldn't be allowed to compete.

"I think we need to discuss our agreement, don't we?" He sounded pleasant enough. And why wouldn't he? He was about to save himself quite a bit of money.

"Mr. Longworth, I'm so sorry about the way things worked out. I had every intention of letting Mira represent the studio in those competitions—"

"I'm well aware of the circumstances, Miss—Rachel. Mira has kept us informed. I understand none of this was your fault."

"And I honestly would have had her compete anyway, regardless of your offer. She's a beautiful dancer, and I fully intend to let her—"

"I'm sure, I'm sure. Please don't fret. I know you have honorable plans for Mira. She's very happy there, working for you. We've talked at great length about it. She told me she wasn't ready to compete at that level anyway."

Well, this sounded like an improvement over their previous father-daughter relationship.

He continued. "Now, this change in our financial agreement isn't the end of the world for you, dear. Despite the circumstances, you're still covered through January's mortgage."

Her heart sank. Yes, he was right. It wasn't the end of the world. But that didn't make it any easier to say good-bye to the possibility of his covering her mortgage all the way through October of next year.

She couldn't hide her sigh. "Yes, I understand. You're right. I'm still very appreciative of your gracious offer. Your help has made it possible for us to enter these competitions and improve the studio's business."

"But you had plans for those additional months' payments, I take it."

She cocked her head. "Yes. I certainly didn't take them for granted, but I'm a planner."

"Which is one reason I'm impressed with you and how you run your business. And, frankly, I'd like to see Mira's place of employment do well. She enjoys teaching, and I'd like to know your studio will thrive beyond January."

Rachel laughed. "I'll do my best. I wouldn't want to insinuate that I can't keep my head above water without your help. I think I can manage the business better than that."

"I don't doubt it. So I'd like to make you a different offer for when your February mortgage payment comes due."

Rachel glanced back at Cruz, who stood at the window and gazed out, apparently deep in thought.

"I'm listening, sir."

"I'd like you to be able to carry on with your plans for the studio, but a deal is a deal. I'm sure you understand."

"As I've said."

"So I'd be more than willing to make an interest-free loan to you for the same amount I would have covered. You'll have to pay me back, but you can pay me in installments beginning at the end of the loan period."

She wasn't sure of the benefit in that, other than postponing money she still had to pay. But Longworth wasn't finished.

"When will the next series of competitions take place?"

She stood up straight. She dashed around to the other side of the desk, pulled out her calendar, and began flipping. "It's…let me see, the local competition will be in late October."

"They have them every quarter, is that it?"

"Well, no. They don't usually have a winter competition."

"I see. And do you feel fairly confident that you'd ask my girl to compete for you if you entered the October competition?"

"We're definitely going to enter, yes, and I'd love for Mira to dance for me."

"Fine. Then let's consider this. You go ahead and keep to your business plan as is for the studio. Even if nothing else, you'll have a good amount of time before you have to pay on your mortgage. And I'll make the same offer to you about the October competition that I did for the July competition. If Mira competes, three months mortgage free. If she wins, another six months free."

"You mean you'd forgive the loan for those amounts?"

"That's precisely what I mean."

"Well, I'd be a fool to say no to that."

"And I don't do business with fools. Excellent. I'll have Miss Prinkle draw up the—"

"But, Mr. Longworth, could I ask you… What does Mira think about all of this? Have you told her about our financial agreements?"

"I told her I'm involved in your business as an investment. She's used to my investing my own money in small businesses. I've made a great deal of my fortune that way."

"I can imagine. But in this case, you're really not making a dime. How is this an investment for you?"

He chuckled. "Miss Stanhope, I'm not a terribly demonstrative man. But I do know what's truly precious in life. My daughter is precious. My daughter is who I'm investing in."

Rachel's smile remained when she hung up the phone. Odd man. But he obviously meant well and was trying to show love to Mira in his own way. She wondered if Mira was satisfied with her father's somewhat distant way of demonstrating his affection. In such situations young girls often—

Rachel's mouth dropped open. Oh, goodness. In such situations young girls often fell for older men.

CHAPTER THIRTY-SEVEN

"Aaron, get your hands out of Amanda's food." Suzanna barely glanced in her little son's direction before catching him in the act. "You have a plate full of breakfast there. Eat your own pancakes."

The two women shared a booth with the twins in the diner across from Rachel's studio.

Rachel, already dressed for a full day of teaching, deliberately allowed some distance between herself and the twins. Especially Aaron, who seemed more prone to spills and splatters. "So, what did the doctor say about the twins?"

Suzanna watched the toddlers before answering. "Huh? Oh, it wasn't a doctor's appointment. Just a quick trip to the clinic. They were due for boosters. I got them there early before it got too crowded." She lowered her voice. "Only a few tears. Not bad."

"Well, I'm sorry for the occasion, but I'm glad you were nearby. I'm going to miss dinner at Mom and Dad's tomorrow. I have too much to do to prepare for next week's trip to New York."

"When are you going up?"

"Probably Friday. I thought about going up a day early, just to enjoy the city a little. But I don't want to take advantage of Connie and Mel."

"What do you mean?" Suzanna pulled a couple of paper napkins from the dispenser and wiped egg from Amanda's cheeks. She removed Amanda's little eyeglasses and cleaned them as well. "Here you go, sweetie." She pushed the glasses back up Amanda's nose and gave it a little tweak. Amanda's grin, coupled with those glasses, made Rachel smile. They really were adorable kids. When they behaved well. And didn't cry. Or smear things everywhere.

She realized Suzanna awaited a comment from her. "What?"

"How would you be taking advantage of Connie and Mel if you went to New York on Thursday?"

"Oh. Because they're taking time off this week to run the studio for me. They have pretty flexible schedules at their day jobs these days, but…you know. I hate to ask for too many favors."

Suzanna nodded. "I guess. But I get the impression they enjoy being there. Maybe they wouldn't mind. Are you and Cruz flying up together?"

Rachel closed her eyes and let her shoulders droop. "That's another thing."

"What?" Suzanna frowned. "Aren't the dances working out well?"

Rachel sighed. "The dancing is perfect. He's a terrific little dancer. But…" She glanced over her shoulder to make sure no one could hear her.

Suzanna leaned in, a small anticipatory smile on her face. "But?"

"He thinks he's in love with me."

Suzanna's mouth silently formed a big *O*. She sat back and hooted. "Hoo boy!"

"Shh!" Rachel's eyes widened. She was glad Fran wasn't working today, or she'd have made her way over to the table in seconds, eager to hear what she was missing.

Suzanna shrugged. "He *is* awfully cute."

Rachel's scowl was meant to discourage. "He's a twenty-one-year-old *kid* is what he is. And here I'm supposed to travel to New York with him and stay at a hotel? It's just… It doesn't look good. I mean, Josh is probably going to let him stay in his room—"

Suzanna put her hand up. "Hold on there, Daisy Mae. Back up the turnip truck. *Josh* is going? Josh as in handsome newspaper reporter Josh? Kiss-at-the-door Josh?"

"Shh!"

"And you're worried about the impropriety of little Cruz going with you?" She chuckled. "Sweet little Rachel and *two* good-looking men on a trip to New York—"

"Oh, stop. The *Tribune* is sending Josh to cover the competition. There's nothing wrong with..." She frowned. "Oh gosh, that does look even worse, doesn't it?"

Suzanna sat back and wiggled her eyebrows. "Not if I go with you."

"You?"

"Yeah. Old married lady on the scene. I'll be your duenna."

"My what?"

"Chaperone, sweetie. Aaron, one more time with the straw and I'm taking it away, I promise you."

Rachel looked at the twins. "What would you do about Bonnie and Clyde here?"

Suzanna shrugged. "Todd owes me a break. He promised ages ago to take the twins for me so I could do something for myself for a few days. And if he can't do it, your mom would probably love to stay with them."

"That's true. She's always hinting about wanting more time with them."

Suzanna bounced where she sat. "Oh, my goodness. Let's do it. I absolutely want to do this. I haven't been to New York since I was in college."

Rachel grinned. "Okay! I like the idea. And you can come to the competition and talk me down when I start going insane."

"I'm your gal!"

By the time they wiped the kids down and paid their bill, she had only a few minutes before she needed to open the studio for the day. They walked out of the diner together and into the already-warm morning air.

On the sidewalk, busy digging in her purse for her keys, she bumped right into Suzanna and laughed at her clumsiness.

Suzanna had stopped in her tracks. Despite the distraction of watching after both of her children, she had apparently looked across the street at the studio before Rachel did. When she met eyes with Rachel, her expression cautious, Rachel frowned. "What?"

Suzanna looked back at the studio, and her eyes followed.

Mira had just been dropped off at work. She turned to wave goodbye, and Josh's Bel Air pulled slowly away.

CHAPTER THIRTY-EIGHT

Several days later Josh waited up front at Doris's beauty salon. The whine of an entire bank of pink hairdryers against one wall nearly drowned out Johnnie Ray's "Cry," playing mournfully on the radio at the front desk. The sandwich sign on the sidewalk out front announced a Wednesday Special, half-price on permanent waves. He could smell enough strong chemicals to take down a rogue elephant. How these women tolerated having that stuff on their heads was beyond him.

Doris hadn't seen him yet because she was so engrossed in her conversation with her client. While she teased and combed, teased and combed, she kept shaking her head as if disgusted with whatever her client told her. Whenever Doris added anything to the conversation, she stopped and pointed the rattail comb toward her client's reflection in the mirror, as if she couldn't express herself and tease hair simultaneously.

Once she finished poofing the woman's hair, combing a little flip at the bottom, and spraying it so still it resembled a helmet, she turned and saw him watching her.

She lifted her eyebrows, smiled, and gave him a little wave. Then she lifted her manicured nail in the air. "Be right with you, Josh."

She held up a hand mirror so her client could check the entire circumference of the helmet, and then the two of them approached the front. Doris turned her client over to the receptionist and hooked her arm in Josh's.

"Going outside for a minute, Linda."

As she had before, Doris pulled out her cigarettes the moment they walked out.

Josh took her lighter and lit it for her. "Promise me you won't ever light up inside the salon, Doris?"

"Why ever not?" She picked a piece of tobacco from the tip of her tongue and sat on the display window ledge.

He looked back toward the salon. "Something tells me the majority of your *customers* are highly flammable, let alone the chemicals in there."

She chuckled. "You know, I *did* set my thumbnail on fire once, lighting my cigarette."

"Yet another reason you should give up smoking."

"Yeah, yeah. You sound like my mother—who smokes like a house on fire, by the way."

He took a seat next to her. "So did you go to that party this past weekend? With Candy's other friends?"

She blew out smoke and nodded. "But you're not going to like what I found out."

"Anything is better than nothing at this point."

"That's exactly what I mean, handsome. I found out nothing."

He huffed in exasperation. "Shoot."

"I'm sorry, Josh. I talked with everyone I could think of who knows her. There were even a few people there who had ideas of where she might be. You know, with friends who weren't at the party Saturday night? But I checked with every one of them over the last couple of days. Nothing. She's just dropped off the face of the earth. I'm telling you, wherever she is, she's got to be getting antsy by now. She hasn't been talking with anyone she knows other than those first calls. No more calls to her folks or Mitzy. No calls to me or anyone I can think of. Teddy must have her so holed up she doesn't even have a telephone."

He ran his hand through his hair. "Okay. Again, I appreciate your help."

"Yeah, I appreciate yours too. I'm not giving up. If you think of someone else you want me to call, you just let me know."

"Ditto. I think at this rate, it won't matter by the time we find her. I mean, it's important for her sake that she break free of Wiley. But as far as legally nailing Wiley is concerned, I'm really losing time. And hope. He's going to have his tracks covered soon, if he doesn't already, and that will be that."

Doris stood and dusted off the back of her skirt.

Josh pulled his wallet from his jacket. "You still have my number at the paper?"

She nodded, and he replaced his wallet in his pocket.

"Okay. Listen, I'm going to New York for a few days, to cover a story for the paper. If you find out anything—anything remotely connected to Candy's whereabouts—do me a favor and call the paper. They'll know where to reach me, and I'll give you a call back as soon as I can."

"Got it." She dropped her cigarette to the ground and stepped it out. "What do you think about my giving the snake another call?"

"Wiley? And saying what?"

She shrugged. "I don't know. Maybe tell him I'm getting worried and does he have any ideas where I might call. Maybe even mention I'm thinking of reporting her as a missing person."

Josh raised his eyebrows. "Now that might be a good idea. Might scare him into action somehow. Anything but the status quo would be an improvement."

"All right." Doris walked to the door. "Let me think on that and I'll try him again. I'll let you know what happens. You have a safe trip."

He laughed to himself. Yeah, safe trip. Safe everything. His job was no more dangerous than napping in a porch swing. He risked more bodily harm getting in and out of the tub than he did working the Style pages.

At least the trip to New York involved spending time with people he enjoyed. One person in particular. The last time they talked, Rachel had seemed a little put out by his lack of attention, but he hoped she would understand. Once he put this Wiley situation to rest he'd be able to be more attentive. A better friend. He hoped her annoyance would be temporary.

He thought about Fran's list of what constituted a "great guy." He wondered if Rachel had such a list in mind. Would he meet any of her qualifications?

If nothing else, she must know he was trustworthy. He couldn't think of anything about his behavior that would suggest otherwise.

CHAPTER THIRTY-NINE

Rachel dropped her mouth open when Suzanna showed up at the line for the ticket counter at National Airport Friday morning.

"Don't worry. They'll be perfect little angels. I promise." Suzanna held two good-sized suitcases in her hands. Aaron held fast to the one on her right, and Amanda did the same with the one on her left.

"Suzanna! What are you thinking?" Rachel looked past them to see if Todd was there, planning to say good-bye to his wife and go back home with the twins. But no, the three of them were on their own.

"Todd got called out of town again—he's actually down at the other end of the airport, at PanAm. And your mother promised your grandmother a weekend at Rehoboth. Isn't your grandma a little old for the beach?"

Rachel pressed her fingertips against her forehead before addressing Suzanna again. "You didn't *have* to come with me. You could have cancelled."

Suzanna's eyes looked slightly wild for a moment. "Oh, no. Uh-uh. Nothing doing. I deserve this trip. Who knows when I'll get this chance again?"

"But what about the kids' tickets? Isn't it too late—"

"Nope. Piece of cake. We're all set."

Rachel drew a steadying breath. She couldn't think of any more arguments. Now she was especially glad she had decided against going up a day early. All she had to do was survive today and tomorrow morning before they began to prepare for the competition.

After eyeballing the twins for stickiness, she gave each of them a brief hug and looked up at Suzanna. "You're going to have to be responsible for the kids, okay?"

Suzanna shrugged. "So what's new? Come on, we'll have fun. I'll take them all over the place while you do your practicing or whatever it is you have to do before the competition, and then we'll cheer you on."

She couldn't imagine the toddlers tolerating the competition. But she couldn't worry about that now.

"So where's Cruz?" Suzanna glanced around them. "And Josh?"

"They're both flying up at different times—"

Before she could say another word, Suzanna squealed, drawing stares from other passengers. She spoke over Rachel's shoulder. "What are you *doing,* maniac?"

Rachel frowned and turned to see Karen running in their direction. No, she was most definitely not coming to wish them a happy trip. She, too, carried a suitcase. And she laughed as if she were getting away with something.

"If you two think you're taking a trip to New York without me, *you're* the maniacs!" She stopped and plopped her suitcase at her feet. She heaved a winded sigh. "Suzanna, when I told Chuck you were going with Rachel—okay, maybe I whined a little—he told me to get myself on the flight and the weekend was mine. Ha!"

She frowned. "What are the munchkins doing here?"

Suzanna smacked herself in the forehead. "Why didn't I think of you? You could have taken the twins so I could go with Rachel."

"Right." Karen rested a hand on her hip. "Or *you* could have just stayed home with the twins so I could go with her." She waved both hands in the air. "Doesn't matter. We'll have a blast." She squatted down and put a big smack of a kiss on each of the twins' cheeks. Then she hugged Rachel, who decided to keep her mouth shut until she felt more constructive. "Won't we have a blast?"

* * * * *

By the time they arrived in New York and got adjoining rooms at the Stratford House, Rachel had to admit the twins were far better travelers than some adults she knew. They hardly fussed at all and they napped during most of the flight.

Suzanna leaned against the front desk as the bellboy loaded their luggage onto a cart. "I guess Karen should take my spot in your room, huh, Rachel? I'll take the second room with the kids. That way you'll be sure to get a good night's sleep."

"Thanks. I really appreciate that." This was turning out all right after all. The rooms, although pricey, were nowhere near as exorbitant as rooms at the Waldorf. Yet they were clean, the carpets were plush, and the fresh linens and room cleansers erased almost all traces of cigarette odor.

They left the adjoining door open as they unpacked, and Rachel soon appreciated the rambunctious company. She originally thought of this trip as purely business, but now it felt more like a short family vacation. The change in atmosphere made her realize how her chronic worrying about the studio kept her from focusing on relaxing once in a while.

Which reminded her. "I'd better check to see if Cruz or Josh have arrived yet."

"Why?" Karen hung up a pair of slacks in the closet. "You think they're going to want to walk the city with us?"

"Walk the city?"

"Yeah, you know, just soak it in. We don't really have time to do serious sightseeing. I figured you all didn't make big plans."

"No, actually, besides the competition, the only plans I made..." She bit on a fingernail. "Oh. Hmm."

Suzanna stood at the door. "What's wrong?"

A knock at the door made them all turn. Everyone watched as she opened it, and there stood Josh and Cruz.

Both men greeted Rachel at once. Cruz spoke so quickly he sounded as if he had already entered some kind of competition. But this competition wasn't about dance. It was all about Rachel.

"Want to see the sights?"

Josh just gave Rachel a crooked, knowing grin and shot a swift glance in Cruz's direction. "Did you get checked in all right?"

Amanda and Aaron swiftly gathered at Rachel's side, and she let the door swing open.

A frown marred Cruz's face, but Josh broke into a wide grin and squatted down to the twins' level.

"Well, hey you two! I'm Josh. Who are you?"

Amanda clammed up, but her brother spoke out confidently. "I'm Aaron." He pointed at his sister. "'Manda."

"Aaron and Amanda, huh? Are you twins, maybe?"

They both nodded.

Josh pointed at Amanda. "And you're Amanda, right? Or are you Aaron?"

"No, *I'm* Aaron!"

Amanda giggled, and Josh looked at Aaron. "You're Aaron? You sure you're not Josh?"

Both of the twins laughed and answered loudly and simultaneously,

"*You're* Josh!"

Rachel didn't realize she was smiling until Josh looked up at her. He returned the smile, stood, and looked past her. He raised his hand in a wave. "Afternoon, ladies."

Suzanna and Karen had the good grace to smile pleasantly at both Cruz and Josh, but to Rachel it was as obvious as the sun in the sky who drew their attention most strongly.

"Come on in, guys," Rachel said to the men. "I might as well fill you in on who's who and how our plans have changed."

*****

But Josh's plans apparently hadn't changed. He still insisted on treating everyone to dinner. In fact, Rachel found herself bowled over by how easily he took charge and made sure everyone had a good time.

Before the dinner hour they took the kids to ride the Central Park carousel and to take a horse-drawn carriage ride around the park. They visited the Fifth Avenue FAO Schwarz toy store, and even Cruz loosened up around Josh and enjoyed the afternoon. They had dinner at a big Chinese restaurant.

Josh addressed Karen and Suzanna before they entered the dining room. He rested his hands on Rachel, and Cruz's shoulders as he spoke. "Now, I hope you gals don't mind if I sit near Rachel and Cruz and monopolize a little of their time? I'm actually supposed to be writing a story about them and tomorrow's competition, so I'd like to do an informal interview, if we can hear each other in there."

"Not at all, Josh." Karen actually fluttered her eyelashes. Rachel closed her eyes and shook her head.

Suzanna leaned down to the twins. "Okay, Amanda? Aaron? Did

you hear Uncle Josh? He needs us to let him ask Aunt Rachel and Cruz a few questions. No climbing on him in there or making too much noise. Be good and I'll get you an extra fortune cookie after dinner."

Rachel stared at Suzanna. She walked near her as they entered the restaurant. "Uncle Josh?"

Suzanna shrugged. "Just a figure of speech." But she glanced back at Josh before giving Rachel a quick wink.

The heavenly scents had reached them well before they even entered the noisy restaurant, and their "city walk" had built up savage appetites in all of them. They ordered what seemed like far too many dishes—egg rolls, wonton soup, Peking duck, moo goo gai pan, orange chicken, garlic pork, egg foo yung, and sweet and sour shrimp—and finished them all.

Despite the fact that Cruz seemed driven to not like Josh all that much, he kept relaxing around him. He hadn't frowned at Josh once by the time they finished their fortune cookies, and he graciously thanked him for picking up the tab.

Rachel watched Josh as he excused himself from the table to use the facilities. She had to admit, he could handle himself all right when he was in his element, and this was clearly his element. He just seemed so… manly. So grown up, for lack of a better description. She still couldn't imagine he had anything romantic going on with Mira. *That* would pretty much cancel out the whole "grown up" idea.

Cruz must have been thinking somewhere along the same lines as her. He leaned across the table so he didn't have to yell above the noise in the restaurant.

"Do you think Mira's upset she didn't get to come up with us?"

Rachel sat up. "Oh. Uh, no. I think she was fine with it. She's looking forward to the fall competition. We're all looking forward to the two of you competing together then."

"Uh-huh." Cruz didn't act as excited about that prospect as she had hoped he would.

By the time they all left the restaurant and made their way back to the hotel, she had talked herself out of swooning over Josh and his wonderfulness here in New York. The man was charming toward her, that was for sure. But he seemed pretty charming with Suzanna and Karen too. And who knew what was going on with Mira?

She had been dealt a bad enough blow by Billy's rejection to last a lifetime. She wasn't about to make the mistake of falling for someone who couldn't be bothered to pursue her more energetically than Josh had back home.

But when they all got out of the cab and he hugged the sleeping Aaron against one broad shoulder and the sleeping Amanda against the other, Rachel felt her heart melt a little. All she could think was, *That is absolutely adorable.*

And the twins were cute too.

CHAPTER FORTY

Josh shot up in bed, disoriented by his surroundings. He sat still for a moment before he realized someone was knocking on the door. That must have been what woke him up. Yes. He was in New York. Two muted horn honks from the traffic below sounded like confirmation.

He heard the shower running in the bathroom. Cruz.

He grabbed his trousers from a chair and slipped into them. He had barely pulled his undershirt over his head when he opened the door and squinted momentarily against the well-lit hallway.

Rachel's gaze, focused on his undershirt, traveled up to his hair. He saw a twinkle of amusement in her eyes, and he reached up to use his hands as combs.

"I woke you." She was bright, perky, and had clearly been up and ready to go for some time.

He nodded and turned on the light. Cruz had closed the curtains before hopping into his bed last night, so the room didn't have a hint of morning to it. "Yeah. What time is it?"

"Ten thirty. How do you sleep so late?"

"Very soundly, apparently." He looked back toward the bathroom. "Sounds like Cruz is in the shower."

"Okay. I don't want to surprise him if he walks out, so I'll go. We're going to go do some girly things until it's time to head to the Waldorf for warm-ups and stuff. Do you mind hanging out with Cruz and getting him to the Waldorf later? Maybe you two could do some guy stuff."

Josh smiled. “Guy stuff. Yeah. We’ll think of something. Duck hunting or javelin throwing. Something like that.”

“I knew you’d come through.” She smiled. “Have fun. Just don’t let him hurt himself.”

“We’re not *really* going to—”

“Yeah, I know. Just, you know, don’t let him sprain his ankle or anything like that.”

“I’ll carry the boy across the street at every corner.”

She lifted her hand, palm up, as if presenting him as a fine example. “As I said, I knew you’d come through.” She turned to leave.

“What time do I get him to the Waldorf, Rachel?”

“Oh. The competition starts at seven. So he should be there by five. And make sure he brings his tux and shoes and everything like that.”

Josh nodded.

Cruz walked out of the bathroom after Josh closed the door. He wore an undershirt and boxers and had combed his dark hair straight back. He lifted his chin toward Josh. “Morning. You snore.”

Josh nodded. “Duly noted. You want to do anything in particular today before you need to be at the competition?”

“We probably better check with Rachel—”

“She just left. They’re doing girly things today.”

“Girly things? Like what?”

“Whatever it is, we’re not invited, and that’s fine by me. Any sights you want to see? You said last night this was your first time here. We could hit some of the standard tourist attractions.”

“All I can think of hitting right now is someplace to get breakfast.”

Josh took a quick shower, and they headed to the diner across the street from the Stratford House. Over pancakes, eggs, and bacon, they made a list—the Empire State Building, the Statue of Liberty, Ellis

Island, Greenwich Village—and planned to visit whatever they could before their time ran out.

Josh paid the bill and tucked the list in his pocket. "Let's stop back at the hotel to make sure we have everything you need for the Waldorf."

"You sure we really need to lug that stuff all over the city?" Cruz grimaced like a put-upon teenager. "What if I forget something somewhere?"

"Between the two of us we should be able to handle that little bit of responsibility, don't you think? Otherwise we risk being on the wrong side of the city when we need to get you to the Waldorf. We'll have more control over that possibility, as far as I'm concerned."

They stopped at the front desk to check for messages.

"Yes, sir. You have one here." The clerk handed a slip of paper to him.

Date/Time: *Saturday, August 25, 11:30 a.m.*
To: *Josh Reegan*
From: *Washington Tribune*
Message: *Please call Doris Spinelli ASAP. Says you have number.*

Josh nearly gasped.

"What's up?" Cruz leaned against the front desk. "Rachel?"

"No. Come on. I've got to get up to the room and return this call."

*****

He couldn't dial fast enough. He got the beauty salon's receptionist and nervously tapped his pencil against the nightstand while he waited for Doris to come to the phone.

"Josh. I'm so glad I caught you."

"What've you got for me, Doris?"

"She's there."

"Candy? Where?"

"That's what I'm telling you. She's *in New York*!"

Josh stood from his bed and nearly shouted. "Where?"

"That's what I'm not sure of. See, I called Wiley like I said I would. Told him I was getting worried because I couldn't find a single friend of Candy's who knew where she was or had heard from her for a month. He tried to shrug it off again, you know? But this time I said I thought I should call the police and report her missing. Get them in on the act."

"Right." He hated to be ungrateful, but he already knew she planned this. He didn't need a blow-by-blow description. He wanted to get out there and find Candy.

"He got all excited then, even though he tried not to let me hear it. He says, 'No, I'm sure that's not necessary. Why don't you just let me make some phone calls and see what I can find out?' I told him I didn't want to wait long, that I was going to call the next day if he wasn't able to help me by then."

"Good. And?"

"So he doesn't call me back. But Candy *does*. This morning. At first she tries to act like she's just taking a little break on her own, that it was all her decision. But we go way back, Josh. I pulled the plug on that little pony show right away. So she admits Wiley wants her to lay low for a while until this whole thing—the thing you started—"

"Right."

"Until that blows over. When I pressed her for where she was, she admitted she was in New York. In Manhattan. But the best I could get was Broadway. Some hotel on Broadway and... Hang on, let me see what I wrote here. I think this is thirty-two, Josh. I wrote it fast, but it's either a thirty-two or a thirty-seven. The little line on the bottom might be a, you know, where I didn't lift my pen off the paper soon enough. I was too busy trying to sound nonchalant to pay attention to what I was writing."

He nearly groaned. This was good news, but his time was limited. "You didn't ask the name of the hotel?" He jotted what little information she gave him on the small pad of hotel stationery on the nightstand.

"Yeah, but she was nervous about talking. Said she already told me too much, that Teddy warned her to just say she was all right and no more. Said to just keep it to myself and that she only told me so I'd stop worrying and stop making a fuss."

Josh ripped the paper off the pad and jammed it into his jacket pocket. "Okay, thanks, Doris. This is terrific. I really appreciate your calling."

"Yeah, well, if you find her she'll probably never speak to me again. But I care more about her well-being than I do about her liking me."

"Me too. I'll let you know if I find her."

After he hung up, he knocked on the bathroom door. "You almost done in there, Cruz?"

Cruz opened the door and finished drying his hands. "Yep. Ready for my tour."

"Grab your stuff for the Waldorf. We've had a change of plans."

CHAPTER FORTY-ONE

That afternoon Rachel awoke and pushed her sleepy body upright. She had dozed off on top of her bed without realizing it. Panic snapped her alert, and she grabbed her travel clock. Phew! Four o'clock. That was cutting it close. She had just enough time to get everyone together, gather up her clothes and gear, and head over to the Waldorf.

Their day had been fun but more tiring than she expected. She deliberately wore her most comfortable, flat shoes, and their little group hadn't covered a lot of actual territory. Neither had they been out long—only a few hours.

But they had visited quite a few shops in the garment district. Just having the toddlers in the mix—well behaved as they had been—tended to make activities more of an energy drain.

She, Karen, Suzanna, and the twins had returned early enough for the twins to get a quick nap so they'd be fresh and happy during the competition. By the quiet in the adjoining room, Rachel guessed Karen and Suzanna had done as she had, fallen asleep wherever they sat.

It wasn't until she moved to rise from the bed and wake up Karen and Suzanna that she realized something felt odd about her hair. She had showered and done her makeup before sitting on the bed. She had opted to wear her hair waved and loose around her shoulders. So what was that she felt?

She reached behind her head and there it was. Something was stuck back there. She tried unsuccessfully to pull it free and recognized by the stick that she had a lollipop tangled up in her hair. And from the feel of it, either she had moved around a lot or someone had struggled to try to remove it before giving up. It was a knotted, sticky mess, in what was now a rat's nest of hair.

She darted her eyes back to the clock on the nightstand. "Oh, no. Oh, no!" She jumped up and ran into the adjoining room. Karen and Suzanna were both lying back on the beds in Suzanna's room, and the twins sat on the floor, playing quietly together with a handful of the Tinker Toys Suzanna bought them at FAO Schwarz the day before.

Aaron looked at Rachel, pointed at her, and said one word. "Lolliplop."

"Oh, my goodness!" Rachel shook Karen, and Suzanna awoke with the commotion. "Wake up, you two!" she said. "I'm in trouble here!"

The two women shook off their grogginess. Suzanna frowned. "What's the matter? Oh, mercy, I fell asleep. Are we late?"

"I'm going to be." She spun on her heel. "Look at me!" Karen and Suzanna both jumped from the bed to study her hair.

"Aaron!" Suzanna aimed her stern voice exactly where it belonged. "Yours was the green one, young man. What did you do?"

Aaron's bottom lip quivered for a nanosecond, but Amanda handed him a little wooden Tinker Toy wheel, and his concern and attention veered elsewhere.

Rachel huffed. "I think it's pretty obvious what he's done. Little stinker can be stealthy when he wants to be."

"I'm sure he didn't mean to stick it there," Karen said. "Maybe he just set it down for a minute while he—"

"Oh, for Pete's sake, that really doesn't matter, does it?" Rachel nearly cried. "What am I going to do?"

Karen pushed her toward the bathroom. "We'll wash it out. It will come right out if we wash your hair."

"We don't have time to wash my hair!" She struggled unsuccessfully for composure. "It's time for us to leave for the Waldorf!"

Suzanna put her hands up. "Okay. Hang on. Let's think for just a second. Don't panic."

"Too late!" Rachel reached up to try again to dislodge the lollipop.

"No, don't do that." Karen took her hands away from her hair and pushed her toward the bathroom again. "We're going to try to only get that part of your hair wet."

"But we won't have time to curl it again. To wait for it to dry again."

Suzanna nodded. "She's right. Okay, so we'll give you an updo. Just wash what you have to, leave it to dry as much as possible on the way to the hotel, and we'll work on it there." She looked at her watch. "You still have more than two hours before the competition."

"But we were supposed to run through our dances..." Rachel huffed out a sigh. "Oh, never mind. Let's just get this thing out as fast as we can."

* * * * *

An hour later the group of them arrived at the Park Avenue entrance to the Waldorf. All three women toted something along as they entered, got directions from the front desk, and crossed the mosaic-laden marble floor of the front lobby.

Karen held Rachel's cosmetics case and shoe bag. She spoke words of encouragement to Rachel, who bore her garment bag over her shoulder and hadn't yet fully calmed down. "We're only half an hour late, Rachel. Not so bad, right?"

Suzanna gripped a toddler with each hand. "Yeah. You and Cruz are so well rehearsed, I can't imagine that half hour making much of a difference."

"We still have to get my hair presentable, though. Maybe someone should go find Cruz and make sure he knows we're here. He might be worried."

Karen nodded. "I'll do that. But first let's get you—"

"Rachel!"

They all turned at once and erupted in gasps, laughter, and all-around bafflement.

Rachel's parents and brother Chuck descended on them. Everyone, including the toddlers, created a small mob of hugs, kisses, and chatter.

Karen, her husband's arm around her shoulder, spoke to Rachel's mother. "I thought you were taking Grandma to the beach."

"She cancelled. Didn't want to make the drive and preferred a quiet weekend at home."

Rachel's dad gestured to her mom. "But Jeanne here was already geared up for a trip, so I thought we should all drive up and support my amazing daughter."

Rachel, standing amid so many supportive loved ones, her hair still a disheveled mess, was struck dumb. Did her father just call her amazing? Had this special effort really been *his* idea? She knew tears threatened to come if she said anything, and when her father looked into her eyes, he seemed to sense that as well.

He stepped through the group so he could squarely face her. "I don't know if I've ever given you enough credit, honey. But I'm so proud of what you've accomplished with your business. I know it hasn't been easy. And whether you win or lose this competition tonight, I want you to know how much I love you. How much I've always loved you. You are a remarkable, strong woman."

The group had fallen silent. When he hugged her, his familiar scent of Aqua Velva sparked memories of past comforting embraces, and a tear or two spilled from her eyes. She heard her mother's quiet sigh of emotion.

What had she been worried about? This was just a dance competition, after all. She had already won something she hadn't even realized she battled for.

Surely nothing could ruin the night now.

CHAPTER FORTY-TWO

"Come on, man, give it up." Cruz's voice had a hint of whine about it, and Josh had to fight against lashing out at him. "We've checked seven places already, man. She's not here."

"She's not *here*." Josh pointed to the lobby floor of yet another hotel. "But she's here." He raised his hand and swirled it in a circle, encompassing, in his mind, all of Manhattan. "I'm too close to give up so easily. I don't believe in coincidences, and I'm not about to ignore help from above. Here, give me your garment bag. I'll carry it for a while."

"I can carry my own stuff," Cruz huffed as they walked back out to the street. "I'm hungry."

Josh checked his watch. "Oh. Yeah. Sorry. I lost track of time. Come on, we'll get some hot dogs over there at the stand."

"Hot dogs? I'll spring for a real restaurant." Cruz patted his back pocket. "I want a full meal."

"Nothing doing. It's almost time to leave for the Waldorf. We don't have time to wait for table service. Buck up. I'll take you all to dinner after the competition."

They walked to the stand, but not without a murmur of dissent from Cruz. "Slave driver." He ordered three hot dogs and stuffed them with chili and cheese.

They sat on a nearby bench to eat. Cruz draped his garment bag over the back of the bench and leaned forward while he ate, bits of chili dropping to the ground. While he seemed absorbed in his food, Josh ate in distraction and surveyed the city block around them.

Eventually, between bites, Cruz said, "So what happened with you and Rachel?"

"What do you mean, what happened?" He stopped chewing and glanced at Cruz.

"You used to come around the studio a lot. You don't seem to be in the picture anymore. Am I right?"

Josh looked back out at the throngs of people. "I've just been busy. Chasing down this story—the one I need to find Candy for—has been a disruption. And then there's my current job at the paper. Writing those—"

"Fashion articles?" Cruz smiled around a mouthful.

Josh looked at him again. "How about we agree not to hassle each other about whether or not each other's job is manly or not? All right with you, dancing man?"

Cruz cocked his head, shrugged, and continued to chew.

Still, just for good measure, he felt inclined to say, "Rachel's terrific. A really special woman."

He thought much more of her than that, but he got the feeling Cruz didn't need any more encouragement to admire Rachel, so he left it there.

Before taking his next bite, Cruz threw another question at him. "So how about Mira?"

Josh nodded. "Mira's an amazing young gal. A guy could do a whole lot worse than fall for her. Kind, humble, beautiful, graceful—"

"Okay, I got it."

Josh heard a hint of annoyance. Either Cruz didn't like Mira and preferred not hearing such accolades or he liked her a lot and preferred not hearing them from him. Just as he was about to ask him which it was, he saw a flash of red hair that made him take notice.

"Hey." He straightened, and his heartbeat doubled. "Hey! There she is!"

Cruz sat up and followed his gaze. "Who, Mira?"

"Candy!" He almost yelled her name, but then he thought better of it. He grabbed Cruz's garment bag. "Come on."

Hot dog wrappers and napkins fell all around Cruz's feet when he stood. "Hang on!" He stooped to pick up everything.

Josh had already started down the street, but he turned and ran back to help Cruz. "Come on, I'm going to lose her."

They took off running. "Just call after her, man. I'm going to upchuck, running like this."

Josh called over his shoulder, "I'm afraid she'll lose herself in the crowd if I call her. There! She went into the Gateway."

They reached the small hotel moments after she entered. Cruz looked at the façade. "We already asked about her here."

"I don't know why I didn't think of it. Of course she didn't register in her own name. Not if Wiley's trying to hide her. This was a total gift from God, seeing her on the street."

Cruz laughed. "You really think God's in the news-writing business, don't you?"

Josh lifted an eyebrow at him. "I *know* He's in the business of fighting corruption. You can count on that, son, and I mean it."

"Okay." Cruz looked embarrassed but still amused. "Sorry. No offense meant."

They rushed through the unmanned lobby and got to the elevator as it shut. Josh stood back and watched the floor indicator to see where she stopped.

"Fourth floor. Okay, come on, come on." Josh tapped his fingers against the wall while they waited for the elevator to return, and then they rode it back up. But once they stepped out on the fourth floor, they faced a hall of closed doors in either direction, with no idea which one Candy was behind.

"Now what, Sherlock?" Cruz looked both ways from the elevator.

Josh pointed down the left side. "You watch that side. I'll watch this one." He looked to his right and yelled once, quickly and very loudly. "Candy!"

Cruz nearly jumped. "Hey! What are you—"

"Watch!" Josh pointed back down the hallway. Within seconds a door down the hall opened, and Candy's head poked out.

She saw Josh and Cruz and her eyes went wide. She gasped and ducked back inside, slamming the door shut.

"Come on." Josh headed toward her room.

"Man, you're crazy. You ever get arrested for disturbing the peace?"

"Not yet. But the day is young."

He knocked on Candy's door. "Okay, Candy, open up. Come on. You've got to talk with me. You know I'm not leaving here without telling everyone where you are. And then what? Your parents are going crazy, looking for you."

They were greeted with nothing but silence for a short time. Then she swung the door open, her lips pursed. "I'm gonna kill that Doris. I *thought* she might be lying."

Josh shook his head. "She wasn't lying. She really is worried about you. Everyone who cares about you is. Can we come in?"

She eyed Cruz. "Who's Mr. Short, Dark, and Handsome?"

Cruz put out his hand. "Cruz Vergara, *hermosa*." The moment Candy extended her hand, he took it and kissed it.

Josh chuckled, but when he looked at Candy, he saw she appreciated the melodramatic gesture. *Women.*

She stepped back to let them in. "Teddy's going to go nuts if he finds out you're here."

"Go nuts? Has he threatened you?" Josh asked. He and Cruz sat in the two guest chairs, and Candy sat on the edge of her sagging, lumpy bed. One glance at the stained walls and worn carpets of the room, one whiff of the sour residue of past residents, sized up Wiley's low regard for the girl. There were no really cheap hotels in this area, but this one was clearly several notches below the quality of its neighboring competitors.

"No," she said. "I mean he'll go nuts on you."

Josh harrumphed. "There's nothing he can do to me. He doesn't frighten me physically, and he can't do anything legally about my talking with you. As a matter of fact, he's the one who needs to be concerned about tampering with a possible witness in an embezzlement case."

Her eyebrows lifted. "Has a case gone to court, then?"

"Well, no. Not yet." Josh frowned. "But that's because you chickened out on doing your civic duty."

She stood up and put her hands up, as if she could halt his judgment. He noticed dark circles under her eyes.

"Come on, Josh, cut me a break. What do you want me to do? Put my boyfriend in prison?" She walked over to the window and turned her back on them.

"Your *boyfriend*? Candy, I don't know what he's telling you, but he *has* a girlfriend. A fiancée, as a matter of fact."

She faced him. "That's a temporary thing. He's going to dump her as soon as he gets promoted."

"Promoted?"

"He's after the county manager's job."

Josh nearly shouted. Sal had been right about Wiley's ambitions.

"He isn't doing enough damage holding the county's purse strings? Now he wants to mismanage the county into complete chaos?"

She shrugged. "He seems to think he'll do a good job. And he says it's the next step to chairman of the county board."

"So explain me something." Cruz spoke, and both he and Candy looked at him as if they had forgotten he was there. He pointed at Candy. "You seem like a really nice girl. Pretty. Classy. What's the problem with you?"

Candy's eyes fluttered with the compliments, but she punctuated the end of Cruz's question with a subtle frown. "What do you mean, what's the problem with me? I'm not doing anything wrong. Just being loyal to my—"

"No, I get that. That's nice too, your being loyal. But why is *he* ashamed of *you*? How come he thinks he needs to be with some other woman to get the job he wants?"

Josh could have hugged the guy. Instead he simply looked at Candy and gently lifted his eyebrows when she met eyes with him.

She looked at her lap. "People in high places have certain expectations."

"Maybe." Josh leaned forward in his chair and rested his elbows against his knees. "But if Wiley has any intention of letting you come out in the open as his girlfriend, fiancée, or whatever he's promised you, what makes you think he's going to consider you more presentable when he reaches an even higher place in government?"

"Well, he..."

"Do you really think that's why he's forced you to hide away from people who really care about you? And from the truth?"

He thought he had her convinced. She sat there in contemplative silence for what felt like forever. But in the end she shook her head so emphatically, she looked as if she were trying to shake all logic—everything he and Cruz had said—right out forever.

"I'm sorry, Josh. I just feel like this is my only chance at real happiness. At someone who loves and—and appreciates me."

He wanted to tell her how stupid that sounded. He struggled to keep calm. He had staked so much on finally finding her and convincing her to do the right thing. For him *and* for herself.

"Hey." Cruz broke into his thoughts. "What time is it, anyway?"

Candy answered before Josh even raised his watch to check. "Ten after six."

Josh nearly swore. Both he and Cruz jumped out of their chairs and said the same thing simultaneously: "Rachel!"

Candy apparently felt compelled to jump up too. "Who's Rachel?"

"I can't believe I forgot about her!" He grabbed Cruz's garment bag. "You were supposed to be at the Waldorf over an hour ago!" They both rushed to the door.

"What's at the Waldorf? Can I do anything to help?" Candy wrung her hands and looked from him to Cruz and back again.

Josh shook his head and opened the door. "My—my good friend's dance competition." He lifted his chin toward Cruz. "He's her partner. This means everything to her, and I've wasted all this time for my own selfish..." He stopped explaining and ran out the door. "Come on, Cruz. You're going to have to dress in the cab."

The last thing he saw before the elevator arrived was Candy standing in the hallway, studying them and biting her nails. There she stood. The end of his city desk career.

CHAPTER FORTY-THREE

"This can't be happening." Rachel stared at Karen and Suzanna, the dressing room noise around her melding into one homogenized buzz. She almost felt she could faint. "Where could they be?"

Suzanna took Rachel's hand, which she had done repeatedly for the past hour. "I'm sure there's a good explanation, sweetie. They know how important this is. They wouldn't deliberately be late."

"I mean, an hour ago I was a little ticked that we were losing last-minute practice time," Rachel said. "But now? I'm actually starting to worry whether they'll even get here in time."

Karen rubbed Rachel's shoulder. "Maybe traffic is just really bad from wherever they were when they started on their way over here."

She struggled to even pay attention to what her sisters-in-law said. "Karen, could you go out there and check again? Check the front lobby and make sure they aren't lost somewhere in the hotel?"

"Sure." Karen rushed through the crowded dressing room and out the door.

Rachel smoothed down her dress yet again. She was going to wear the fabric away at this rate. She grabbed a tissue and blotted her forehead. "What time is it, Suzanna?"

"It's only a few minutes since you asked before."

She looked Suzanna in the eyes. "I realize that. I just need to know."

Suzanna checked her watch. "Six thirty."

Rachel groaned.

"Look, take a seat, will you?" Suzanna pushed her down into a chair in front of one of the mirrors and put on a smile. "Your hair ended up turning out beautifully, didn't it?"

Rachel said nothing. She stared at her hair. She had actually been worried about being late because of Aaron's lollipop. That seemed eons ago.

Suzanna kept talking. "And see? That worked out all right. We worried for nothing. So let's not—"

"That's it." Rachel nodded. "That's it. We need to pray. When I worry I always have to remember to pray."

"Absolutely." Suzanna bobbed her head. "You go on ahead." She rested her hands on Rachel's shoulders and closed her eyes.

She had hoped Suzanna would do the honors, but now she realized she was the one who needed to adjust her focus. She closed her eyes and took a deep breath.

"Okay, Lord, You—You know all things, and I can't see the things You can. So I'm asking You to please calm me down about this. Please help me to focus on Your will tonight. If it's Your will, please get Josh and Cruz here right now. But if that's not Your will, please help me accept that." Her voice got small and fast. "Although I really don't understand why You would let us get this far just to not be able to compete." She sighed and slowed back down. "And, Lord, please help me to not go crazy mad on Josh when I see him. Please help me to not hate him. Please keep me from taking off my shoe and knocking him over the—"

"Okay. Amen, Lord Jesus," Suzanna blurted. "Amen."

She felt Suzanna's squeeze on her shoulders and realized she needed to be done praying for the moment.

When Karen returned she looked as concerned as Rachel felt.

"What?" Rachel said. "What's happened?"

Karen shook her head and glanced at Suzanna before answering. "Uh, nothing's happened. There's no sign of them yet. But I'm sure they'll be here any minute. Try to relax."

Rachel stared at the makeup table before her. She tried to tell herself it wouldn't be the end of the world if they didn't get to compete. She knew that. Hadn't she just told herself winning didn't matter, after talking with her father? They could compete again—rather Mira and Cruz could compete again—in the fall. But they were so close. Winning wasn't even an issue at this point. Just getting to compete was a big enough deal to boost the studio's reputation. Getting kicked out for unprofessional behavior? That was a different matter altogether.

She heard Suzanna whisper, "You've *got* to be kidding me." The quick shushing from Karen caught Rachel's attention. She spun around to see the two of them smiling awkwardly at her. They looked as if they had just heard she had only hours left to live.

"What?" She stood up and spoke loudly enough that the group next to them turned to stare. "Come on, tell me. Something *has* happened."

Karen took in a deep breath and released it, pursing her lips. "No, nothing's happened to Josh and Cruz, as far as I know. It's just—"

"Just what?"

Suzanna pulled her hands together and grimaced as she spoke. "Karen saw Billy in the crowd out there."

She felt a lump of emotion form so quickly, she put her hand to her throat. "Why is he following me like this? He's like the Grim Reaper or something." She sank down in her chair. "Maybe it's best if I don't get to compete tonight. I don't want him to have any opportunity to embarrass me again."

Karen shook her head. "No, don't say that. My guess is he's here because he knows he made a huge mistake about you. He probably hopes he can win you back again."

"Still," Suzanna said, "his behavior is pretty creepy. He came all the way to New York to watch her?"

Karen frowned and made big eyes at Suzanna. Then she stepped back toward the door. "I'm going out there and ask Chuck to go talk with him. If Billy tries anything, Rachel, you know your big brother's going to shut him up or tackle him to the ground. Don't you worry about Billy for another second." She dashed through the crowd.

She envisioned her brother and Billy rolling around on the floor, taking down spectators, judges, other competitors. She grabbed the tissue box from the makeup table and tried to fan herself with it.

"It's so hot in here! What time is it, Suzanna?"

Suzanna sighed and checked her watch. "Twenty minutes left."

Rachel tossed the box back on the table and pressed her fingers to her temples. "I should have known better than to trust him. Why did I think he cared about me or my needs? How could I have fallen for another self-centered, selfish, self-*obsessed* guy just because he pretended to think I was special? Whatever he's doing right now, it's more important to him than what he promised me. He's just another guy looking to further his own desires without thinking of others. Nowhere near as trustworthy as he seemed. And obviously without a bit of respect for what I do, even after all this time."

Suzanna rubbed Rachel's back. The affectionate gesture was the last straw, and she couldn't keep her eyes from welling with tears. She yanked several tissues from the box and tried to stop the tears from destroying her eye makeup. When she looked up at Suzanna, she saw pure sympathy in her eyes.

"Sweetie, I didn't know you'd actually fallen for him."

Rachel frowned. "What are you talking about? Fallen for who?"

"Josh. Isn't that who you were talking about? You weren't talking about *Cruz,* were you?"

"Good night, no. I was talking about Josh. But I haven't *fallen* for him. Why would you say that?"

How Suzanna could muster *any* amusement in her expression right now was beyond her. But without a doubt that sympathetic look changed ever so slightly, and she felt like a child when her sister-in-law actually gave her a little pat on the shoulder.

"Oh, honey. We'll talk about it later."

CHAPTER FORTY-FOUR

"Hey, hey, what's he doing back there?" The cabbie pulled his cigar from his mouth and adjusted his rearview mirror. "Get your pants back on, there, fella."

"Please hurry." Josh sat up front with the driver. He leaned forward in his seat, as if that would propel them faster. "He's just changing into his tux. He's late for a dance competition. He won't have time to change once we're there."

The cabbie eyed him. "You're dancers?"

"He's a dancer. I'm a reporter." He ran his hand through his hair. "An idiot reporter."

The driver nodded. "I've had a few of those in my cab from time to time." He leaned out his window and blasted his horn at a driver who cut in front of them. "Moron!"

Josh watched him turn his attention back to the traffic without the slightest bit of stress in his expression.

"So why the confession?" the cabbie asked.

"Pardon?"

"You're a self-proclaimed idiot. How do you figure that?" He cocked his head back, toward Cruz. "Have anything to do with running around with the fancy fella back there?"

Josh frowned, looked back at Cruz, and then looked at the driver again. "He's not a fancy fella. What are you talking about? He's a dancer. He teaches dance. Nothing emasculating about that, if that's what you're insinuating. The kid's talented."

"Thanks, Josh," Cruz piped up from the back. Until then, he hadn't realized Cruz could hear them. He hadn't even bothered to comment on the cabbie's making fun of him. Maybe he got that attitude a lot.

Certainly he had made assumptions about dance being a less-than-masculine pursuit. He and Rachel had clashed about that often enough. When did he change his mind? Maybe just from getting to know Mel and Cruz?

He shook his head over his own ignorance. Yet another time he had shown disdain for Rachel's business.

As if he read Josh's mind, the cabbie asked again, "So why'd you call yourself an idiot?"

Josh frowned at him. "Why are you so interested, anyway?"

"No reason." The cabbie shrugged. "Part of the job. I'd go berserk if I didn't ask people about themselves. Don't let the glamour of my surroundings fool you. I get bored."

Josh chuckled. At least the guy took his mind off the stress of the moment. But now he thought again of how he'd let down Rachel. "Hurry, okay?"

"I'm hurrying, pal. You want to actually get there, right? So keep your pants on." He looked in the rearview mirror. "Both o' youse." Another glance at Josh. "What'd you do that's so boneheaded?"

"Ugh. There's this fantastic woman—"

"Ahh, I knew it."

"You knew what?"

"It's always a woman." He pointed to a snapshot he had taped to his dashboard. The picture showed the cabbie with a portly brunette and two teenaged daughters. "I gave up my dreams for that one right there. Twenty-five years ago."

Josh nodded. He had to ask. "What was your dream?"

"Private eye. But I needed something more stable. More respectable. Something better suited to a family man, right?"

Josh smiled. "Right."

"So. You give up a dream for this fantastic woman?"

"That's just it." Josh sighed. "I may have just ruined one of *her* dreams, looking out for my own. I've been chasing a news story that could mean…well, kind of a promotion from my current job. And I let it distract me enough that I forgot about getting Cruz here to their dance competition when I was supposed to."

The cabbie turned momentarily to include Cruz in the conversation. Cruz was trying to find himself in the rearview mirror to fasten his bow tie.

The cabbie grunted. "So Cruz, how come you didn't just get *yourself* to the Waldorf? You're a grown man, right? You know how to hail a cab, yeah?"

Cruz looked blankly at the driver for a moment before turning to Josh. "Man, Josh. He's right. I was so wrapped up in what we were doing too, that didn't even occur to me. I didn't have to stay with you and Candy."

"Who's Candy?" the driver asked. "Are you telling me there's already another dame in the picture? 'Cause I can tell you right now, son—"

"She's the news story I was after." Josh checked his watch and slapped the hand rest before he calmed enough to speak again. "I didn't realize I kept Cruz away too long, or I *would* have sent him ahead. That's why I'm an idiot. I didn't give Rachel one thought once I got that call from Doris."

The cabbie looked at Josh, who quickly spoke. "Also part of the news story."

With a whistle, the driver said, "Sounds like quite a story you got there. Candy, Doris, Rachel—"

Cruz spoke up. "Rachel's not part of his story."

"Probably never will be, either," Josh mumbled. He leaned forward again and put his head in his hands. He combed his fingers through his hair and sat up. "You know…what's your name?"

"Leo."

"You know, Leo, I've been writing these human element stories, about stuff like jukeboxes and burger joints. Fire departments and grade school graduations."

"Don't sound all that human to me."

Josh pointed at him. "That's just it. My editor forced me to find something human about all of them. So what I really ended up writing about was what people remember when they hear certain songs and about folks who care about serving others. You know, about things like unsung heroes and trailblazers. And the whole time I'm doing it, I'm moaning about how I'm not doing what I consider important. And Rachel… She just kept encouraging me about what I was doing and saying all kinds of supportive stuff about the job I wanted to get back."

"You're right." Cruz sat forward and leaned his arms on the back of their seat. "She…I guess she really…likes you a lot."

"*Liked* me is more like it. The one time she leans on me, and what do I do? I completely let her down. Just so I could chase the story that would get me back on top. And you know what? I didn't even get the story. The gal I needed for the story refuses to talk."

"That's Doris?" Leo asked.

Cruz answered. "That's Candy." He frowned and tapped Josh on the shoulder. "But what about Mira?"

Incredulous, the driver looked at him. "Mira? There's *another* one in this mix? Is she part of the news story, too, or does Mira *like* you like Rachel does? Or did."

Josh shook his head, looking out the window. When would they ever get to the Waldorf? He jerked his thumb toward the back of the cab. "No, Mira likes him."

The sudden silence drew Josh's attention away from the window. He looked at Leo, who kept eyeing the rearview mirror, a grin on his face. Another glance to the back of the cab, and he tried to rewind. "Wait. What did I just say?"

A confused smile sprouted on Cruz's face. "Mira likes *me*?"

"Oh, shoot." Josh smacked his forehead. "All right, Cruz. You didn't hear that."

Cruz laughed. "I thought she liked you, Josh."

"Me?" Josh laughed too. "I'm old enough to… Well, to be her much older brother, let's just say that." A thought occurred to him, and he pounced on it. "That would be as awkward as you and, say, *Rachel*."

Cruz looked like he was working mental puzzles for a moment, and then he nodded. "Yeah. Me and Rachel. She's way too old for me."

They pulled up at the Waldorf.

"Of course she is." Josh couldn't help the tug at the corners of his mouth. He handed the fare to Leo, who narrowed his eyes as he smirked at him. Josh grinned back.

Maybe Leo would have made a decent private eye, after all.

CHAPTER FORTY-FIVE

Despite the fact that she was short a partner, Rachel lined up with the rest of the dancers. She held out hope that Cruz would appear at the last moment.

Karen and Suzanna gave her hugs as they prepared to leave the staging area.

All three of them turned when they heard a stirring at the front of the room. Rachel thought she heard someone mention her name, and she stepped out from the lineup. Was he finally here?

Mira spotted her and ran toward her.

Mira?

"What are you doing here?" Rachel asked.

Mira giggled. "I came to support you! My goodness, I didn't think I'd get here in time."

Rachel accepted her excited hug and spoke quickly. "Is Cruz with you?"

Mira pulled away. "Cruz? No. I literally just got here. My father had a meeting up here and let me fly with him in his client's private jet. Connie and Mel let me leave early. I hope you don't mind." She looked around the room and finally registered the situation. "Oh, no, Rachel. Where is he?"

Suzanna sighed. "We're assuming he's with Josh."

"Josh isn't here either?" Mira's eyes widened. "But that doesn't make sense. He was so..." She abruptly stopped speaking.

Whatever she had planned to say was apparently private or inappropriate. She couldn't tell which, and at this point she didn't care. He had let her down.

Karen took Mira's hand. "Come on, we'll explain. They want us out of here."

As Suzanna and Karen led Mira away, she called to Rachel over her shoulder, "I'm rooting for you!"

Yeah, a lot of good that was going to do. It was Billy Nawta all over again. At least this time she wasn't deserted on the dance floor, in front of everyone and in the middle of the competition. But standing here, alone, surrounded by all the dance couples, wasn't much better. People kept looking at her, pity or scorn in their eyes. No one said anything, not yet. But she stood out like the town wallflower.

She was going to get a reputation as the dancer who kept losing her partners.

One of the competition organizers walked into the room, upbeat but officious. Gray-haired and still built like a ballet dancer, she spoke as she walked down the line, casting glances at each couple.

"We're all ready, right, ladies and gentlemen? We have a huge, excited crowd waiting for you out there, one of the largest I've seen for this particular competition...."

She stopped when she reached Rachel. She leaned to look beyond the line, as if she thought Cruz might be hiding or something. Then she finally rested her eyes on Rachel.

"Where's the young man?"

Rachel swallowed and then sighed. "He's late."

The woman lifted up the reading glasses that hung on a chain around her neck. She looked at her watch and then peered over her glasses. "Are you saying your partner isn't here? At all?"

Rachel steeled herself, to keep her lip from quivering. All her hard work. Everything—

No. She wasn't going to do this. She had prayed for God's will, and she was going to cling to that. Somehow this was His will. She squared her shoulders and gave the woman a nod.

"That's what I'm saying. Something has happened to him—I don't know what. But he isn't here."

She and the woman both looked around them. Everyone within hearing had turned to watch what was happening.

The woman removed her glasses and spoke like a schoolteacher. "Eyes front, please, ladies and gentlemen." She gently pulled Rachel out of the line and spoke to her quietly enough to keep it private.

"These things happen, dear. In all of my years of experience, I've had my share of disappointments. I know you've worked hard to get this far. But if your partner isn't standing beside you in this line by the time I finish my inspection, I'm going to have to ask you to stay behind when the dancers take the floor. I mean, I won't ask you in front of everyone. I'm asking you now. Understood?"

Her gentle way of handling the situation was nearly her undoing. Rachel nodded. She always wept when she was down and people showed her kindness.

"Understood."

"Let's have you go to the back of the lineup, then."

Considering the fact that there were only seventeen couples competing, she resigned herself to the inevitable. She barely reached the back of the line before the organizer did.

And when the woman met eyes with her at the end of her inspection, Rachel appreciated the sadness there. "I'm sorry, dear."

She simply nodded before the woman turned away and spoke

to the sixteen couples who *had* made it to the Waldorf in time to compete.

"All right, everyone. All the best to you. Follow me, please, and keep it quiet."

Rachel waited for them to leave before she let herself cry. She lowered her head.

I know this isn't earth-shattering stuff, Lord, but You know how much it meant to me. You know how hurt I am. I tried to forget how it felt when Billy accused me and stranded me on the dance floor before. But here I find myself stranded again. This embarrassment is kind of hard to forget. Whatever reason things worked out this way, please help me to be gracious and grown up in how I react. I know my life is blessed. But I hope right now You don't mind if I indulge myself just a little.

She wiped her tears with the back of her hand and walked out of the staging room in time to hear the announcer call the dancers to the floor. The ballroom was far cooler than the staging area had been, but experience told her the dance floor would heat up soon under the glitter of the chandeliers and the warmth of the competitors' efforts.

She was aware of people around her giving her double takes as she stood on the periphery of the crowd in her elegant dress. Still, people lost interest in her as the couples were introduced.

She took a deep breath. She would at least be gracious enough to watch the dancing and cheer on the competitors.

By the time the first dance was about to begin, she felt enough strength had seeped in to enable her to let the disappointment go. At least for now. She thought of herself as a spectator and focused on the dance floor.

So when something caused a scuffle just behind the judges' table, she was as shocked as everyone else.

CHAPTER FORTY-SIX

Josh blinked slowly and nodded as several people associated with the competition tried to stop him from reaching the judges' table.

"Yes, yes, I understand." He flashed his press card at them. He pulled Cruz along behind him, a firm grip on his arm so he wouldn't lose him in the shuffle. "Press coming through. Excuse us. Press coming through."

He had known better than to try to get Cruz back to the staging area. By the time they got there, it would be too late. Better to just storm right to the front of the crowd and reach the people with the power.

Everyone around them started talking the moment he and Cruz passed through. He felt like Moses parting a babbling brook. He could hear from the announcer's tone that the competition was about to begin. He had to reach the judges before they allowed a single step to take place. He thought he might be able to get Rachel and Cruz in there, regardless of the circumstances, if he could talk to them before anyone actually began to dance.

So he did what he had to do. At the risk of embarrassing himself, he simply called out to the judges' table, which he had almost reached.

"Hold the competition, please, ladies and gentlemen. Hold on just a moment, please."

The babbling swiftly turned to rumbling, which panned out from his self-made epicenter.

The man in the middle of the table—most likely the head judge—turned and frowned at him. As soon as he and Cruz were near enough that the judge didn't have to shout, he addressed Josh, indignation bubbling from his lips as vividly as his words.

"Young man, whatever do you think you're doing? This is a dance competition, not a boxing match! A little decorum! Please!"

He and Cruz broke through the crowd and stood behind the table.

"I'm really sorry about the intrusion, sir." Josh looked up and down the table. "Please excuse my poor manners, ladies and gentlemen. Given the circumstances, I didn't know what else to do." He put his hand on Cruz's shoulders. "This young man and his lovely partner have been preparing for this competition for months. They're a beautiful thing to watch on that dance floor. I know a lot of people here have seen them dance. They won the Virginia something or other in ballroom dance just a few weeks—"

"*Excuse* me!" The man in the middle of the judges' table pushed away but didn't stand. He faced him and Cruz. "I don't care *what* the couple accomplished before today. If they're not qualified, they're not qualified."

"Oh, but that's just it." Josh held up his hand. "They're *more* than qualified. And the only reason they're not out there on the floor right now is because I got in their way. I was supposed to deliver this talented young man here two hours ago. But I got so wrapped up in chasing down a news story, so focused on my own business that I forgot all about what I promised. I let my friends down. That's the only reason he's late. And that's the only reason he and his partner aren't out there. Yet."

He saw a thin, gray-haired woman lean over the table to speak quietly with the head judge. She slipped on her reading glasses and pointed to a roster on the table as she spoke.

The judge frowned as he listened and then turned back to Josh. "Well, I'm sorry. They weren't ready when they needed to be, so they've been disqualified."

He heard an actual groan in the crowd around him. Someone even said, "Oh, come on." He took heart in that.

He tried a different tack. "I understand you want to follow the rules, sir. But you haven't actually started the dancing yet. Which is a good thing, because I was sent here by the *Washington Tribune* to cover this competition. I happen to be one of the lead reporters for the Style section, and my editor is very keen to feature this competition for our national reading audience."

He glanced around them, trying to will the crowd to support him in his efforts.

"I'd much rather write a story about the thrill of a last-minute save and fantastic performances by *all* your competitors than about the bad taste left in everyone's mouth over your disqualifying two excellent dancers who were both here before you even began the competition."

Josh looked up, scanned the crowd, and raised his voice. "As a matter of fact, where's my photographer? Freddie? You here?"

A flash startled the head judge and everyone around him. Freddie stepped out from the crowd, smiled, and held up his camera. "Got a nice one of you there, judge!"

Many members of the crowd laughed.

The judge stared at Josh for a moment before he turned to his colleagues at the table. They swiftly conferred, heads shaking and bobbing, hands waving with exasperation and resignation.

"Come on, judges." Josh spoke to them, despite their having their backs to him. "Let them dance."

Someone from the crowd echoed his words. "Yeah, let 'em dance."

Several more people took up the phrase. Before he knew what was happening, the crowd, enjoying every minute of the drama, began to chant in Rachel and Cruz's defense. Even people on the other side of the room, who couldn't know what was going on, got into the act. Cruz nudged him and lifted his chin toward the dance floor. The competitors had even taken up the chant.

"Let them dance! Let them dance!"

The judge stood and held up his hands. The noise swiftly died down, but the judge couldn't be heard without his microphone. He sat at the table and pulled the mike closer to himself.

"All right, all right. Please, everyone behave. We feel it's only fair to penalize the latecomers by fifteen points in our overall scoring"—he turned to glance at Josh before returning to his mike—"*despite* the reason for their tardiness. That said, we have decided to let them dance."

The crowd cheered, and Cruz was slapped on the back by everyone as he made his way to the dance floor.

He stood alone for a moment, and the judge finally leaned into his microphone. "And where is your partner, sir?"

Josh felt a shudder. Had she left? Had he done all of this, only to lose her friendship—and anything else they might have developed—anyway?

A stir started at the far corner of the ballroom. He peered into the crowd and saw people making way and encouraging someone in their midst. Finally Rachel emerged, and the room broke into applause for her.

Even from where he stood, he could see she had been crying, and his heart broke. He had done that to her. Before this evening was over, he had to figure out how to make it up to her.

Still, by the time she made her way to Cruz, who took her hand and gave it a gallant kiss, a shy smile had found its way to her lips and her eyes.

He knew she might not ever forgive him, but right now that didn't matter. She was happy again. That was enough for him.

CHAPTER FORTY-SEVEN

It had dawned on Rachel as she watched Josh's intrusion across the room: yet another man had chosen to disrupt an otherwise elegant and perfectly organized event in order to turn the spotlight on her in some fashion. She nearly ran back to the staging area to avoid another shameful exit under hundreds of pairs of eyes.

Yet something had compelled her to stay. Something told her this interruption was an entirely different matter. Involving an entirely different kind of man. With entirely different motives and feelings about her. As Josh argued with the judges it became clear. His every effort was focused on supporting her.

By the time Cruz made his way to the dance floor, she realized that Josh wasn't only a better man than Billy had ever been. He was also a better man than *he* had been when they first met. He had embraced what was important to her so unselfishly that he risked ridicule and public, physical expulsion in order to make this situation right. The self-important man she met in front of her studio a couple of months ago would never have considered such a gesture, war hero or not. He had been a man given to nobility on the grand scale, but certainly not on the small, human-element scale.

That understanding brought a smile to her face as she made her way onto the dance floor.

Because of the hubbub when Cruz and Josh arrived, she thought the crowd seemed to pay particular attention to Cruz and her when the competition first got underway. She hoped Cruz didn't notice the same thing. She didn't want him getting nervous.

But not only did the attention seem to give him confidence, something else gave him a sureness in his movement that she hadn't noticed before. He seemed genuinely happy, and she hadn't been aware of any lack of happiness in him in the first place.

The first dance—the waltz—came to an end and the couples lingered, waiting for the judges to confer and the next dance to be called. Rachel kept her eyes on the judges' table but spoke softly to Cruz.

"So where *were* you two?"

"Josh got a lead on that story of his. His office called about the girl he needed. The one who went missing."

Rachel gasped. No wonder. "Did they find her?"

The next dance was called. The quickstep.

"Later," Rachel said. They definitely needed their wits about them for this one. But after a while she had to smile. This was the dance Cruz had claimed as his weakest when she first hired him. Now? He had it all down pat. He made perfect weight changes throughout, and his timing was as tight as a second hand when dancing the chassés. They both got huge grins on their faces when they finished.

"That was even better than Virginia Beach." She gave Cruz's hand a little squeeze.

He was about to say something back when his eyes opened wide at someone in the crowd behind her.

Rachel glanced behind herself and back at him. "What?"

"Mira's here!"

Rachel smiled and tried again to spot Mira in the crowd. "Yeah, her father flew her up here in a private jet. Can you believe that?"

She wasn't sure if he even heard her. He had a goofy grin on his face, and he repeated himself.

"Mira's here."

Rachel peered into his eyes. Something had changed. He looked away from the crowd and saw Rachel studying him.

"Rachel, what I said before. About—"

"Ladies and gentlemen. Please prepare for the foxtrot."

They stopped talking and readied themselves. They had always done well with the foxtrot, and tonight was no exception. Once they began, their rise and fall was flawless, as far as she could tell. They were like gentle waves across the dance floor.

She realized she felt no nervousness whatsoever. She no longer felt a burning need to win this competition in order to succeed with her studio or impress her father or even to get Josh to give her credit for excelling in something he hadn't once appreciated.

She was having fun. It had taken the panic of thinking she wouldn't get to participate to make her simply appreciate dancing for the sake of dancing. She hadn't enjoyed the art like this for...well, since she opened her own studio.

By the time the dance ended and the contestants were sent back to the dressing rooms to change for the tango and the Latin dances, she was at total peace with however the night turned out.

Cruz waved to Mira as they left the floor. He spoke to Rachel before they went to their respective changing rooms. "Rachel, what I was going to say... I'm sorry for throwing myself at you back home. For saying I was in love with you."

She waved off his comment. "Don't worry about it, Cruz. I knew it was just—"

"After listening to Josh talk about you on our way over here, I realized I wasn't anywhere near as serious about you as he is."

She breathed in and tried not to let her breath shake as she exhaled. She didn't know what to say.

"And then when he told me Mira likes me—"

"Mira likes *you*? I mean, Mira likes *you*! Yes, I suspected that all along."

They parted company in order to change, and she couldn't seem to move as swiftly as she needed to. Suzanna and Karen dashed into the changing room just after she slipped into her dress. They practically squealed when they found her.

"So were you floored by Josh's big speech?" Karen's eyes positively twinkled.

Rachel shook her head, still processing what Cruz had said. Josh was serious about her? "I—I didn't hear his speech. I just saw him and Cruz, but—"

Suzanna broke in. "I'm telling you, Rachel, it was like something out of a movie. The man was *driven*. I think he would have stood on his head and squawked like a chicken, right there in front of everyone, if it would have helped convince those judges to let you dance."

"Very passionate." Karen nodded. "You want your hair down a little to go with that sultry dress?"

Doggoned if she wasn't missing every romantic thing Josh was doing or saying about her. First to Cruz and then to half of the people in attendance tonight. But not to her.

"Rachel?"

"Huh? Oh. Yeah, let's let it down. Maybe pin it up on one side?"

"Five minutes, ladies!" The gray-haired lady walked among the women. She caught Rachel's eye and gave her a little wink. "Don't you be a second late getting out there, young lady." Her smile was like a mother's. "I'm glad it's working out after all." She leaned forward and whispered, "It's a pleasure watching you dance. You remind me of myself at your age."

Before she could respond, the woman moved on.

Suzanna spoke softly. "Too bad *she's* not a judge tonight."

Rachel smiled. "Doesn't matter. Whether we win or lose, this night is turning out perfectly. I'm enjoying myself."

"And don't you worry about that troublemaking Billy Nawta," Karen said.

"Karen!" Suzanna said. "Are you *trying* to make her worry?"

Before Rachel even had a chance to frown, Karen spoke again. "All I'm saying is Chuck talked with him. He's going to behave. He hasn't attended these things—your competitions—to make trouble. He told Chuck he realizes he made a terrible mistake about you." Karen finished pinning Rachel's hair and picked up a can of hairspray. "I think he's hoping to woo you back again. Hold your head still a minute."

Rachel closed her eyes and sat still while Karen sprayed. "I don't want him anywhere near me. I'm willing to forgive the guy, but I prefer to do it from afar. I don't care how much he regrets what he did. He's not stable."

She stood, and the three of them headed for the door so she could join Cruz in the staging area. She waved to her sisters-in-law and shot a quick prayer up before she found Cruz.

You know how grateful I am, Lord. You know. Thank You for helping me relax and enjoy tonight. Please keep my focus on You and on simply enjoying this gift You've given me.

When she and Cruz walked to their place on the dance floor, she met eyes with Josh. As good as she was feeling, her heart hurt when she saw him. Despite his being surrounded by several hundred people, he gazed at her with the look of a seriously lonely man.

CHAPTER FORTY-EIGHT

Josh watched Rachel while she and Cruz traveled the dance floor with some of the most elegant and, frankly, steamy dancing he had ever seen. He watched her, knowing he had blown any chance of developing a deeper relationship with her in the future.

And for what? Now that he'd failed to convince Candy to come out of hiding, he'd be stuck on the Style section, possibly forever. Yes, he had figured out how to highlight the people involved in his Style articles, but he knew where his heart was with reporting. He had felt sure that was where God wanted him. Apparently not. Apparently there was something else God wanted him to learn.

So he'd make do with human interest stories, and he'd make do without Rachel. He hated the idea of going back home.

He watched her every move, storing the images away. He would bring them to mind whenever he sat at his desk, moaning and griping about what a bonehead he was.

When the dancing was over and the judges conferred, he actually started to get his hopes up. Maybe, if she and Cruz won, she'd be willing to give him another chance. They had certainly been the strongest dancers out there, and he didn't think he was being biased. They just looked great to his untrained eye.

So when the announcements were made, he was as attentive as a defendant awaiting a verdict. The second runners-up were announced. Not Rachel and Cruz.

The head judge, who had come around to the front of the table for his announcements, waited for the crowd's cheering to quiet down.

"Now before we announce the first runners-up, we want to tell you this was a very difficult decision. There was a difference of only a few judging points between this couple and the winners. Very tight competition. Without further delay, our first runners-up are"—he faced the dancers—"representing the state of Virginia, Rachel Stanhope and Cruz Vergara!"

Josh's shoulders slumped along with his spirits. Everyone around him whooped and cheered. Rachel and Cruz hugged on the dance floor. Brave soul that she was, she put on a big smile and almost looked happy. But he knew better.

He didn't hear the names of the winners. What did it matter? The judge's comment about the minor difference in the points only made it more clear that the late penalty inflicted on Rachel and Cruz—thanks to Josh—was their undoing. *He* had been their undoing.

The moment the trophies were handed out, well-wishers stormed the dance floor. At first he held back. His selfishness had truly made him the outsider here, and he still marveled as he watched Rachel pretend to be pleased. One of the judges chatted with her for a moment before she accepted hugs and kisses from her family and friends.

But he felt a nudging—a spiritual nudging—to face Rachel. To walk right up to her and apologize and ask for her forgiveness. He didn't want to ruin her moment by representing the face of failure for her, but somehow he knew he was meant to address this right now. If she chose to chew him out in front of everyone, well, he had that coming.

He waded through the crowd far less gallantly than he had when he and Cruz arrived this evening. By the time he reached her, an older man held her in a bear hug, and she had her back to Josh.

"Your mom and I are so proud of you, honey," the man said. He pulled back, and he saw that the man's eyes were moist. "You were even better tonight than before. I'm ashamed I haven't given you more credit, Rachel. I had no idea. No idea how stunning you could be on the dance floor. No wonder the studio is working out for you." He looked at the woman beside him. "I think maybe your mom and I should take a few lessons."

Rachel and her mother laughed. Rachel pointed at her father. "I'm going to hold you to that, Dad."

Her father glanced up at Josh, which caused Rachel to turn around. She raised her eyebrows and looked ready to speak.

"Rachel, I—"

Another woman's voice interrupted. "Josh! There you are!"

Both Rachel and he turned their heads and came face to face with Candy. She was breathless and flustered. Her red hair, windswept and tousled, made her look reckless and even a little flashy.

He frowned. "What are you—"

"I had to find you! Good thing you said where you were going when you left." Candy took a moment to look at Rachel.

He noticed Rachel look away from Candy and then at him, a question in her eyes. Great. Now she would think he had another woman in his life.

He couldn't read her expression, but she nodded and started to turn away.

"No, Rachel, it's not—"

"Hey," Candy said to Rachel. "I'm sorry I didn't see your whole shtick. But you are a *gorgeous* dancer. You and Cruz looked so good together."

He recognized Rachel's smile. It was most definitely her polite, uncomfortable, I-want-to-get-away-from-you smile. The one she gave him when they first met and he ranted about the pointlessness of what she did for a living.

"Thank you." Once again she turned toward Mira, who stood on her other side.

Josh put his hand on her back. "Wait, Rachel—"

But Candy interrupted again. "Look, Josh, I wanted to find you because I've changed my mind. I'm going to go back to Washington. I'll verify the information I gave you before about Teddy."

He almost didn't register what she said, but he saw Rachel stop, midturn. He looked back to Candy.

"What did you say?"

"You convinced me. I'm telling you, when I saw how worked up you were over letting your girl down here, well, something just clicked in me, you know? *That's* the way a man in love acts. Not the way Teddy's been. He's using me. He's ashamed of me. And he messed around on me with that so-called high-class dame. Everything he's done has been for him. Not a thing for me. He doesn't care about me the way he should. Like you obviously care about…"

Rachel faced Candy now, all ears. It was all he could do not to say to Candy, "Go on, please."

Candy met eyes with Rachel. "About you. He was torn up pretty bad when he saw he was late for your thing here. Called himself selfish. Had a real fit and ran out with Cruz like they were on fire and looking for a watering hole. And he thought he was running away from any chance at making his story about Teddy stick. I realized that after you left, Josh. I'd love to have a man throw that much effort into doing the right thing for me."

He saw a flush rise in Rachel's face. She looked at him and opened her mouth to speak. But she was grabbed from behind by a man sporting a huge grin.

"My talented baby sis!"

"Chuck! Put me down, silly." Rachel's laugh was full of delight.

Candy put her hand on Josh's arm. "I'm heading home tomorrow, just as soon as I can get a flight. And I've got a little surprise for you." She tapped her temple. "I'm not completely stupid. I tore out a few sheets from the back of Teddy's second set of books when I got the chance. They're tucked away at my apartment. A little insurance, you know? If you need something concrete, it doesn't matter if he's destroyed everything else. I think what I have will do the trick."

Josh grinned and put his hand over Candy's. This was almost everything he wanted. "You're a gem, Candy. Thanks. Give me a call at the paper when you get home?"

She nodded. As she stepped back she gave him a conspiratorial wink and got Rachel's attention again.

"I'm going, but I wanted to say congrats." She cocked her head in Josh's direction. "It's not often a girl hooks one like that. I wouldn't be too quick to throw him back if I were you."

Josh quickly found someone else in the crowd to face before Rachel had a chance to see he had heard Candy's comment. Suzanna stood near him, holding Amanda. Amanda's eyes lit up when she saw Josh, and she put her arms out for his embrace.

He truly did like Suzanna and her daughter, but he doubted very seriously that they had ever seen his smile quite this bright.

CHAPTER FORTY-NINE

Rachel failed to respond to Candy's admonishment. What do you say to a comment like that—don't throw that one back—especially when it's made almost within hearing of the fish in question?

She turned to see Josh talking with Suzanna. He held Amanda in his arms and looked pretty happy. Actually, he looked pretty happy with *himself*. Maybe he *had* heard what Candy said. There was no denying the effect Candy's news had on Rachel's ever-improving opinion of Josh. But she couldn't let him get off scot-free. This moment was way too opportune.

She bent to look around Josh and eyeball Suzanna. As soon as they made eye contact, Suzanna put out her arms to take Amanda back. "I think someone else wants your attention." She widened her eyes at him. "I'm praying for you, buddy."

He turned and faced her, a subtle smile on his face. She slowly folded her arms over her chest. "That was quite an entrance you made. Could have gone either way. I mean, these judges can be a bit touchy. They might actually have banned me and Cruz from dancing today *and* from future competitions, thanks to your antics."

"Really?" Josh's expression could only be described as horrified. "Man, Rachel, I'm so sorry. About all of it. I truly did plan on getting Cruz here well in advance. We would have headed over here shortly after getting a bite to eat if I hadn't spotted Candy on the street. And then I was...I was like a dog after a rabbit. I was so single-minded I lost all sense of time. It really was selfish." His smile had completely vanished. "And I made you lose."

Okay, she couldn't let him carry that one. She uncrossed her arms. "No. You didn't. Look, Josh—"

"But that fifteen-point penalty. The judge said the results were only a few points apart. If I hadn't gotten you penalized—"

"No." She rested her hand on his arm, and at once she realized how much she missed touching him. She stared at his strong forearm—his shirtsleeve rolled up to expose the warm skin where her hand lay—and then she looked at him. He, too, was looking down, and then he darted his ocean-blue eyes up at her. She heard the slightest release of breath from him, full of relief.

"Josh, one of the judges spoke to me right after they gave us our trophies. She didn't want me to think the penalty destroyed our chances. She said the points were close, but not *that* close. We would have been runners-up, anyway."

"So my getting Cruz here late wasn't that big a deal?" His grin was hard to resist.

Rachel arched her brow. "Let's not get carried away. It was a huge deal. You just seem to have heaven on your side today."

He laughed. "If that's the case, I know God has a crooked sense of humor. He's been having a lot of fun with me today."

"Yeah, well, He's had a lot of patience with me." She noticed Josh glance at something over her shoulder. She turned to see Cruz speaking with great animation to Mira.

Rachel smiled at Josh. "Well, it looks like Cruz finally took my advice and started giving Mira some attention. Sometimes it takes a while for subtle comments to get through to you guys, doesn't it?"

Josh's eyes crinkled with some private amusement. "Yeah. Subtle. That's the way to get through to us guys. I'm glad whatever you said finally sank in."

Rachel studied him. Despite what Cruz said, despite what Candy said, she struggled to accept that anything she had done, subtle or otherwise, had turned Josh back toward a romantic interest in her. They had experienced too many petty clashes, often due to her being overly sensitive. He had become a good friend, she was sure of that. But their relationship was far from what Candy had described. A man in love? She didn't think so.

"Hey, Rachel." Karen bounced up to them and laughed. "Your dad is so revved up about how well you did tonight."

"I know!"

"It's like you've awakened some happy beast or something," Karen said. "He wants to take all of us to dinner to celebrate." She smiled at Josh. "You should come with us, Josh."

"Oh." He eyed Rachel. "I don't want to horn in on a family celebration."

"Nonsense," Rachel said. "Didn't I horn in on Mary's birthday party? You have this one coming." As soon as she said it she regretted it. If she had wanted to push the friend idea, she couldn't have phrased her invitation any less romantically. Why hadn't she just asked him to come? For her? "I mean—"

"Yeah, you should come, Josh." Karen gave him a pat on the arm. "Mira and Cruz are coming. They're not family, either. Just friends."

Oh, lovely. Just friends. Rachel should write it on a sign and hang it around his neck.

She heaved a sigh and looked him in those gorgeous blue eyes. "Josh, please come with us. Come with *me*. I want you there with me."

It took mere seconds for his expression to change. That was one infectious grin he had.

"Then I'd love to go."

"Oh, *no*." The dread in Karen's voice turned Rachel's head.

Josh chuckled. "I'm going to try not to take that personally."

"No, not you." Karen shook her head and then glanced at Rachel. "Billy Nawta, twelve o'clock."

"What?" What was Karen talking about? Just hearing his name brought the same dread to Rachel's voice. "What do you mean?"

Karen stiffened as if she were a Cold War spy. "He's over there. At twelve o'clock. Well, my twelve. Your nine. And…I guess Josh's three—"

"Oh for goodness' sake, Karen." Rachel looked around until she saw Billy in the thinning crowd. He was engaged in a fairly animated conversation with Chuck. Maybe that wrestle to the floor was still a possibility.

Karen spoke, apparently unconcerned about what Josh might know or think about Rachel's old boyfriend. "I asked Chuck to tell him to stay away from you, but that doesn't seem to be going well. I think he's hoping to eat humble pie and beg you to take him back."

Rachel shot a glance at Josh. He studied Billy, his eyes narrowed in thought, before he met eyes with Rachel.

She answered Karen's comment without taking her eyes off of Josh. "Absolutely not interested."

The twinkle in Josh's eyes just about made her swoon, but she managed a mischievous smile instead.

Karen continued speaking, oblivious to the silent exchange going on before her. "Ah, good. He's walking away from Chuck. Oh, no. He's not. I mean he is, but he's walking this way. I think he's coming here to—"

Josh closed the gap between Rachel and himself. "I think we might be able to put a stop to that." As if they had just finished a dance, he wrapped one arm around her waist, cupped the back of her head, and dipped her back. He bent to her and kissed her as if they had kissed this way hundreds of times. Warm, soft, and impossible to resist. Rachel's arms were around him before she took her next breath.

She barely heard Karen's awkward comments, which faded as she left them. "Uh, yeah. That worked, kids. He's gone. Pulled a one-eighty and, yep, off he goes. Yes, sir. I'll, uh, see you two later."

Josh pulled away and smiled at her. "I don't tend to be overly cautious, but I think in this case we might want to be sure he gets the picture."

Rachel feigned serious agreement before she pulled him back to her. "Why, Mr. Reegan, you read my mind."

CHAPTER FIFTY

Josh opened the passenger door of his Bel Air and extended his hand. Rachel slipped her hand into his and stepped carefully from the car. She lifted the hem of her evening gown so it wouldn't graze the pavement.

Two weeks had passed since their adventure in New York, and she loved how familiar, yet thrilling, she found the touch of Josh's hand around hers.

When she stood facing him, his intense blue gaze crinkled at the corners with the amused pleasure she was growing to appreciate more and more.

"You look like you have mischief in mind," she said.

He handed his keys to the valet and looped her arm through his own. "I think you just bring that out in me. Nothing to worry about."

"Oh, I'm not worried. I think I was actually looking forward to a little surprise or two. I'm coming to expect them from you. This invitation, for example."

"I would have invited you earlier," he said, "but I wasn't sure if *I* was even going to attend. I've had a fairly bad attitude at work until recently." He grinned at her. "Not that anyone would notice."

"You? Bad attitude? Nawww."

They walked toward the entrance to the Mayflower Hotel, one of her favorite places in Washington. She saw their reflection in the glass doors before the doorman opened them. Between Josh's sleek tuxedo and her pale pink gown, they looked like something out of a Hollywood film.

Inside the lobby a discreet sign, nestled within the potted palms, indicated their destination:

The Washington Tribune Gala
1951 Awards for Excellence in Journalism
Grand Ballroom

"And, to tell you the truth," Josh continued, "before New York, I didn't know if you'd be willing to go out with me. I hadn't been terribly attentive."

She simply smiled. No sense in telling him she didn't need more attention than he gave her before New York. She knew herself better than that.

The ballroom nearly roared with the energetic conversations of all of the evening's attendees. Still, the string quartet in one of the balconies had been miked sufficiently enough that she was able to hear notes of their music blended in here and there with the rest of the sound.

"Josh, this is beautiful!"

A pink glow suffused the room, and warm lights shone up from the ground to accentuate the ornate marble pillars along the ballroom's periphery. The dinner tables surrounding a spacious dance floor were adorned by elaborate arrangements of exotic, vibrant-colored flowers. Their fragrances mixed with the delicious scent of whatever was being served for dinner this evening.

At one end of the room, on a stage, she saw the setup for a big band, in front of which stood a podium and a dais.

"Yeah," Josh said. "This is the big event of the year at the *Tribune*. I'm glad Lou didn't assign me to cover it. I'd much rather enjoy this evening with the most beautiful woman I've ever met."

He leaned down and gave her a quick kiss. Very much like that first kiss at her door. Rachel trembled with the thought of that first evening and the fact that it had eventually brought them to this point. She loved that she hadn't known then what a happy new couple they would become. They had so much to learn about each other, and she relished the adventure.

"Speaking of Lou," she said, "what's the status of your job, now that the paper has gone after Wiley again?"

She could tell at once that his surprise was pretense.

"Oh, didn't I tell you? Must have slipped my mind. This afternoon Sal offered me my old job back at the city desk."

Rachel gasped and reached up to give him a hug. "Josh! Congratulations!" She pulled back and gave him a playful smack on the chest. "I can't believe you kept that to yourself all day! Oh, I'm so happy for you!"

He wrapped his arms around her, his smile beaming. "The funniest thing, though. After all of this time finding the human element in my stories, I… Well, I decided to stay right where I am."

She gasped again. "Writing for the Style section?"

"You say that like it's a bad thing." He frowned.

"Oh. Well. No, I don't think it's a bad thing. It's just—"

"Just what?" He lifted his brows at her, his eyes wide. Innocent.

"I just always pictured you, I mean, I never pictured you writing those pieces forever."

"Those pieces?"

"You know, about topics less serious than what you were doing on the city desk. I always *liked* your Style articles, don't get me wrong. But I…" She couldn't quite figure out *what* her problem was with his staying with the Style section.

He almost looked hurt. "Are you saying you think my current work is frivolous compared to the city desk's hard-hitting articles about real-life problems?"

She hesitated. Why was this starting to sound familiar?

Josh pressed his hand against his chest, feigning devastation. "Do you mean you think my work isn't a real contribution to society because it's about things like parades and rare coins and—and the *arts*?"

Rachel narrowed her eyes at him and let her mouth drop open. She pushed away from him. "That is *not* even funny." She struggled to keep her smile from forming.

He started laughing. "Just wanted to see how those shoes fit on you for a minute or two." He pulled her to himself again. "Of course I took the city desk job. I like to think I've softened up since I've known you. But I haven't gone soft in the head. I *love* the city desk."

The evening progressed quickly, and she got the chance to meet many of Josh's coworkers, which included some of the most famous news journalists in Washington. Josh had known beforehand that he wasn't up for any awards, so the couple's evening was relaxed and nothing but entertaining.

"Next year, though," Sal said to her, "this guy's going to be a contender. If the work you did tracking down your sources on the Wiley story is any indication, Reegan, I think you're going to be quite the star at the *Tribune*."

Despite the fact that Josh humbly took the praise in stride, she could tell Sal's assessment meant a lot to him.

When they were alone again, she whispered in his ear, "He acts a little like a proud father. I'll bet your father would have felt the same."

She saw quiet gratefulness in his eyes.

After an elaborate dinner, from creamy lobster bisque to decadent blackout chocolate torte, the *Tribunes'* publisher and editorial staff presented the evening's awards in the paper's different fields of journalism. She paid special attention to the reporter who won for work on the city desk. God willing, she would sit here next year—or some subsequent year—and listen to Josh's name being announced at that point in the evening.

The band took the stage after the awards ceremony, and she was thrilled to hear how sharp they were. They switched from romantic waltz pieces like "Remember" to an old Cuban cha-cha song she recognized as "Havana Moon." They played the big band songs of Glenn Miller and the boogie-woogie sound of Jackie Brenston's "Rocket 88." She couldn't help feeling a little itchy to get out there and dance, but she knew Josh wasn't a big fan.

As a matter of fact, Josh had excused himself from the table quite a while ago, while Rachel was chatting with Sheila, his city-desk assistant, who sat on her right side. Rachel straightened in her chair and attempted to search the crowded ballroom for him.

She became aware of warmth over her shoulder and turned her head so swiftly, she almost banged heads with Josh.

"Oh!" She laughed. "There you are. I thought—"

He gave her a goose-bump-inducing kiss right next to her ear and whispered to her. "I think this is our dance."

She turned in her chair and realized he was serious. His hand was open to her, and he looked awfully confident for a man who didn't dance. She returned his smile and let him lead her to the floor while the band began to play.

The delicate piano introduction to "Unforgettable" brought a smile to her face.

"Oh, I *love* this song, Josh!"

He embraced her in a perfect close hold. "Yes, I know. That's why

I asked them to play it." He looked past her and affected the haughty, far-off expression ballroom dancers often adopt during competitions.

"Be nice, now," she said. "We're not going to make fun of each other's jobs tonight."

She saw the tug of a smile before he announced—as she often did in class—which dance they were about to undertake. "The foxtrot." And he proceeded to firmly lead her around the dance floor in a nearly perfect foxtrot.

A number of other couples shared the floor with them. But once people noticed that she and Josh were doing actual choreography, they pulled back and enjoyed the performance.

The band's lead singer might not have been Nat King Cole, but he had a rich, mellow voice that couldn't have been more romantic. In her heart, this moment couldn't have been more romantic.

She felt she could start crying at the slightest provocation. Josh had been frank about his disdain for dancing. Frivolous, a waste of valuable time, even somewhat emasculating. Yet for her he had found a way and taken the time to learn—

"Mira!" She said it out loud. "That's why you were spending time with Mira!"

He finally looked into her eyes and gave her his wonderful, natural grin. "She's a patient teacher. You've got a good girl there."

Rachel swallowed the lump that kept trying to form in her throat. "You don't know what this means to me, Josh. Did you learn any others yet?"

He chuckled. "Are you kidding? It took me an entire month just to learn this one well enough so I could fake my way through it without counting." His expression became more serious. "I was an idiot to ever belittle what you do. Please forgive me for that."

She squeezed his hand. "Thank you." If she wasn't careful she was going to fall in love with this gorgeous man.

"Ever since that first day at your studio," he said, "I saw you teaching steps to the kids during their classes. But it wasn't until you and Cruz danced in that first competition that I appreciated how all of that work resulted in…well, in some pretty terrific dancing. It made me want to learn. So I could do it with you. And it impressed me—how hard you worked to make something look so good."

"I guess it's pretty common," she said, "to see beautiful art, or read riveting articles, or see a couple—a couple of people who seem perfect together—and forget about the work and commitment behind that perfection. But it has to be there."

He held her a little closer. "I've never been afraid of hard work, Rachel. And when I want something…now that I want some*one*, there's no one more committed than I am."

She smiled. "I think I've seen a bit of that commitment, yes. You certainly never forgot what you wanted with that corruption story of yours."

He returned her smile, that mischief in his eyes. "If you thought *that* was unforgettable, you ain't seen nothing yet, young lady."

The song slowed to a close as Josh gently dipped her back and finished with a soft, lingering kiss.

As the couples around them applauded their performance, she felt a tear escape from the corner of her eye. She understood now. *This* is what she wanted all along. She hadn't been afraid to dance again. She had been afraid to love again.

God had known how she and Josh would change each other's lives and hearts. And as she returned Josh's kiss, she knew His was a blessing she would never, ever forget.

QUESTIONS FOR DISCUSSION

Josh and Rachel don't get off to the best start when they meet, thanks to Josh's negative comments about "the whole artsy thing." What are some of the elements in Josh's past that molded his attitude?

Where do you stand on Josh's viewpoint of the arts versus "the dark places and events of the world," especially during our own lifetime?

Rachel takes offense at Josh's remarks when they meet and when he voices similar beliefs further into their relationship. Is her reaction appropriate, or does she seem overly sensitive to you? What is it about her background that might have influenced her reactions to Josh's apparently low esteem for her profession?

Rachel is thirty-two years old in this story. Is it reasonable for her to still care as much as she does about her father's opinion? Do people typically outgrow such concerns, do you think? If not, why not?

Rachel's friend and employee Betty announces she has to leave her job quite soon after she learns she's pregnant. This story is set in 1951 and thus reflects the belief that physical activity like dancing might prove dangerous to perfectly healthy pregnant women. What are some other facets of everyday life in the fifties that you think have undergone change over these past sixty years? Do you consider the changes improvements or deteriorations? Explain.

Rachel and Josh relate to the toddler twins Aaron and Amanda in different ways. How might their respective family dynamics have led to their differing approaches to children?

This story features a number of successfully married couples: dancers Connie and Mel; Mr. and Mrs. Chambers; Rachel's parents and both of her brothers' marriages; Josh's sister Bree and her husband. What are some of the qualities of those relationships that you think contribute to marital success? Which of those qualities do you identify with when you think of your own relationship with your husband or significant other?

If you had to choose one way Rachel opens Josh's eyes and one way Josh does the same for Rachel, how would you describe it?

Romans 8:28 tells us that "all things work together for good to them that love God." How does this apply to Josh's concerns? To Rachel's?

How has Romans 8:28 proven true in a circumstance that initially caused you great concern?

Soul-stirring romance...set against a historical backdrop readers will love!

Summerside Press™ is pleased to present our fresh new line of historical romance fiction—including stories set amid the action-packed eras of the twentieth century.

Watch for a number of new Summerside Press™ historical romance titles to release in 2011.

Now Available in Stores

Sons of Thunder
by Susan May Warren
ISBN 978-1-935416-67-8

The Crimson Cipher
by Susan Page Davis
ISBN 978-1-60936-012-2

Songbird Under a German Moon
by Tricia Goyer
ISBN 978-1-935416-68-5

Stars in the Night
by Cara Putman
ISBN 978-1-60936-011-5

The Silent Order
by Melanie Dobson
ISBN 978-1-60936-019-1

Nightingale
by Susan May Warren
ISBN 978-1-60936-025-2

Coming Soon

Exciting New Historical Romance Stories by These Great Authors—

Margaret Daley...DiAnn Mills...Lisa Harris...and MORE!